The Pig Feeder

'Secret of Enniskillen'

Kevin Thomas Quinn

Contents

*In memory of the victims
of the Enniskillen Bombing*

'Love is the only Truth'

ACT I

Chapter 1

Soldier's Nightmare - Nightmare Saighdiuiri

'Look out,'

Bang!

Something flies through the air. We only realise what it is, as it lays there, twisted limbs. A leg over there, an arm here, no legs, no fingers. Distorted face but the eyes stare through. Body parts strewn.

Unidentifiable chunks of flesh hang from the branches of the trees.

So much blood that you can smell it. The smell is clean but unpleasant. The smell of rotten eggs from the blown out intestines of its victim. Smell of bodily fluids. Disfigured face reveals itself, sliced and ripped apart but the eyes stare through. No limbs, no understanding. Desperate shouting, no response.

Disfigured face but the eyes stare through.

Army clothing blackened and steaming from the incendiary. Jocky was his name, a soldier through and through. Now he lays there dying. What can he do?

'Look out,'

Bang !

Another one flies over.

'It's an ambush.' A voice shouts, 'We've been fucking set up. Run!'

Bullets whizz past like wasps buzzing.

Buzz ! Buzz ! Nipping, hissing, missing past.

Screams and shouts, distance faces, distance voices.

Organised chaos, battle field business.

Through the woods they run on foot chased by the Hun

The hunt is afoot, the foxes are strung, The hounds on their heels, the game has begun.

Bullets whizz past like flies fleeing from the mortuary belly.

How they wish they were back in the mess watching telly.

The mist slips through the woods like a ghostly shadow, dancing in a wooded cathedral.

The trees huddle together like a silhouette on the rural landscape.

Standing to attention like timber soldiers on parade, rigid and Unyielding.

We see a figure emerge.

Out of the mist runs John Doyle, a SAS British soldier in full battle dress with rifle in hand. Behind him follows his comrade, Kevin.

Looking from left to right they desperately search for an escape plan.

There is an explosion nearby.

This deafens them, temporarily.

With repeated explosions they continue to be ambushed.

The two soldiers are running as fast as they can. Amidst the sounds of the pursuing enemy, it is not long before John hears Kevin shouting in pain from over his shoulder. John turns around to see Kevin injured in agony on the ground. John immediately grabs Kevin saying,' I've got you mate.' John starts pulling Kevin along the ground from behind. Dragging Kevin unceremoniously backwards in a seated position. John runs frantically forwards pulling his comrade. There is another explosion behind John.

John is not phased and keeps going, as his priority is to get his mate to safety.

John is still running, pulling Kevin along saying, 'We are nearly there Kev.'

As John turns his head around to look at his mate, he is shuddered to see that Kevin's lower half of his body is missing completely blown away

Kevin is obviously dead.

John in denial, turns his face back around ignoring the fact that his mate is dead. John keeps on running pulling the lifeless carcass of his friend behind him.

Oblivious to reality, John says, 'It will be ok mate, We are nearly there. It will be ok Kev.'

Suddenly, the scene changes and John finds himself naked and in a bath.

John has seemingly woken from a nightmare.

John can only assume that he has fallen asleep while taking a bath and dreamt the whole horrific scene.

John sighs in relief realising this.

John stares up at the bathroom ceiling with his head lying back on the bath taps.

As he gathers his senses his mind is alerted to the fact that something is touching his leg.

John with a sense of urgency sits up in the bath causing the water to spill over the bath onto the floor.

John looks down to see he is sitting in a bath full of red coloured water. Coloured red from blood. There are various body parts in the bath.

Hands, feet and human remains unidentifiable to the eye, floating and swaying around in the bath.

The body parts knock into John as the water moves.

John lays there in terror.

John is frozen stiff with shock, unable to move.

John starts to see bubbles rising between his legs. John nervously looks at these bubbles. Suddenly, a severed human head surfaces up from the depth of the water. A disfigured face reveals itself. The severed head floats around on the surface, as it does so the eyes stare through at John.

In the pandemonium, John jumps up.

Suddenly, John finds he is back in his bedroom on his bed. John sits up. There is silence, apart from the rapid breathing of John's breath.

John realises it was all a nightmare.

Rubbing his face and wide eyed in disbelief. John sits on the side of his bed. John gets up and walks into the bathroom. John is naked, and nervously takes a double look at the empty bath as he walks past. Just to double check his bath is not full of blood and floating body parts from his nightmare. The bath is empty.

John lives on the borders of Northern Ireland and the Republic, in a remote isolated old cottage.

John is tall and well-built. Six foot two with wavy dark hair and piercing blue eyes. John is a ruggedly handsome man.

John was in the army and a leader not a follower. An alpha male. A man that has dug a few ditches in his time and if you messed with him, he would put you in one. John has been discharged from the army in ill health. Stood down from the army physically but not mentally.

John has withdrawn from life and wants to be left alone.

John stands in front of the Bathroom mirror taking a long look at himself.

John pulls out a handgun out of nowhere. Placing it to the side of his head, against his temple.

John closes his eyes and pulls the trigger. The gun clicks but nothing happens. John then pulls the trigger again and again repeatedly, still nothing. The gun just keeps clicking over. In despair, John puts the gun back down by the bathroom sink. He lowers his head down in quiet desperation.

There is silence. Suddenly, a figure appears in the mirror over John's left shoulder. It is his army colleague Kevin, who had been blown up in his nightmare. This man is now standing behind John in the bathroom.

Kevin says, 'John, you know there's no bullets in that gun.' John looks demoralised. Kevin continues saying, 'You know you have taken a vow never to kill another human being. That includes you too mate.'

John raises his head and looks up at Kevin.

Saying nothing John turns his back on the mirror and walks out of the bathroom despondent.

October 1993

John walks into the kitchen and begins to make breakfast.

Meanwhile, an elderly man is driving out of Belfast city.

Belfast has been occupied throughout history since the Neolithic period. Nomadic tribes crossed over the frozen Irish sea from Scotland to Ulster, during the Ice Age. These nomads were the influx of a new group, called The Gaels or Gaelics. The first permanent settlements in Belfast were built in the Iron Age.

The original settlement of Belfast was only a small village. based around the marshy ford, where the river Lagan meets the river Farset.

Belfast was part of the Gaelic kingdom of Dál Riata from around 500 AD to the late 700.

Meanwhile, the purr of an old car, cuts through the chorus of birds singing in the morning air. This old man continues driving into the countryside, he drives for some time, through narrow country lanes until he reaches the isolated old cottage.

Back in the kitchen. The kettle is beginning to boil, there is a cherry tomato plant on a windowsill. John is lovingly pruning it with a little scissors. He does this with much delicacy and care.

The sound and smell of sizzling bacon and eggs permeates from the cooking pan.

John has an old record player in the corner of the kitchen on a table. There is a big pile of vinyl records next to the record player. Removing the vinyl out of an album sleeve, John carefully places it on the record player and flicks the switch at the side. John then manoeuvres the needle over and onto the record. The sound of classical music starts playing. A string quartet.

John fills up his plate with bacon and eggs placing it onto a large wooden kitchen table. With a cup of tea and plenty of tomato sauce. John begins to eat his food.

John lives in an old forgotten cottage on the outskirts of nowhere. Outside the cottage has white stoney walls, unevenly plastered. The slate pitched roof is worn and tired, sporadically covered in moss. The building creeks from the passage of time. Built way back from a time long forgotten by living memory.

The cottage sits in a flat pasture of land, desolate and surrounded to the west by woods.

Set out in the wilderness three miles from town, on the borders of Northern Ireland and the republic.

There is a knock at the door. John opens the front door to be confronted by the elderly man who has been driving. The man seems to know John. The old man's car is parked outside. John and the elderly man walk outside and go around to the back of the car.

The elderly man opens the boot to reveal a lifeless body of a man. There are marks and bruises all over the body. The body is naked.

The man's face is concealed as there is a black plastic bag wrapped and taped around the man's face.

This startling scene does not even surprise John or the elderly man. John leans into the boot and hoofs the dead body onto his shoulders. The elderly man gives John a brown paper envelope.

John nods at the elderly man and then walks back into the house. The elderly man proceeds to get into the car and drive away.

John enters the kitchen with the dead body. John unceremoniously plonks the body onto the kitchen table besides his breakfast plate. John calmly sits down, takes a slurp of his tea and squirts more bright red tomato ketchup all over his bacon and eggs. John then continues eating his breakfast as blissful as a hummingbird in a tree.

There is classical music filling the air in the background.

John finishes his breakfast and washes up his dish, drying and carefully placing the plate and cutlery away in its proper place. He regimentally does this so everything is in order, ship shape and Bristol fashion.

John attends to the dead body which has been previously ignored up to now like an uninvited guest. John puts the dead man onto his shoulder and walks over to another door in the kitchen. John balances the body with one hand while he uses the other one to turn the door handle. John then enters the room and into darkness.

John flicks a switch which lights the room to reveal bare brick walls like an old forgotten outbuilding, not touched for years. A mouldy scent perfumes the room like a discarded damp rag.

This room is very sparse, containing only a large wooden butchering table, which is centrally positioned.

On the wall are butchering utensils all carefully and precisely hanging up. These utensils are of varying sizes and have different uses from meat cleavers to long pincers to small scissors and razors.

John lays the body onto a black plastic sheet which covers the wooden butchering table. John then takes a long sharp piercing instrument from the array of medieval like cutlery on the wall. John then starts stabbing the body randomly all over with the sharp skewer. With the exception of the head, which he leaves alone, saving it from this degrading affliction.

John puts down his skewering instrument and proceeds to unwrap the man's face from the plastic bag that had obscured his features. This unwrapping reveals a tortured face with cuts and bruising. As the dead man lays there, he has an open mouth. It is difficult to see if the eyeballs are present as the eye sockets are so swollen, black and blue.

John then takes an unlabelled bottle of whiskey. Lifting it up to the heavens, John takes a swig and salutes all his fallen military colleagues.

He puts the bottle down then picks up a pair of scissors. John then proceeds to cut the dead man's hair as short as he possibly can. John then uses a razor to shave the remaining hair off the head. With a bowl of water by his side, John then shaves the deceased's head and face. Shaving it free from any hair including eyebrows and eyelashes. The dead man's mouth has now closed.

John opens the man's mouth with his finger's and places a piece of wood in the mouth to keep it open. After this John takes a pair of pliers and pulls out all the teeth. One by one dropping them into an old empty oxo gravy tin. The teeth make a tapping noise as they are dropped inside the tin box.

Once all teeth and hair are removed John wraps the body in the plastic sheeting and ties it with rope.

After this morbid preparation of the body John picks up the carcass and opens another door.

The door opens out to daylight. The outside light pierces the darkness of this makeshift abattoir.

John walks outside with the body on his shoulder.

It is raining outside, and the sky is grey. John proceeds to walk down a small country lane. The rain is hitting John hard, pelting John relentlessly at an angle. The rain is stabbing the wind and air as it falls hard.

John gets to the end of this small lane to find an old wooden hut on a side verge, just off the trail. John opens the door to the hut and enters. Inside there hangs other large plastic wrapped parcels of human remains. These body bags are vertically hanging from the ceiling in this temporary mortuary.

As the door remains open, flies escape from the hut. There is a very strong pungent smell of rotting flesh and decaying bodies. The smell does not affect John.

Once inside, John lifts the rapped body off his shoulder and up onto an old metal hook screwed into a thick timber beam on the ceiling. John lets go of the body, it sways and knocks other hanging bodies. The other wrapped up dead bodies sway from side to side.

Various bodies have maggots and flies on them, some of the plastic has broken to reveal rotting carcasses. These are John's previously prepared dead bodies. John stands and watches the various body bags swaying. They move backwards and forwards at various tempos but collectively as if in time to music. John takes a perverse sense of amusement watching the bodies sway back-and-forth.

The scene reminds John of the swaying motion of his friend's body which he found hanging once upon a time.

Johns' friend had been a serving British soldier in Northern Ireland during the troubles. His friend committed suicide by hanging himself. His friend was unable to cope with the things that he had experienced whilst there. The images of his army mates who had been murder by the Irish republican Army had led to his suicide. John was the one who found him. This traumatic event of discovering his mate's suicide had never left John. So, seeing IRA operatives dead and hanging in this makeshift mortuary pleased John. Like pulling the wings from a fly or treading on ants. This gave John a childish dark sense of amusement. Seeing the enemies of his dead comrades swinging aimlessly, hung from the ceiling. In John's mind it was some kind of justice.

John then proceeds to cut slits in the hanging body bag that he has just hung up. This action disturbs more stagnant body bags, bobbing around from the ceiling.

Blood starts pouring and oozing out onto the floor, from the freshly cut body bag.

The floor is thickly covered with hay and straw as the blood falls onto it, the straw soaks it up.

John picks another older body bag hanging up. Putting his arms around the wrapped body bag. John heaves it up off from its resting place and down onto his shoulders.

Once the body is balanced on his shoulder John kicks the hut door open to show the outside, still raining heavily. John leaves the hut of horror. Walking back up the lane with the raindrop's pitter pattering off the plastic of the body bag on his shoulder.

He enters back into the cottage via the butchering room of which he came from.

John lets the door close behind him, shutting the light out and the darkness back into this butchering boudoir.

John puts the body down on to his butchering table and opens the bag. John retrieves a large meat cleaver from the wall and proceeds to hack and chop at the body in a clumsy haphazard manner making the carcass into smaller pieces. One at a time, John throws the pieces into a large bowl, as he cuts away chunks of flesh.

John sees a rat scurry away into a corner

John then picks up the bowl and walks back out the same door leading to the outside. John walks a short distance in a different direction than previously. John arrives at a pig pen to where his pigs live. John rolls the fleshy contents of this heavily weighted down bowl into the pig pen for the pigs to eat.

The pigs spring into life and with excitement start chomping at the meat.

The Pigs eat like they have been starved and now have a feast in front of their eyes.

John talks to the pigs encouraging them to eat, saying 'Come on, dinner.' John then walks away back into the butchering room and shuts the door behind him.

John is The Pig Feeder, disposing of the dead bodies of Irish Republican Army (IRA) Operatives for the Ulster Defence Association. (UDA). The UDA captured, interrogated, and murdered these IRA operatives. The UDA then deliver them to John who processes them and feeds them to his Pigs. A simple way to get rid of any evidence. Even though John is now a retired British soldier. John feels he is still playing a part by disposing of his old enemy. In his mind, it helps him feel he is still fighting against the Irish Republican Army.

Chapter 2

The Romper Room - An Seomra Romper

On the first floor in a house somewhere in a Street in South Belfast, a white wooden door opens to reveal an empty room darkened at the edges and dimly lit. We cannot see who or what is inside this space.

The centre of the room is lit by an old hanging light.

Suddenly, a woman is thrown into the light. She is a slim, petite female with long brown hair, a classically attractive woman, dark olive skin and dark eyes. She has a Mediterranean look about her. The woman is bleeding from her mouth and nose. She is wearing nothing.

Without warning, a fist appears from out of the darkness, punching the woman in the face. Already on her knees, the power of the blow sends her down onto the floor.

The beaten woman raises her head from the floor with trepidation. She realises that the floor she is laying on is covered in plastic sheeting.

This woman visibly shakes in the realisation that the sheeting is in readiness to wrap up her body, after she has been interrogated, tortured, and executed.

Before the woman has time to move. Another separate woman steps out of the darkness into the light. This woman also unleashes a torrent of punches and kicks upon the women on the floor. The victim screams and shouts with sporadic groaning as she absorbs the force of the blows on her body.

The attacking woman stops as if to gather her breath. This female attacker is large in stature with porcelain like skin and red hair, the woman has piercing blue eyes, like an angel.

Once the attacker has gathered her breath, she starts again kicking and hitting the woman on the floor relentlessly.

The female attacker stops her violence and begins walking around her victim, like a vulture preparing to swoop on her prey.

The female attacker then reveals a hammer in her hand She pats the hammer in her hand intimidatingly, then talking to the woman on the floor says, 'You Catholic Scum. IRA Bitch. Welcome to the romper room. We are members of the women's Ulster Defence Association. We are known as the notorious

Heavy Squad. We are going to give you a proper rompering. The whole Heavy Squad Treatment for you. I am your interrogator.'

The female interrogator says, 'I have a gift for you. Are you willing to suffer for your Catholic religion and your saviour, Jesus Christ?

The interrogator disappears into the darkness of the room. She quickly returns saying, 'I have made you a crown to wear, to show everyone just how proud you are of being catholic. A crown just like the Crown Jesus wore.'

From the darkness in the room the UDA Interrogator reveals a wreath made from barbed wire. Holding it in her hands it is reminiscent of the crown of thorns worn by Jesus Christ at his crucifixion.

The female torturer continues to talk saying, 'This crown is made of old, rusty barbed wire and has been taken from the Peace wall along Cupar Way. That wall separates the Protestants on the Shanklin Road from the Catholics on the Falls Road. I have painstakingly and lovingly twisted and mangled the wire into this lovely crown for you to wear upon your head.'

The other second interrogator grabs the victim and holds her firm in readiness to wear the crown of steel thorns.

The female victim tries to move and wriggle to escape but she is restrained too tightly by the other interrogator. The victim tries to resist but is too weak to put up a fight.

The main female interrogator who is holding the barbed wire crown goes to place it on the woman's head but then stops and says, 'For the last time are you going to tell me where your brother is? The prisoner is silent.

The interrogator in a sarcastic voice continues saying, 'Do Bee. Do Bee. Do ! It's a rompering for you. Now be a good girl and tell me. Where is your brother too?

The victim doesn't speak. The interrogator changes her tone to one of anger saying, 'We know about the Battle at Newry Road with the British Helicopters. We know your brother was there, so where is he?'

The room is deadly silent. That same kind of silence before the gallows hatch opens or same silence before the guillotine falls, a silence that beckons on the arrival of the grim reaper.

The IRA woman looks up at her interrogators but resigns herself to her fate and remains silent. She lowers her head back down in acceptance of what is coming.

Gazing into space, the victim awaits to be fitted with her crown of steel thorns.

The interrogator stands over the woman and with the spiked crown proceeds to place the crown of barbed wire onto the victim's head. Pushing it down into her scalp and forehead to the hellish screams and yells from the recipient. Blood starts to sprout and ooze from the woman's head. Running down her face over her eyes, nose, and mouth.

The main interrogator smiles as she keeps pushing the crown down harder and harder, until the barbed wire crown is firmly embedded into the victim's head. The interrogator's assistant releases her grip from the woman and the female victim collapses back down onto the floor.

The crowned victim tries touching the barbed wire in the hope to remove it off her head, but the pain is so horrific to the touch that it is impossible to remove. The murderous crown has been embedded so deeply into her head.

The main interrogator struts around the room after her latest inflicted torture. This sadistic interrogator is difficult to see as she creeps around the dark edges of the room, like a spider on its web.

This barbarous monster then comes back close up to her victim of prey saying, 'If you tell me where your IRA Brother is, I'll end it quickly for you. All this pain and suffering will end with just one bullet. But if you don't cooperate, I'll start first with your toes then work my way slowly up until you will be begging me to kill you.'

The tortured woman now semi unconscious and half dead struggles to look up at her female interrogator.

The prisoner's body is beginning to fail and she has difficulty controlling the basic functions of the bladder and bowel.

There is a smell of bodily excrement which flavours the room as the victim starts to deteriorate and lose her bodily functions.

There is no bedside manner for a human being tortured and about to be killed.

This woman's body is now surviving only on pure will and fortitude rather than biological function.

The victim is now covered in blood but she manages to raise her head to look up at her interrogators. The victim smiles at her tormentors and in a final defiant voice shouts, 'One United Ireland'

This infuriates her interrogators who explode in a torrent of blows onto their female victim. The attack pauses as the two interrogators return now with house bricks in their hands. The two interrogators repeatedly deliver fatal blows to their prisoner.

As the door of the romper room begins to slowly shut. We are saved from the horrific scene of the defiant woman's final demise. It unfolds to its morbid predicted conclusion.

The night has progressed into darkness and there is now silence in the house of torture somewhere in Belfast. A young boy enters the rompering room and switches on the light, this lights up the female who had been interrogated earlier.

The woman's lifeless body is on the floor but oddly, it is placed in a crucifix position. It then becomes clear the woman has been nailed to the floor as if simulating a crucifixion. The nails banged through her hands and feet. The young boy appears to be only a teenager, he nervously raises his hands, to reveal he is holding a rifle. The boy then aims the gun at the female body, closes his eyes and shoots.

We hear a gun fire one solitary bullet then silence. The resonance of the shot rings out for a split second through the building, then silence. The job is done and a life is taken.

Chapter 3

Secret of Enniskillen - Run Inis Ceithleann

John stumbles over rubble and bricks. Smoke blinds John's view and chokes his throat. John loses his footing and trips. His hands touch the rumble to steady himself. The bricks are hot to touch from the explosion. In shock and disbelief John pushes himself on searching to help people. The site looks like a scene from a Hollywood disaster movie. There is devastation everywhere, body parts litter the area. John cannot see any completely intact human bodies as he searches to help in this hell. John scrambles over the debris, desperately scanning for survivors in this alien landscape.

As he searches John feels something soft underfoot. John looks down to realise he is standing on a hand. John immediately steps away, releasing the hand. The smoke clears to reveal a head which is covered with rumble. John reacts to this immediately, quickly clearing the debris to reveal a face. To his horror, John is looking at the face of a young girl in her twenties. Her face is blackened with dirt and smoke, her eyes closed as she lays motionless. Most of her body is underneath the rumble only her top half protrudes from the bricks and concrete. There is lots of dust blowing around as it is windy. Black smoke from pockets of fire momentarily blows across both John and the girl then clears.

John reaches his hands out towards her to clear some more of the debris. Her eyes open suddenly startling John who takes a step back in shock.

The young girl's eyes are a beautiful light blue like the sky on a summer's day. They sparkle out of the darkness of the soot and grime and they stare intently at John. The young girl is calm and silent just looking at John in quiet amazement.

She mutters to john in a soft southern Irish accent saying,' 'Why?'

John looks at her speechless.

The girl struggles to breathe and coughs but steadies herself. She then again repeats her question to John saying, 'Why?'

John is dumbfounded and cannot find an acceptable answer to give to this young girl.

Before John can speak, this angelic girl asks, 'Why do I have to die?'

This profound question mentally paralyses John, leaving him crippled beyond words to answer.

Speechless without words, the only words John can think of saying is, 'You are loved and always will be.'

Suddenly, there is noise behind john. A man scrambles over the rumble hurrying over to John and the girl. He is covered in dust and his clothes are ripped and cut. Obviously, this man has been in the initial blast. He is an older man and says, 'Please help my daughter. I am her father. I found an ambulance over there.' In panic the man continues saying, ' Please, will you help me carry her over to the ambulance.' John instantly nods to the father.

The father looks at his daughter and knees down at her side to hold her hand. The girl smiles and whispers to her dad. John turns away to give them some privacy. The father and daughter have a private conversation only that they are privy to. The father lowers his head and gently kisses his daughter's cheek.

John turns back to see this young flowering spirit, not yet blossomed into the full bloom of life, has her eyes shuts. The young woman tilts her head to the side and dies.

Her father keeps holding her hand even though he knows she has gone. In his mind he hopes it may give her some comfort as she departs this world. Desperate to give his daughter some solace, to show her humanity amidst this evilness. Tears stream from her fathers eyes. The tears roll down onto his daughter's face. Her father holds his daughter's hand, as it is warm and he will not let go of it. John knows that the father must let her go and release her hand but the dad struggles to do this. John knows that the father must do so to pick the girl up and get her out of the rubble.

Without needing to say anything the father takes an intake of breath and lets go of his daughter's hand. John then bends down and pushes the broken concrete and bricks from off the girl. John and the father scoop the lifeless girl's body up and carries her over to the nearest ambulance.

There is pandemonium all around, as the public and emergency services deal with the aftermath of the bomb explosion. John and the father bring the girl in their arms to the back of the open ambulance. A busy paramedic signals to them to place her on a stretcher. The paramedic quickly examines the girl, instantly realising she is dead. The paramedic shakes their head at the father to signify the girl is dead. John says nothing but looks down in sadness. The father hugs his daughter with his head on her shoulder, sobbing uncontrollably.

John finds a blanket nearby and brings it over to the father. The father lays the blanket over his young daughter's body, covering her face with it.

John tries to imagine he is dreaming this nightmare, but the horror is real. John looks to the skies and unceremoniously releases a scream of anger saying, 'Traitors'. John's voice is prolonged and fills the air that can be heard to the heavens. John drops to the ground on his knees and into darkness.

There is light as John opens his eyes.

John is back sitting in an old armchair in the living room of the cottage. John looks around to see Kevin snoring in a similar old armchair behind him. John realises he has been asleep and dreamt this nightmare.

Kevin wakes up from his sleep. Kevin is looking at John in contemplation still not fully awake yet.

The room is very quaint, little has been changed since the original elderly couple lived there before John.

Kevin is a short, stocky man with a brown gingery beard. He has a broken boxers' nose which punctuates his granite face. His tough look matches the roughness of his shaven head. Kevin has an aura that gives off a strength about him. Kevin is johns' best friend.

Kevin is wearing combat army camouflage trousers and an olive green military woollen combat style pullover jumper.

John says, 'I was having a nightmare. I was back at the bomb site after the explosion. I remember the young girl and her father. I remember carrying her dead body with her father.'

Kevin looking at John sadly says, 'I know, I will never forget it either.' Kevin then says, 'Afterwards the girls father publicly forgave the terrorists.'

John says, 'I cannot imagine, how he was able to forgive those murderers. I will never forgive them.'

Pausing to gather his thoughts Kevin says, 'They fucked them.' John continues saying, 'They completely fucked them'

Kevin replies saying,' They fucked us all, John.'

Kevin then continues saying, 'We had those bastards and they made us let them go. They knew they would bomb and kill, and they made us let them go.'

Kevin continues saying, 'Our own people, our own superiors, let the bombers go free to kill innocent people. Eleven innocent civilians murdered and 63 injured.'

John says. 'Murdered by who? the bombers? or the Government?

'Our own superiors knowingly stopped us from killing the bombers when we could have eliminated them. The British Government deliberately allowed the IRA to slip through our fingers and murder those innocent people.' Kevin says, 'It is all fucked up and no one knows about it. The families of the innocent people killed. They do not know the truth nor do the public.

John says, 'You are right Kevin. The British Government and counterintelligence, knew we knew their secret.' John pauses then says, 'The Secret of Enniskillen will never be told. It will die with us.'

Kevin says, 'That is why they sent us on that mission and informed the IRA. So, the IRA knew we were coming and could ambush us.'

John says, 'They wanted to silence us as we knew their secret, we know too much.'

Kevin says. 'After allowing IRA bombers to kill innocent people. The British Government then tried to kill us because we knew the truth'

John says. 'It is a truth that would bring down the Government if revealed. We were becoming too much of a risk to them.'

Kevin says,' Yes, especially after you sent your official complaint to Army headquarters.' When the military high command ignored your complaint. You then sent your anonymous letter to the Tánaiste in Ireland and the Irish Minister for Foreign Affairs. That sealed our fate when the British Government found out you had contacted the Irish government, we were dead men.

John says, 'I only told the truth.'

Kevin says, 'Yes, I don't blame you mate. But you must have known the British Government would want us dead after that letter.'

Kevin continues saying, 'You told the Irish Government that basically, the British Government and counterintelligence knew that the IRA were going to bomb the cenotaph in Enniskillen on Remembrance Day. Furthermore, you stated in your letter that you were part of a group of SAS British soldiers that had intelligence on the IRA Terrorists plan. That you informed your commanding officers and unbelievably were forced to stand down under the orders of your superior command..

The IRA Terrorists then went on to explode their bomb at the cenotaph, killing and injuring innocent civilians. Finally, you stated in the letter that the British government knowingly did this for political reasons. The British Government thought that allowing the IRA Terrorists to continue with their bombing mission, would create a public outcry. So as you can imagine the British government was pissed off with you.'

John says,' as I said early. I was only telling the truth about the Enniskillen bombing.'

John continues saying, 'The government got what they wanted as the public sympathy, especially in America, would turn against the Provisional IRA after the bombing. The powers that be also thought the outcry after the bombing would help pass through a new Extradition act in parliament. Which they did get passed as a result of the bombing.

Kevin says, 'The British Government could argue their new Extradition Act was justified after the Remembrance Day Massacre in Enniskillen.'

John says. 'Well, I don't regret sending it. It was the truth and sometimes the truth is uncomfortable and creates repercussions'

Kevin says, 'You can say that alright, as far as the British government were concerned, that letter signed our death warrant. I wouldn't mind but the letter did not even get released to the press. No one ever found out the secret of Enniskillen.'

John says, 'Yes, The Irish and British Politicians all closed ranks and covered it up, when necessary, they all stick together.'

John continues saying, 'I tried my best to get justice for the innocent civilians blown up on that day. It should have been avoided, we had those IRA Bastards in our sights, we could have eliminated them.

Kevin says, 'We should have killed them when we had the chance. We should have taken them out of the equation.

John says, 'We were ordered not to capture those IRA Bastards even when I threatened to overrule our commanding officers' orders. But our senior command threatened to court martial all of us if I refused their orders. I didn't want that for you and the boys. I was not going to allow them to court martial you, Jocky and Tom.

John continues saying, 'I didn't care if I got a court martial but not you boys' John pauses in thought then says, 'I will regret it for the rest of my life. I should have disobeyed the order and killed the those IRA terrorists. I should never have agreed to allow them to continue and explode that bomb at the Remembrance ceremony.

John continues saying, 'I should have disobeyed, and we should have taken those Bastards out.

Kevin says, 'It is not for you to shoulder all the blame, we all allowed it to happen. There is blood on all our hands. We could have changed it. We could have stopped it'

Kevin continues saying, 'But we didn't.'

Kevin is silent for a few seconds looking at John in despair. Kevin then says, 'We put our trust in our superiors and they fucked. It is not only us.'

'The public put their trust in the British army and in governments and they fucked them too. Purely for political reasons the British Government and our own military superiors betrayed everyone.'

John interjects in an angry tone saying, 'To knowingly allow the IRA to explode a bomb killing innocent people, they should all be ashamed of themselves. It would have been worse. Thankfully, the other bomb the IRA terrorist cell planted that day, failed to go off. Only failing because the wire mechanism disconnected from the bomb.

They had planted the secondary bomb further up the road. If it had detonated it would have killed multiple innocent casualties in the procession that later marched down that road. That procession included the girl guides and the scouts. Even children's lives are meaningless to the ambitions of the IRA and the establishment.

Our own British Politicians allowed terrorists to succeed. Resulting in multiple casualties, innocent people killed. Lives snuffed out and expendable to the powers that be. They are no different from terrorists. We had been fighting an unwinnable war because they are all the fucking same. They both have disregard for human life.

Kevin says, 'They fucked us mate'

John says, 'Yes Kev, they completely fucked us mate.

John continues saying, 'To top it off, our superior commanding officers then send us on a mission, knowing we would be ambushed by the IRA. It's as if our superior officers liaises with the IRA when it suits them. The lines are blurred mate. Who are the good guys anymore ? I am confused. We didn't have a chance on that mission. Our own British intelligence knew the IRA were mob-handed there and they still sent us anyway to be butchered.'

Kevin says, 'We were fucked from the outset and jocky died'

John says, 'Jocky got killed and you were injured. I don't know how me and Tom escaped injury'

Kevin says, 'The Enniskillen bombing should never have happened. That IRA terrorists cell should have been illuminated, especially the leader. A particularly vicious evil psychotic IRA extremist. There were eight members of the cell and she was the commanding officer.

John says, 'The leader of the terrorist cell. She was known as 'The Queen Bee.' She was nicknamed as previously she specialised in killing off duty British soldiers in honey traps. Utilising her good looks and flirtatious charms. She would meet off duty British soldiers, in bars and pubs and give them the impression she wanted to fuck them. She would lure the poor unsuspecting off duty soldier back to an IRA house where they would be tortured and killed. She was responsible for the deaths of many British soldiers. This murderous activity helped her excel up the promotional ranks in the IRA. Eventually, commanding her very own IRA Terror cell.

This woman was ultra-motivated at killing British soldiers. Motivated after one of her friends' family was murdered in the

Bloody Sunday Massacre. Her friend's family member was one of the thirteen killed by the British Army's Parachute Regiment on 30th January 1972 aka the Bloody Sunday Massacre.

As a young girl she was present on that day. She saw first-hand the horror and explicit violence enacted on the civil rights demonstrators. One of which was her friend's family member. She then took up the fight against the British. She saw her fight as equivalent to the French resistance against the Nazis in World war two. In her eyes, the British soldiers were no better than the Nazis, occupying Ireland with their internment.

Kevin says, 'Bloody Sunday was a massive recruitment motivator for the IRA. After that happened, hundreds of new recruits wanted to sign up to the IRA and fight the British army.

John continues saying, 'We had that bitch in our sights and allowed her to go free. We could have picked all of them up easily before that morning on Remembrance Day. But our bloody commanding officers allowed her to go free to kill and she is still free today.

Kevin says, 'I have heard she lives in America now'.

John says, 'Yes, I bet she acts as if butter wouldn't melt in her mouth. She is probably married to a politician or lawyer and seen as an upstanding pillar of the community.

Kevin says, 'Yes, she probably a preacher's wife, holier than thou and righteous'

John says, 'Fucking Hypocrite'

John looks at Kevin and says,' We lost Jocky and you nearly died because of those Bastards.'

Kevin in contemplation says, 'You know John, there is one thing I have come to realise about religion.'

Kevin pauses in a sombre mood then continues saying, 'My father was an outgoing man, had many friends and everyone in the street liked him. They thought he was the salt of the earth, he always had time for the neighbours for a laugh and a joke But I saw his other side, his dark side when he had a drink in him, he would find any excuse to beat the fuck out of me after he had finished beating my mum unconscious You know what ?

John does not speak, shocked by kevins revelations.

Kevin continues saying, 'My dad was a vicar. He was a well-respected man of the Church of England. He was a man of the cloth as they say. He was the Vicar of our church. He performed his ministering with great enthusiasm for his parishioners. Every Sunday without fail my father would pray for forgiveness for the sinners of his flock whilst giving out the holy sacrament aka the bread and wine.'

'He did everything perfectly, well-dressed, ironed shirt, pressed trousers. Even carried an ironed handkerchief in his pocket with his initials on it, That is how organised and proper he showed out to the outside world. But at home behind closed doors, he was a dishevelled, violent, drunk. When he was drunk, he loved picking a fight with me. Trouble was I was only nine years old. I was just a kid. I didn't have a chance to fairly defend myself. As I got old and bigger there came a time when I was a teenager when I was stronger than him. I knew one day I will get my chance to fight back and win. So I bided my time. I had been practising fighting at a martial art club, I used my paper round money to pay for it. Then when I was fifteen my father, the vicar, drunk as usual, picked a fight with me. But this time I was ready for him. The time had come for revenge. So, one night he came looking for me to use his fists on but I was waiting for him.

I beat the fuck out of him. I beat him so badly that it paralysed him. I wanted to disable him so he could never hurt anyone again, especially my mum. I said he must have done it when drunk.

All those years of abuse at his hands. It all came back to haunt him, as I bashed him up every way possible. I bent that bastard in half and threw that cunt around like a rag doll and a Hail Mary and an amen to that.

Kevin pauses as he feels his anger resurge as he relives his past.

Kevin then continues says,' I learned that religious people aren't necessarily good people and religion is as good as the people who preach and practise it. So I say live and let live. I take as I find, and I don't hate no one just because I'm told they are supposed to be my enemy by my government. I joined the army like you, to get a life out of the streets of London. I go to fight only because I signed up to it and I fight to protect my mates.

The IRA or UDA or any group of people killing others in the name of religion are fraudsters. They say they are protecting their religion but they are nothing but bullies using that as an excuse to do evil. It's not because of religion that killing happens but by self-appointed hypocrites using religion as an excuse to bully and kill.

Kevin continues saying, 'Do you know the Catholic and the Protestant crucifix and rosary beads are not much different from each other? The cross is still the same. The difference is just in the number of beads. The Protestant or Anglican rosary beads have 33 beads and the Catholic rosary beads have 59 so they are very similar. It just comes down to the number of beads. The difference is 26 beads, that's all it comes down to. So, with only that small difference why is there so much killing, hatred, and division amongst two groups of people who fundamentally share the same cross of Jesus Christ and the same God. We are all the same, just people living on this planet together.'

Kevin ponders his thoughts then continues saying, 'Some say we are all human beings having a spiritual experience. I say we are all spiritual beings having a human experience. Love is the only truth. It is the same Jesus we all pray to. Just a different way we look at it with the same faith. It is just a different way we arrange it, just like the Rosary Beads.

So, I come back to my original point. Religion is manipulated by murderers and politicians to do bad things in the name of God.'

John who has been listening intently to Kevin says, 'You are right Kevin, love is the only truth. It is all fucked up. The right thing was to stop those IRA terrorists before they killed 11 people and injured 64. The Godly thing was to stop them.'

Kevin says, ' And we did not. So we are just as much responsible for their deaths as the government who ordered us to stand down and allow them to do it.'

John and Kevin are silent at this conclusion.

John says, 'It was never admitted, but the gardai did detect suspicious activity and arrested several suspected IRA men in Monaghan on the morning they bombed the Remembrance Day ceremony in Enniskillen.

Three men from Co Tyrone on the run from the RUC and living in Monaghan were stopped in a car in Monaghan hours before the explosion. The men were questioned and released but later intelligence reports suggest that they were almost certainly involved in the bombing, according to the officers.

'Queen Bee,' the leader of the terrorist cell, was also known by the gardai to have arrived in Monaghan the morning of the bombing. Yet, the Gardai did nothing even though they found it suspicious. They failed to detain anyone.

Kevin says, 'Well perhaps the gardai were told to stand down and ignore them just like we were ordered to do. It wasn't only us that were ordered to allow them to go free to perpetuate their atrocity.

Kevin continues saying, 'After the bombing our intelligence found out that 'Queen Bee' had driven west from Enniskillen after they had finished planting the bomb in the building owned by the Catholic Church beside the Cenotaph. Estimated at around 10.43 a.m. on Remembrance Sunday.

Kevin continues saying, 'Yet, she was allowed to escape even though our intelligence knew exactly her whereabouts.

John says, 'I realised I had been lied to by our superior commanding Officers. We had surveillance on that terrorist cell days previously. We knew they were planning a bomb attack and we did our jobs informing our superiors. Our superior commanding officers knew a bomb attack was imminent but deliberately allowed it to happen resulting in the deaths of innocent people.'

Kevin says, 'We had been used as pawns in a political game of chess to create this explosion at Enniskillen on Remembrance Day. Our superior officers knowingly refusing to stop a known terrorist attack, to stir up political animosity and public anger back in England and in America against the Irish Republican Army.'

John says, 'This IRA bombing was not an isolated incident during those times things were done to stir up tensions between the feuding Catholics and the Protestants. The powers that be, allowed murders of innocent people on both sides to take place if it benefited them. The IRA and UDA were prepared also to sacrifice innocent lives for their own political gains.'

John continues saying, 'I feel guilty for not preventing the IRA terrorist cell. We had them in our sights, complete intelligence on them from our surveillance. Under orders of our superiors, allowing them free to carry out this murderous atrocity on innocent civilians.

Kevin says, 'I have anger towards my so-called honourable leaders who lied to me. Their betrayal has had a dramatic emotional and psychological effect on me. Jocky being killed in an assassination attempt on our team ordered by my own government.

Kevin says, ' Now, it's only me, you and Tom who are still alive.

John says, 'I felt guilty for the murder of innocent people so I vowed never to take a human life ever again.'

Kevin trying to console John says, 'It was not us, we were just doing a job under the illusion, we were fighting the enemy as British Soldiers,'

Kevin and John are silent again. John is in deep thought as he knows that this vow never to take a life again prevents him from taking his own life. That is why he felt he was still involved in the fight against the IRA by disposing of the bodies of the IRA Operatives that the UDA interrogated and executed.

After their own government set them up in an IRA ambush. John's team were never the same again. Jocky was dead and Kevin injured. Tom left the army and worked with the UDA.

Tom introduced John to the UDA high command. Tom became a go between for the UDA and the British Army. A deal was struck that John would dispose of the dead IRA operatives, discreetly by feeding them to pigs.

In the deal Kevin, who was too injured to do much, was allowed to live with John in the safe house. The UDA would set them up in an isolated cottage on the borders of the republic to perform the disposals. So, john became the pig feeder.

In the deal with the UDA, John explained to them that he would never kill for the Ulster Defence Association, only dispose of the dead bodies. The UDA took up John's offer. John disposed of the dead corpses in the only efficient way he knew, feeding them to Pigs.

John says to Kevin. 'I need a drink.'

John exits the room and comes back ten minutes later carrying a tray with two cups of tea and biscuits.

Kevin says, 'That was not the drink I imagined but it's fine.'

They both take a biscuit and have a slurp of tea.

Kevin says looking at his biscuit, 'Oh yes, chocolate digestives are the best'

John admiring his biscuit says, 'Of course Kev, rich tea biscuits are too dry like a camel's armpit and normal digestive biscuits are okay but chocolate digestives take the biscuit if you pardon the expression.'

They both laugh like kids.

Kevin says, 'I like to dunk my biscuit in my tea and wait just until the biscuit is soft enough to hold as much tea as possible. But without breaking off and losing it in my cup.'

John says, 'I always stick to the five second rule. Any longer than five seconds dunking your biscuit and you are risking losing it into your tea. More than five seconds and you are dicing with death with your chocolate digestive.'

Kevin changing the subject says, 'Talking of seconds and dicing with death. Do you remember the three second rule, back when we grew up in South east London?'

John replies saying, 'Of course, I have never forgotten it. I still stick to it even today.

Kevin says, 'If you are out walking in the street and someone looks at you for more than three seconds then it is like fighting talk in South east London.

John says, 'When we were growing up, I would never look at a stranger in the street for more than three seconds without the prospects of confrontation. Back in the day in south east London if i am looking at a man in the street for more than three seconds, I am officially classed as staring him out. That's fighting talk back then. There is a high probability I am going to be pulled up and confronted, normally with the question, 'You got a problem mate ?

Kevin laughing says, 'South East London unwritten code. Do not stare at anyone more than approximately three seconds unless you want trouble. If it is a woman that was different but definitely not a man. You do not stare for too long at someone without there being consequences. If you are minding your own business when you're walking in the streets in London, you never look at anyone for more than three seconds. If you're not asking for trouble and minding your own business. Plus, you don't know who you are staring at. There were some proper gangsters around our way.'

John interjects saying, 'Yeah, a lot of plastic ones too. All mouth and no trousers but the real ones were proper hard bastards.'

Kevin continues saying, 'I remember the three second rule, once when I lived in Kent outside London for a couple of months on detachment with the regiment. I couldn't cope with people staring at me when I was out walking around the town. These people completely had no idea of the unwritten rule of London. People would stare at me for more than three seconds, I felt like everybody was out looking for trouble. It was difficult not to get aggressive to these country bumpkins. In London, if you mind your own business, you don't stare at people for too long, unless you know them.'

John and Kevin both laugh.

John says, 'Yeah, I remember the three second rule Kev.'

As John is speaking, he pulls his biscuit out of his tea and manages to eat it while it is soggy. Enjoying the biscuit John says, 'You cannot beat a Biscuit and a cup of tea.'

Kevin says, 'You mean, you cannot beat a Chocolate digestive and a cuppa.'

John puts his cup back down onto its saucer and places it on a small side table beside his armchair.

Chapter 4

The Pig Feeder - An Friothalai Muice

It is early morning and John and Kevin are already up. John and Kevin are in deep conversation.

John says, 'One of the best ways to get rid of a human body without leaving any evidence is, John pauses for dramatic effect then says,

'Feeding the body to Pigs.'

'To Feed a body to pigs, in particular hogs or big pigs is the best way to get rid of a body without a trace.'

John is in the bathroom on the toilet having a crap.

John is talking to Kevin who is leaning in the doorway of the bathroom listening intently.

John, still seated, wipes his backside as he continues saying, 'These pigs will eat virtually anything and leave no trail apart from.' John interrupts his own conversation as he simultaneously stands up and pulls his trousers up saying, 'Teeth and hair, they will eat everything apart from teeth and hair.'

Kevin has been listening closely to John then says, 'So, what do you do with the teeth and hair?'

John now pulls the toilet chain and continues saying, 'I burn the hair in the open fireplace in the front room. It makes a strong burning smell but it's the quickest way.

John pulls up the zip on his trousers and stands in front of the wash basin washing his hands. Kevin says,' And what about the teeth, what do you do with them?

John says, 'Football.'

Kevin says,' What do you mean, Football?'

John continues saying, 'I fill an old football with them, so it rattles. Then, I put the football in the pig pen for the pigs to play with. The pigs love it. They play around with the ball with their snouts, as it rattles with the teeth inside.

John continues saying, 'I think it breaks up the monotony for them between meals. It is like a football match, sometimes the way they fling that old ball about with each other. It is like they are really enjoying themselves.

Kevin grins, saying, 'It's a bit like watching West Ham.'

Kevin starts laughing saying, 'Get it ? West Ham, Ham, as in Pork, as in Pig.'

John does not laugh as he is in deep thought reminiscing about something.

Kevin has stopped laughing at his own joke and seeing John staring into space says, 'What are you thinking about John ?'

John says, 'I am thinking about my dad and how much I miss him.' My dad always loved pigs all his life and it was pigs that ended his life.

Kevin says, 'How do you mean ? Pigs killed your dad?'

John in a melancholy mood says, 'When I was growing up my dad had some pigs on his allotment. Me and my dad always looked after them. We fed them and cared for them for years.

One day my dad was mucking out the pig's pen. He always did this early in the morning before he went to work. He had a massive heart attack and died right there in the pig pen.

It took hours to realise that something was not right. My dad had not turned up to work. I was only nine years old. I was just a kid. When I got home from school. I heard that my dad was missing and had not been at work. I just knew he would be at the pig pen. I ran all the way straight to the allotment and that was where I found him.'

John is staring aimlessly into space as if reliving that memory all over again in his mind. John then continues saying, 'When I found my dad there was not much of him left. The pigs had eaten most of my dad, just leaving the scalp and his torso. There were parts of him scattered about the pig pen. I will never forget what I saw that day for the rest of my life.'

That terrifying scene disturbed me for years. I refused to talk for six months. I completely retreated into myself. My dad was such a loving, kind man, and he was all I had after my mum died. But now he was gone and I was alone. I was put into foster care and eventually met you Kev and we became best buddies.'

Kevin smiles at John saying, 'Damn right! Brother.'

John and Kevin smile together in recognition of their lifelong friendship.

John then continues saying, 'I had counselling but was never the same again. At first, I had anger and hatred for those pigs. But as time went on and I grew up, I came to the realisation that these animals had the right idea on life.'

This comment shocks Kevin who says, 'What do you mean?'

John continues saying, 'Even though my dad cared and gave affection to those pigs. When it came to it, sentimentality and emotions meant nothing. Those pigs just saw my father as a piece of meat. They viewed my dad as food to survive on.'

John continues saying, 'The practicality of survival is the only priority for those pigs. No emotions, just cold-blooded decisions.'

John continues saying, 'The pigs had no emotional attachment in life and that attitude appealed to me.'

Kevin is still stunned by John's thoughts but continues listening as John continues saying, 'I eventually respected the pigs for their unemotional attitude to life and learned to adopt this mental mindset myself. Ultimately this led me to be the cold-blooded, calculating killer that I became. This resulted in me enrolling into the British army, which led me to be a member of the SAS. It was my personal mantra in life as a human being for many years. No sentimentality or emotions, just survival. No emotions, just practicalities as a cold-blooded killer. The results that come from that is the only thing that matters'

John pauses for a moment in a reflective mood then says, 'However, I took on a new attitude to life after allowing those IRA bastards to detonate that bomb at Enniskillen. After seeing a young girl die in front of me, killed by the blast that I could have prevented, it changed me. My time in Northern Ireland opened my eyes and changed my opinion on life. Every human being on this planet has a right to life. Everybody has the right to live in safety and peace. After Enniskillen, I received an epiphany vowing never to kill again. I have stuck to it ever since.'

There is a ring on the doorbell, and this disturbs John and Kevin's conversation.

John opens the door to be confronted by the same old man who previously delivered the dead body of an IRA Operative.

He is back with more deadly deliveries. The weather is typical, and the rain falls heavily on the ground and on the old man.

The rain soaks into the old man as he stands there. The rain does nothing to affect the old craggy looking stone-faced pensioner.

Like the grim reaper's personal delivery man for the dead, he opens the boot of his car to reveal three more dead bodies.

This time two men and a woman lay in the boot of the car. They are all naked and with black bags over their heads. They are slumped like rag dolls over each other.

They are all covered in cuts and bruises. Their skin is discoloured from the effects of torture.

John takes the bodies inside with the help of the old man. They struggle with the male bodies, but the woman is quite light to carry.

Kevin watches in the background, through a window in the cottage.

John takes another brown envelope from the old man. No words are exchanged from the wrinkled faced corpse courier, this old man's face as old as the jagged rocks of Ireland. A face well-worn in from time. His skin has a patina to it and The old man shows no emotion and says nothing.

The man leaves and john and Kevin are left stand over three corpses laying haphazardly on top of each other on the kitchen table.

Kevin says, 'Come on then, they won't prepare themselves for dinner'

John picks up one of the men, heaving it up onto his shoulder. The corpse is of a large man. John staggers into the butchering room with it.

John uses all his strength to manoeuvre it onto the butchering table. Dropping it down with a big bang, as it lands it shakes the table.

John grabs his butchering apron which is made of worn out brown leather. The apron is marked and stained from use. The brown leather appears blackened in some areas where the blood has soaked into the leather deepening and discolouring the colour. The kind of leather apron that would not look out of place on Jack the ripper himself.

John talks to his army colleague Kevin as he prepares the dead man for disposing. John likes to describe the process of how he prepares a dead body for feeding to his Pigs. How feeding a dead body to pigs is the best way of getting rid of a dead body.

John says, 'As you know, a Pig eats everything apart from hair and teeth.

'For that reason, the large bones of the body need to be broken into small pieces to help the pig digest the bones. Have no doubt, they will eat the bones if prepared correctly.'

Preparation is the key, so I always have a black plastic sheeting already on the butchering table, that I lay the body onto. This way I can wrap the prepared body into a bag so I can bring it down to the hanging hut, as I like to call it. I hang the body to improve the tenderness of the meat for the pigs to eat. The process is called ageing, it allows the enzymes in the body to break down the proteins and improve the eating quality.

John pauses thinking to himself then saying, 'I digress, where was I ? Yes, the plastic sheeting or bags. As I was saying, it must be strong plastic, not like some plastic sheeting you can buy which is too thin and will not hold the weight of the body parts. No cheap bags, you need to buy the more expensive heavy duty plastic bags in the shop. Cheap is no fun when you have to clean up all the intestines off the floor because they fell out of the bag when it split. I know from experience when I have bought cheap before and have paid the price, if you pardon the pun.

Nowadays, I always spend that extra and get strong bags. It pays to spend that extra on your plastic body bags.'

At this point John stops and looks around and notices Kevin is not there in the butchering room.

John is alone. John is not fazed by this and continues talking to himself in a slightly delusional fashion.

John seems to repeat himself saying, 'Plus, the strong sheeting keeps everything clean. Strong plastic bags keep all the body parts, entrails, blood, and fluid, nice and tidy. You are better off buying the heavy-duty plastic bags in the shop, they are a little bit more expensive but in the long run more cost effective. The thin plastic bags can break, and you must then double up the bags, so you don't really save yourself any more money buying cheaper.'

John continues saying,' The body must be shaved, and teeth and dentures removed. As previously mentioned, pigs cannot digest teeth or hair, which is about the only thing they cannot eat.'

John cuts the body in various places on the corpse to drain the blood. John says, 'Draining the blood away makes less mess when the pigs eat the body.'

Blood starts to pour out onto the table. The blood then drips onto the floor off the table. John stops and again looks around, this time Kevin is back in the room and quietly listening. John, seeing Kevin is back, says, 'Don't worry about that blood, I will mop that up later.'

John continues saying to Kevin, 'I hang the body after cutting the main veins, so blood drains out. Blood can be poured into the soil outside or poured into the pond at the bottom of the lane. To properly drain it, I hang the body in the hanging hut. There, the remaining blood will run out into the hay on the floor.'

Whilst cutting and piercing the body John takes a bottle of whiskey and takes a swig from it. John lifts the bottle to the heavens to salute his fallen comrades who were killed in action by the IRA. John pours some of the alcohol over the dead body as a kind of ritual. As if a respectful salute to his opposing enemy.

Kevin is now watching this from over John's shoulder.

Kevin says, 'I remember Jocky, he always swore that Scottish whiskey was the best whiskey. He always made us have a swig before we went into battle. It helped when we needed extra Dutch courage and as Jocky would say salute to the Gods of War.'

Kevin continues saying, 'I will never forget the way he looked at me when he got fucking blown up when we were ambushed by the IRA.'

Kevin in a sombre voice says, ' Jocky never made a noise just stared at me straight in the eyes, not even blinking. He looked at me as if to say fuck me this is it, I'm dying and just like that he went without even closing his eyes. Jocky, his eyes just stared through.

Kevin looks down saying, 'I will never forget that Jocky. He was hard as fucking nails. A proper geezer.'

John is quietly listening to Kevin's story and then takes a second swig from the whiskey bottle saying, 'Yes, cheers to you Jocky, this one's for you,' John half-heartedly raises the bottle looking as if he is still in shock at the thought of his mate Jocky dying.'

As John finishes swigging the bottle. John angrily stabs the lifeless body with his other hand. It is as if John is taking out his frustration on the body, for the death of his comrade.

John then looks at the dead carcass laying in front of him and puts the bottle of whiskey down beside him. John continues with his butchering skills on the dead body.

John continues to stab and cut the dead body. John talks saying, 'No one understands what we had to go through. I mean civvies, normal people, they think we are like characters in a fucking war film, not fucking human beings with feelings. I know we signed up to this and took the queens shilling but we are human beings, seeing our mates blown up and killed.

John continues saying, 'They think we are unfeeling fighting machines.' As John says this, John snips the dead man's ear off with a pair of scissors, chucking it in a big bucket on the floor. John continues, saying, 'We have got feelings too.' John continues to snip the other ear off, throwing it also into the bucket on the floor.

John continues saying, 'That is what we get drilled into us at training school, that we are machines. That is done only to give us the confidence and the bravado to get the job done. John pauses his conversation and picks up a large hammer then says, 'I mean, what we had to see changes you.'

John then hammers the dead body repeatedly to the crunch and the crack of breaking bones.

John says, 'I don't feel like a person, more like a fucking alien. I mean it leaves you mentally in limbo with a multitude of feelings. I feel lost, sad, angry, and ashamed.'

Kevin says, 'what do you mean? Why do you feel ashamed?'

John continues saying, 'I mean, that I survived, and my mates did not. They were good people, you know heroes. Not a fucking, fuck up like me.' John says, 'I deserved to die and they didn't nor did the innocent civilians murdered on the 8th November 1987. I will never forget Enniskillen on that Day.'

Kevin, now also in a sombre mood says, 'If you call it being alive.'

John nods his head as he continues with his preparation of the dead body.

Kevin says,' Your right mate, we are not alive. I died when we allowed those Fucking IRA Bastards to blow up innocent people. I don't want to live, not after that.'

Kevin continues saying, ' We are just dead men walking mate'

John nods again in agreement.

John then continues with a club hammer in his hand. John starts to hammer down on the corpse's head to break the bones of the skull, yellow fluid and pieces of brain seep out of the broken skull. John puts his hand into the open hole in the dead man's head. The brains are in pieces after the trauma it has received from the hammering. John carefully pulls all the main pieces of brain out and throws it into the bucket.

John starts repeating himself again saying, 'Breaking up the body like this helps the pig's digestive system. It keeps the pigs bowel movement regular as clock work. Breaking up the big bones so the pigs can chew easily. This process tenderises the body.'

John then hacks at the body with a meat cleaver. John places the entrails and flesh of the dismembered carcass into what looks like a builder's rubble bucket which is still on the floor.

John picks up a large axe then pauses looking at Kevin.

John, feeling philosophical, says, 'I do not fear death, I embrace it. It will be my release.'

John then swings the large axe up in the air and with one swipe chops the dead man's head clean off in one precise swoop. The head makes a thud as it rolls onto the floor.

John is completely calm and oblivious to the fact, he just cut off a man's head.'

john says, 'I am alive and they're dead, it's not right.'

John picks up the severed head and drops it in the big bucket on the floor, containing the other body parts.

John then picks up the bucket which is heavily weighted down by now from human remains.

Kevin says, ' I thought you were going to wrap the body in the plastic sheeting like a body bag to hang the body up in the hanging hut. Instead, you have chopped it into pieces. John, looking detached from reality says, 'I changed my mind.'

John kicks the door of the butchering room open which leads outside to the pig's pen.

John walks out into the light towards the pigs to feed them with the bucket of human parts.'

John tips the contents of the bucket into the pig pen. The screech of excitement from the pigs as they chomp and gnaw at the human remains with glee.

John and Kevin both lean on the wall of the pig pen looking at the pigs.

Kevin says to John, 'Do you have names for them?'

John says, 'Who?'

Kevin says, 'The pigs'

John says, 'Fuck off, what do you mean like Pinky and Perky?

Kevin says, 'Well, yeah you know, I just thought you would give them their own names.'

John replies saying, 'Seriously fuck all that. There is no sentiment with these bastards.'

John continues saying, 'These pigs don't give a fuck about you or me. They are void of emotion, they see you and I as just meat.' Their survival is the only incentive over anything and anyone. Unemotionally hard as nails. There is no sentimentality with these swine. They are here to do one job. and that is fucking eat everything and anything to survive.'

John continues saying, 'Mate, if me or you got ill and fell in there, they would have no problem in eating us alive, if we lay there long enough. They do not care, we are all the same to them, just walking meat.'

Kevin is shocked into silent thinking. Kevin then says, 'Then best I don't fall in there and laughs.'

They both start laughing with amusement as they continue to lean on the wall of the pig's pen.

John says, 'They would make easy work eating you mate. You need sixteen pigs to finish the job in one sitting, so be wary of any man who keeps a pig farm. They will go through a body that weighs 200 pounds in about eight minutes. That means that a single pig can consume two pounds of uncooked flesh every minute.'

John continues saying, 'This breed of pigs here are called Poland China.'

Kevin interjects saying, 'That sounds like a high-class prostitute.'

John smiles saying, 'You may joke Kevin, but these bad boys are one of the biggest breeds of pigs you can get. They weigh about 800 pounds of pig.'

John says, 'I starve them for a few days then feed the chopped up corpses to them and they love it. It is like a feeding frenzy. They eat everything up, no problem. No mess, just a nice clean job. I had sixteen pigs here at first but one died so there are only fifteen now but that does not affect how quickly they dispose of the evidence.'

John continues saying, 'The Poland China breed originated from Texas in the middle 1800s they are a tough breed. They can survive anywhere tough as old boots these bastards. The Poland China pig was bred between 1835 and 1870 in Ohio, America. They cross bred a Polish pig with a Big China hog so that is how they got the breed's name.'

Kevin says, 'That is an unusual pairing of nationalities.'

John says, 'This breed has the record for the heaviest pig ever. His name was Big Bill and this hog weighed approximately 2500 pounds. It lived in Tennessee in the early 1920s. These breeds of pigs are hard bastards. They will survive in any environment.'

John continues saying, 'My dad had some when I was young. They were the ones that ate him when he had his heart attack and died. They just saw him as meat and food to feed on. No sentiment, no emotions. So, when I had the opportunity to make myself useful and help the UDA dispose of their IRA dead bodies, I was the right man for the job.'

Tom made the UDA aware I had some previous knowledge and expertise in pig farming and the opportunities that go with that. Through Tom the UDA asked me for my services in waste disposal.

With my advice they set up the human waste disposal system at this cottage. I suggested getting Poland China breed pigs to eat the dead bodies from my own experience with them. They are the best eating machines they will happily eat anything and everything,

So, here we are using pigs to dispose of IRA Operatives once they have been interrogated, tortured and executed.

My conscience is clear as I am not taking a life, only disposing of the dead bodies. I see it as a waste disposal. I get some revenge on the IRA for Jockey. So, I take out the trash.

So, that is how this has all come to be, with me and you living in this cottage.

Kevin says nothing.

Chapter 5

The Resurrection - An aiseiri

A female body lays on its back on the kitchen table. It is silent. The quietness of the room makes the kitchen feel like a chapel of rest, for this departed soul.

After some time, the serenity of this chapel is broken with the clank of the latch on the cottage front door. John returns from outside.

John is still wearing his butcher's apron covered in blood from preparing and feeding the previous dead body to the pigs.

John heads straight to the table and scoops the woman up in his arms.

John carries the woman into the butchering room and lays her on the butcher's block. The deceased female is laying on plastic sheeting which John has already prepared as part of his routine.

The plastic sheeting to prevent any bodily waste and bits of flesh being discarded and causing a mess.

John begins his work and looks around to pick his weapon of choice to stab the female carcass. John has his whiskey bottle at hand for another toast to a fallen enemy.

John takes a steel skewer from his array of utensils. John holds the metal skewer in his hand to cause a downward blow and puncture the woman's body. John lifts his hand to strike the first incision into the dead woman. John concentrates and aims the sharp point of the skewer to land directly between the women's bare breasts.

As John holds his fist up in the air ready to plunge it down. Something jolts John's mind, it freezes johns' hand in the air. Holding the pointed skewer up straight, ready to stab this female corpse.

Kevin appears behind John from out of the darkness of the room saying, 'What is wrong John?'

John ponders his thoughts saying, 'I am not sure, something isn't right.'

John continues saying, 'I just have this feeling as if something is wrong. A gut feeling, a weird feeling has come over me.'

John puts down the skewer and says nothing but just listens. The room is silent. John tilts his head, so his left ear can focus its attention. John thinks he hears something.

Kevin again says, 'What is wrong?'

John says, 'Wait, I am listening.'

The silence gets more prevalent, as they both keep quiet.

Kevin says, 'What is it?'

John looks down on the corpse and slowly lowers himself down to the level of the dead body, still laying on the Butchering table.

Kevin nervously repeats his question saying, 'What is it John?'

John holds his hand up to Kevin. As if to say stop talking as johns' eyes are fixated on the head of this dead woman. The dead woman lays stretched out in front of John.

Johns' eyes are wide open as if his senses are heightened.

John pinpoints his attention on the face of the dead woman. Her face is still masked with a plastic bag over her head. Unbelievably, John sees the plastic is moving very slightly. It can only be noticed, if you are specifically focusing your attention on it.

John is stuck rigid, focusing on it with shock and disbelief. John stares in amazement. Ever so slightly he sees the layer of plastic wrapped around the woman's mouth rising and falling.

The silence is overwhelming. Suddenly, the corpse jolts up as the dead woman takes a big inward gulp of air from inside the plastic bag. This is a gulp for life.

John, who is crouched down close to the body, falls backwards onto the floor with surprise. John lands on his backside, then immediately jumps up to his feet. The dead body lays back down on the butchering table.

Now, seemingly alive the woman is struggling to breathe. The plastic bag over her face is severely restricting her mouth to breathe. As she fights for life, the rest of her body is motionless, just her head struggling to breathe.

John is frozen for a second. His brain is trying to make sense of what is happening and what to do. His mind pushes his brain into gear, and John instinctively grabs to break the plastic and allow the woman to breathe. As John does so, the woman gladly gathers in as much air as possible. Gasping for life. The woman still with her eyes shut, lays back down motionless on the butcher's table. Alive and breathing the woman is calm and breathing regularly.

John and Kevin are silent just looking in shock at this living, breathing corpse as alive as a newborn lamb in springtime.

They both are thinking it without needing to say it. 'What the fuck do we do now?'

Kevin, who is standing behind John says, 'It's Fucking alive!'

John says, 'She! is Fucking alive you mean, it's a female, a woman and she's laying there alive, resurrected from the dead.'

John quickly runs out of the butcher's room into the kitchen. John goes straight to the final masked corpse on the kitchen table. John rips the plastic bag off its head to see if that dead body is still living. However, it is obviously dead as half its face is missing.

John runs back into the butchering room where Kevin is still standing, watching over the corpse, which has miraculously rises from the dead.

Kevin looks in amazement and says, 'John, what are we going to do with her?'

John thinks for a few seconds processing his train of thought then says, 'Nothing, I'll just do nothing.'

Kevin says, 'Nothing ! you can't do nothing, you have a living and breathing IRA Operative in your custody.'

John says, 'I'm not going to kill her, you know that Kevin.'

Kevin says, 'Yes, I know you took a vow never to kill again, so just let the Ulster Defence Association know and let them deal with it.'

John shaking his head says, 'No, If I do that, I'm sentencing her to death as they will just send someone down here to kill her.'

John continues saying,' It would just be like killing her myself but without getting blood on my hands. No, I'm not doing that.'

Kevin says, 'If you let her go, she will inform the IRA and they will know where we are and come and kill us.'

John says, 'Yes, that is true and that is why I'm going to do nothing.'

Kevin says, 'John, if you do nothing, you know she will probably die of her injuries without medical attention.'

John says, 'If we take her to the hospital or doctor, it will get back to the IRA and the UDA and they will both come down and kill us twice over.'

John and Kevin pause as they both consider the problem. After thinking it over, John turns to Kevin saying, 'Well then, there's only one thing to do, I'll have to nurse her back to life and keep her here under lock and key, until I figure out what to do with her.'

John continues saying, 'That is if she survives.'

Kevin in deep thought looks at John and says, 'Yes, I suppose that is the only answer for now.'

Johns' attention turns away from Kevin and back to the woman. John lifts her up in his arms. John carries her out of the butchering room and away from death. John brings her to safety into his bedroom, laying her on his bed.

Kevin has followed John into his bedroom saying, 'So, I guess this will be the makeshift recovery room?'

John nods to Kevin as he covers the woman with a blanket.

Kevin rubbing his hands and head nervously starts to appear uneasy saying, 'I need some air to process this.'

Kevin walks out of the bedroom.

John hears the front door of the cottage open and close as Kevin disappears.

John goes into the kitchen where the final dead body is still laying on the kitchen table. John picks the corpse up and carries it into the butchering room to process the body for the pig's dinner.

As John enters the butchering room, the door closes behind him. This shut the rest of the world out. The only evidence to indicate John is in the room is the sounds of the hammering and thumping, as John prepares the pigs' supper.

Chapter 6

Salvation – Slanu

Some time has passed and it is evening in the cottage. The woman given salvation from death, is laying in John's bed and still alive.

John is looking at this vulnerable human being laying helpless in front of him.

Without his care, she is condemned to die of her injuries. Injuries inflicted while in the custody of the Ulster Defence Association.

As John looks at his patient, he systematically examines the woman's body for injuries. John stands over the woman and scans her body with his eyes, area by area. As he looks over her body, he also feels the woman with both hands, searching for any broken bones or bumps.

John assesses the woman from head to toes. John rolls her from side to side checking the woman underneath, then rolls her back flat on the bed. Once John is content that he has completed his assessment, John sits down.

He knows it will not be easy nursing her back to life. John is committed to his convictions that there will be no more loss of life where he is concerned.

John is seated on the edge of the bed and places a notebook on the bedside table and takes out a pencil from the bedside draw underneath. John starts writing in the book.

Kevin is back in the cottage from his time out on his own. Kevin is now seated at the back of the bedroom in an armchair.

Kevin is curious about John's notebook saying, 'What are you doing mate?'

John says, 'I am writing down notes of the woman's medical condition and triaging her injuries.'

Kevin, intrigued, says, 'So what is wrong with her?'

John, still seated on the side of the bed, looks at his notes and says 'Well, she has a broken left leg.

Broken right upper arm, dissociated index finger and thumb on the right hand.

Dislocated thumb on left hand.

Multiple bruises and lacerations to her face and body.

Incisions and lacerations around her head and scalp.

Broken right cheek bone.

Deep cut to the bridge of her nose.

Chipped front tooth.

Missing various teeth, top and bottom.

Cigarette burns to the left cheek of her face and to both breasts including her nipples.

Additional cigarette burns to her back and both legs.

Bruises and swelling to left side of her head.

The lower part of her left earlobe is missing and signs of infection on the remaining fleshy tissue on the ear.

She has a high fever and rapid, slight, pulse.

'More importantly she has a bullet wound between her lower left shoulder and her left breastbone. The bullet has gone straight through with the exit wound at the rear between her left shoulder blade and spine. Luckily missing her major organs.'

John pauses for thought then continues saying, 'My assumption is probably the bullet was meant for the woman's heart, when they went to execute her, at the end of her torture. Obviously, the UDA operative got sloppy and careless, not hitting the heart area correctly or maybe they just were a bad shot, fortunately for her.'

John says, 'They must have used a rifle to shoot her which is unusual.'

Kevin says, 'How do you come to that conclusion, Mr Sherlock Holmes?'

John says, 'Well, the bullet made a deep but narrow wound in and out, for both her entry and exit wound in her body. A bullet does not cut the human tissue as it hits the body but in fact, crushes the tissue causing a cavitation in the tissue. The difference is size, and depth of the cavitation is caused by the diameter, mass, material design and velocity of that bullet.'

John continues saying, 'Judging the bullet wound, a rifle bullet would most likely be the size hole and design to her flesh sinus of the wound. A bullet half diameter like a hard solid copper alloy material aka a rifle bullet. A rifle bullet, only crushing the human tissue directly in front of it as it penetrates, would match the bullet wound.'

John continues saying, 'A rifle bullet causes a deep narrow channel to the wound. Hence, it exited her body missing her vital organs, luckily for her. Any other bullet type would have created a bigger area of damage on entry and exit and affected her major organs which would have killed her.'

John continues saying, The rifle bullet made a more temporary cavitation than permanent as the human tissue flowed around the bullet causing a deep and narrow wound. Just like the one we see on this woman. So, I conclude, she was shot with a rifle.'

There is silence.

Kevin is staring at John with an open mouth then bursts out laughing. Kevin says, 'Fuck me John, I wish I had never asked you.'

You are a bloody anorak, A specialist on bullets. In fact, I would go as far to say you're a bullet trainspotter.'

'I bet you collect the numbers of your favourite bullets.'

John, breaking from his concentration, laughs too saying, 'Screw you.'

Still laughing, Kevin says, 'You should go on mastermind, specialising in the secret life of bullets. You sad fucker.' Kevin continues to laugh even louder.'

John smiles then says, 'Did you not learn anything when we were at basic training.'

Kevin says, 'No, not really. I was too busy getting drunk with Jocky and shagging women.'

John laughs saying, ' How you passed I will never know,' John closes his notebook.

Kevin says, 'So, what is the prognosis Dr John?'

John pauses for a moment then Looks at Kevin saying, 'Basically, in medical terms, She is proper fucked.'

Kevin is silent for a few seconds.

John says, 'There is one thing I have noticed Kevin.'

Kevin, intrigued, says, 'What?'

She also has what I would call crucifixion wounds. Kevin is silent as John continues saying, 'This poor soul has had large nails banged through her hands and feet. There are large holes in them. She also has a wound to her side and marks to her head, like puncture wounds as I explained earlier.

Kevin is shocked, as if this has some significant meaning.

Kevin says, 'We have seen them before John, and we all know whose trademark interrogation that is.'

John says, 'Yes, regrettably I recognise those wound marks as the handy work of the crucifer.'

Kevin concurs saying, 'Yes, there is only one interrogator in the UDA that does that to her victims.'

John says, 'Yes mate, only one monster that does that to people. I would recognise those crucifixion wounds anywhere. No one else would do these crucifixion wounds on victims. Only she would be so sadistic and obsessed about Jesus Christ and the crucifixion, to do this. No one else would dare imitate her particular interrogation style, for fear of her retribution. As she likes to think that this specific evil torture was her trademark and no one else's.

Kevin says, 'There are monsters everywhere you look. Just like the female leader of the IRA cell that we let go to kill innocent people at Enniskillen. Another monster.'

John says, 'Yes, I agree mate. Now we must live with the guilt for the rest of our lives for not stopping that evil bitch and her gang of murders blowing up the cenotaph.

Kevin says, 'I had heard after the Enniskillen bombing, she escaped to America because of all the animosity around the bombings even from some of her own people.

John says, 'There is evil on both sides and we were stuck in the middle of it.'

Changing the subject Kevin says, 'Is your patient going to live?

John ponders for a few seconds then says, 'She will live mate because I'll make sure of it. I promised myself there would be no more death and no more collateral damage when I am involved.'

Kevin nods in agreement saying, 'We have seen too many dead people. No more mate. Not for us.'

John says, 'The next 24 hours are critical whether she pulls through or not . If she does, then her injuries will take about 2 to 3 months to heal.

Kevin says, 'What are you going to do if she does not make it?'

John looks at Kevin saying, 'Well, then she will be dinner for the pigs.'

John and Kevin are silent as they reflect on their dilemma.

John realises he will need to use his army medical training, if he wants to save this woman's life. He previously honed his medical skills in the field of battle.

John is fully aware that it would be too risky to take her to a hospital or to a doctor. If it was discovered she was alive either by the UDA or the IRA, all their lives would be in danger.

John breaks the silence saying to Kevin, 'For this type of bullet wound. I will use petroleum jelly to keep the wounds from becoming infected. It is better than using alcohol. I find it heals slower when I use alcohol. It will heal a lot quicker with Petroleum Jelly.'

John feels excited at being useful again. John says, 'I still have the medical equipment from the regiment, from our days on operations. I still have loads of stuff from our army days. In my mind, I still feel I am in the regiment. It is like I never left. In my heart I'm still a soldier.

Kevin nods in agreement saying, 'I know how you feel. I feel the same way too brother. Once a soldier, always a soldier.'

John says, 'I need to set up an intravenous drip for her. She has lost a lot of fluids. She needs to get those fluids back quickly, if she is to stand any chance of pulling through. I need an intravenous drip. Let me see what I have in my storeroom.'

John goes out of the room.

Ten minutes have passed before John returns. John enters the room with a large, camouflaged bag which he dumps on the floor.

John starts taking out tubing and a plastic container.

Kevin sits up in his chair intrigued at what John is doing.

John searching through his bag says, 'I have no supply of Intravenous fluids, so I'll need to make it up, homemade style.

John says to Kevin, 'Can you remember what we would use to make homemade intravenous fluid?'

Kevin instantly replied saying, 'To make your own intravenous fluid you need six teaspoons of sugar. A half teaspoon of salt. One litre of clean drinking or boiled water and it cooled and stored in a fridge.'

John says, 'I am impressed Kevin, you did learn something at army training.'

Kevin grins saying, 'Me and Jocky always used it to help our hangovers, after a heavy session on the booze. It is perfect for rehydrating the body which in turn soothes a hangover.'

John smiles and raises his eyes to the heavens in disbelief at Kevin's comment.

John says, 'What are you like? You and Jocky were always getting up to mischief at the training centre.'

John then turns his attention back to his patient and starts to set up a makeshift Intravenous Drip.

John starts talking to himself to remind himself what to do, saying, 'Right, to assess her responsiveness to the intravenous fluid therapy, she needs to be laying down horizontally. I need to raise her legs 45 degrees, so the blood returns to the centre of the body. If the blood pressure increases within 30-90 seconds, the patient is likely to respond positively to the Intravenous fluid.'

Kevin has fallen asleep in his chair. Oblivious to johns' medical ramblings.

Even though John sees Kevin asleep in the chair. John continues to talk his way through the medical procedure, saying it out loud to himself.

John props the woman's legs up with bed pillows and at the same time stretches over and holds the woman's wrist. John uses his watch to take the woman's blood pulse. John waits patiently, timing her for 90 seconds. John smiles saying to himself, 'That's my girl, yes, now we are getting somewhere.'

John is happy with the woman's responsiveness and lays the woman's legs back down.

John then takes various objects from his bag.

John continues to describe his actions out loud saying, 'Now, to create an IV bag. I get a large clear plastic bag. Insert a syringe into a corner of the bag, piercing the bag. Then, I remove the plunger of the syringe. John does the actions as he talks.

John continues talking to himself saying, 'Once this is done. I connect the tubing and valves to the syringe and with a sterile needle attach it to the end of the tube.'

John continues saying, 'Then, I fill up the clear plastic bag with homemade intravenous fluid until the bag is 75 percent full. I then tighten the opening of the bag and hang the bag above the level of the patient. Gravity will then create downward pressure on the intravenous fluid and push it into the patient's vein.'

John stops talking as he concentrates inserting the needle into the blood vein of the woman's arm. John is nervous doing this but does it with ease.

John smiles at himself proudly, saying, 'You still get it, John.'

Once done john opens the release value on the tubing. This is to allow flow of fluids into the woman's body to rehydrate her.

John again holds the patient's wrist and times her blood pressure for 90 seconds.

John smiles and says, 'Yes, it's working.'

Johns' excitement stirs Kevin to wake up from his slumber. Kevin, blurry eyed, sits up saying, 'What's happened?'

John says, 'It has worked.'

Kevin, still half asleep, says, 'What has?'

John says, 'The IV Fluid.'

Kevin, impressed with John, says, 'Well done mate.'

John says to Kevin, 'I will need to straighten her broken bones next, so they can heal correctly.'

Kevin says nothing. He seems to have fallen asleep again in the armchair.

John carries on talking, as if Kevin is listening.

John takes the bed covers off from over the woman.

John looks at her broken leg and lays his hands on it. John positions himself lower down the bed, so he can have a straight view of her legs.

John grabs hold of the woman's left ankle and slowly pulls and tugs at the limb until it is straight. Obviously painful, the woman groans, even though unconscious. This sign of pain does not phase John, who is in deep concentration. John is on a mission to straighten the woman's broken leg.

John manipulates the limb until he is sufficiently satisfied it is straight. Amidst the moans of his patient, John ensures the leg is set correctly.

Now the woman's leg is done. John moves on to the woman's fingers and thumbs. John straightens them one by one. The woman repeatedly groans with each manipulation of the bones. Even though still unconscious the pain is felt.

Once John has completed his bone manipulation, he checks his patient, to evaluate his handy work. Pleased with his progress, John ensures the female patient is comfortable before leaving the room. John returns with bandages and gauges, as well as a pair of scissors.

John then proceeds to bandage the woman's broken limb. John wraps the limb with gauze roll bandage until the leg is completely wrapped.

John exits the room returning with a bucket of water and a bag of builder's plaster powder. John places it next to the bed and opens the bag of builder plaster powder. John then tips the contents of the bag into the bucket of water and proceeds to stir it up.

Kevin appears over John's shoulder saying, 'What the fuck are you doing now?'

John, not fazed by Kevin's comment, continues to stir. Eventually, John replies saying, 'I am making a plaster cast for her leg.'

Kevin, 'What! Are you joking with me? You're using builders' plaster?'

John says, 'Yep' as he continues stirring the mixture.

Kevin says, 'Have you gone out of your mind? That is for plastering walls, not for medical stuff, like broken bones.'

Kevin laughs saying, 'Fuck me, I have seen it all now.'

Kevin walks away and disappears from sight.

John lays a separate cover sheet under Philomena's leg and finishes stirring the plaster mix. John then puts his hands into the bucket and scoops out a handful of plaster. John begins rubbing it all over the woman's bandaged leg.

John smooths the plaster mix all over the leg until it is sufficiently covered to johns' requirements.

John then leaves it to dry.

John enters the bathroom and washes his hands. John then cleans up the bedroom and returns the bucket back into the kitchen.

Kevin is now back and sitting in his chair at the back of the room.

John comes into the bedroom with a razor and shaving foam in his hands.

Kevin says, 'Now what are you doing?'

John says, 'I must shave her head. I need to get to her wounds on her scalp and stitch them up.'

Kevin says, 'Well, it makes a change to shave the head of a person who is not actually dead.'

John kneels next to the woman's head and gently cuts her hair with a pair of scissors. John cuts it in chunks until her hair is short enough to shave.

John patiently shaves her head. He then washes her bald head and pats it dry with a towel.'

Once her head is dry enough John then attends to the puncture holes and lacerations inflicted to her scalp.'

John is aware of the wounds to her hands, feet, and the side of her body. This is reminiscent of the crucifixion torture treatment by a prominent figure in the Ulster Defence Association. Nickname,' The Crucifier.'

John treats the injuries from the barbed wire crown placed on her head. Inflicted in the romper room whilst prisoner with the UDA. John knows too well the crucifix wounds that he sees on this woman, as the work of a infamous female interrogator, the crucifier. She was one the chief interrogators. John knows all about the woman called the crucifier and her sadistic depraved party trick, of crucifying her victim after interrogating.

The crucifier became notorious for her crucifixion techniques which involved placing a steel barbed wire crown on the victim's head. After that, the hands and feet would be nailed to the floor and finally the side of the victim's body would be pierced with a knife or sword. Mimicking, in the bible, when Jesus Christ was interrogated and crucified on the cross. The woman in front of John has obviously been interrogated by the crucifier. John is now desperately trying to save this woman.

John attends to the wound on the side of the woman's body. Once done, John treats the puncture holes in her hands and feet, where nails had previously been hammered. John stitches these wounds carefully and gently.

John is amazed how this woman has survived the type of injuries she has sustained.

Kevin is in his armchair, watching in silence as John treats the woman.

John uses his army knife and army suture kit to repair her wounds. His suture kit is basically, the medical sewing kit for the human body. John, still talking to himself, says, 'I will stitch up the wounds that need stitching, I will need to remove the stitches around the 5th or 7th day. John clears and cuts away dead flesh and infected skin around the woman's injuries.

John sews up the deep cuts and lacerations on the woman's body hoping that he can save her life.

John, satisfied with his stitch work then moves on to the other wounds not needing stitching but needing cauterization. Cauterization is the burning of the wound to prevent bleeding and stop infection. John leaves the woman for a moment, going into the kitchen.

John turns on the gas hob of the cooker. John gets a sharp knife and proceeds to heat the knife up on the flame of the hob.

John examines the knife to see if it is hot enough. With a sense of urgency, he returns to the woman.

John knees down next to the woman who is still silent being semi unconscious

With precision and in deep concentration John lays the red-hot knife onto the lacerations he previously stitched. John uses the heated knife to burn the flesh which seals up the wounds.

John then pours his whiskey alcohol over the cuts then lights the alcohol with his lighter. Flames briefly cover the wound in the hope it will sterile the damaged area.

John looks over to Kevin saying, 'I must keep all her wounds clean and dry. If a bandage becomes wet or dirty, I must replace it. If this happens, I must remove the bandage and wash the area with soap and water. Use a wet cotton swab to loosen and remove any blood or crust before applying a new bandage. It is important to be disciplined in this to avoid any infection.

Kevin is silent but listening.

John cleans the woman as she has messed herself with urine and excrement due to being unconscious. the woman is naked and John puts an incontinence pant on her.

Kevin says, 'Where the fuck have you found those big knickers.

John says, 'Luckily, I came across a pack of incontinence pants I found that must have been here from the elderly couple that lived at the cottage before we moved in.'

Kevin smirks saying, 'I take it they are new pants and not used?'

John says, 'Very funny, of course they are new pants.'

John says to Kevin, 'Her flesh wounds should heal within 10 days, if they do not get infected. I'll check the wounds daily for signs of infection. I will also need to check her for numbness in her extremities. If her wounds bleed for longer than 24 hours, they could be infected. Swelling of the wounds, redness or the wound oozing pus is a sign of infection. We can only wait and see now, if I have done a good job.'

Kevin says,' Well you have done your best John. The army trained you well brother. I think you have done a great job.'

John continues to monitor the woman and feels her head and body noticing she has a fever.

Concerned about the fever, John uses a wet cloth to cool the woman down. John repeatedly wipes the woman's forehead with a wet cloth.

John ensures the woman has a light covering over her in bed so as not to overheat her body. The woman seems comfortable and in deep sleep for the night.

John takes up his seat next to the bed for his usual night-time vigil, watching over his patient.

Kevin has fallen asleep in the other armchair at the back of the room and is snoring.

ACT II

Chapter 7

The Troubles - Na Triobloidi

The morning comes and the dawn peeps through the curtains in the cottage. The air in the bedroom is stale from the previous night's sleep.

John opens his eyes, still sitting in an upright position in his chair, from his night vigil over his patient.

John had been up in the night mopping her brow for her fever.

Her screams and cries during the night from nightmares were terrifying to hear. John physically held her during the night to try and comfort her. The woman seemed to get some solace from John holding her.

John looks over at the woman who is now sleeping and seemingly comfortable after her difficult night. John leans forward in the chair to feel her forehead. This confirms her fever has greatly improved. John feels a sigh of relief at this positive news, a fact which gives John great satisfaction.

John turns around to check on Kevin who is still asleep in his chair at the back of the room. Kevin is still snoring but at a much quieter level than previously during the night.

John takes the bed cover from off the woman to check her wounds. After examining the wounds, she seems to be in good condition with no obvious signs of infection.

John takes her incontinence pants off. He then cleans up the excess spillage of urine and excrement that seeped through her pants during the night.

John finishes cleaning her up. As John places new incontinence pants on her, he hears the woman whispering some words.

Her words are indistinguishable, but she starts to move her head as if she is waking up.

john comforts her by saying, 'It's ok, you're ok, relax, take it easy'

The woman is becoming more conscious. She is aware of John nursing her but is so weak that she cannot speak. She doesn't move much, just looks around confused about where she is.

The woman realises the reality, that a needle is in her arm, and this panics her. The woman reaches to remove it. John seeing this, grabs her hand preventing her from removing the needle

John holds her hands and says, 'Easy, it is ok, you're safe. let me do it.'

The woman is struggling to speak and agitated

John smiles at her and says, 'Really, it is ok, your safe just relax.'

The woman calmly lays her head back into the bed, she is too weak to do anything

John removes the needle and moves the homemade IV Drip away from the bed

The woman mutters saying, 'Where am I? Who are you?'

John says, 'You are in a safe place and I'm a friend, just rest.'

John continues sayings, 'What is your name?'

The woman says, 'Philomena.' The woman too tired for any further conversation changes her gaze from John. The woman looks up at the ceiling and closes her eyes to sleep.

John seeing this covers the woman with the bed cover and leaves her to sleep. John walks out to the kitchen. In the kitchen, john takes a square tin from off a shelf and carries it over to the kitchen table.

John reaches into the tin ,removing two painkiller tablets and lays them on the table. John picks up a knife and starts crushing up the painkillers on the table surface. John uses the side of the knife to do this.

John then scoops up the granules of the tablets.

John fills a glass with water and brings it to the table. John then scoops the granules into the glass and stirs with a spoon. Holding the glass, John walks back down the hallway and into the bedroom.

The woman is awake lying horizontally on the bed staring at the ceiling in thought.

John approaches the bed with the glass of water in his hand.

John says, 'Drink some water it will help.'

John puts the glass up to the woman's mouth saying, 'just take a few sips it will help with the pain.'

The woman raises herself up in the bed to tries to drink John supports the woman's head and holds the glass of water with his other hand. The woman sips the drink. She coughs, it has been sometime since she has drunk fluids. The woman drinks a few further sips with John still holding the glass for her. This rehydration seems to perk the woman up. After gathering her thoughts, she asks john, 'Who are you and where am I?'

John pauses thinking what to say then answers saying, 'My name is John and I'm a pig farmer. I found your body by the roadside and took you in. Since then I have been helping you back to health'

Johns' eyes look down uncontrollably feeling guilty for his lies but unsure what truths to tell her.

John asks, 'What is your name?'

The woman says, 'Philomena.'

The woman looks around the room taking in her surroundings Then she says, 'Philomena Martinez.'

John says, 'Will you have some soup, Philomena?'

Philomena nods at John who smiles and exits the room for the kitchen.

Philomena becomes more aware and is now fully conscious.

She realises she is naked apart from wearing incontinence pants. Obviously, she also realises that John has seen her naked as her wounds have been attended to. The thought of this makes Philomena feel uncomfortable and vulnerable.

Philomena understands that this man has rescued her for some unknown reason. Philomena's memory is now coming back. She remembers lastly being in the romper room. She realises she has escaped from death as her previous interrogators tried to murder her.

Philomena lays back still in a state of shock trying to gather her thoughts

She remembers she was last in the hands of the UDA. She is straining to remember everything but remembers being tortured and beaten. Her thoughts are disturbed by John opening the bedroom door. John returns holding a tray with a bowl of soup and bread.

John says, 'I have some soup.'

John places the tray on the bedside cabinet. John picks up the soup bowl and with a spoon he goes to feed the woman.

Philomena is horizontal but raises her head up to the spoon. She is unsure of John, but this is secondary to her hunger. She lets John feed her. John also helps her drink so more water from the glass. Philomena takes her time to swallow her drink as John helps her to hold the glass. As she does so, they lock eyes which seems to momentarily give them a sense of connection. Just seconds but enough for both of them to feel something. An attraction that they both quickly ignore but subconsciously has registered between them.

After Philomena finishes her drink she says in a weak voice, 'Can I use your phone? I need to call my brother?'

John is nervous but he tries to stay calm saying,' There are no phones, and the cottage is very isolated' John pauses then continues saying, 'Just rest for now and I will help you get to your family or friends, I promise.'

John leaves the room only to return in seconds with a ladies nightdress in his hands. John says, 'I got you this to wear. I hope it fits. I think it will, it's new. I found it in one of the cupboards, must have been here when I moved in. I will leave it next to the bed for you to put on.'

Philomena is unsure of John but she knows there is little she can do because of her injuries. Philomena tentatively smiles at John, then lays back in the bed to rest.

Philomena knows she is too weak to do anything.

John takes the tray with the empty soup bowl back to the kitchen. Philomena has now fallen asleep.

Meanwhile, john is washing up the bowl at the kitchen sink

Kevin appears from over his shoulder saying, 'So, when are you going to tell her?'

John says, 'Tell her what?'

Kevin says,' Where she really is and what has really happened to her.'

John says, 'What do you mean?'

Kevin continues saying, 'That she was really presumed dead after being tortured and supposedly murdered by your colleagues, the UDA. To top it all, she was delivered here as a piece of meat to a makeshift human abattoir. Waiting for you to chop her to be eaten for dinner by porky pig out there.'

John is silent, thinking what to do.

Kevin continues saying, 'Oink! Oink!'

John shouts, 'Kevin that's enough.'

Kevin smiles and disappears from over his shoulder.

Philomena sleeps into the night. John sits by her bedside watching over her until he falls asleep too.

For the next few days Philomena sleeps most of the time.

John continues his daily routine to feed and hydrate her. John checks her wounds for infection and monitors her temperature.

There are few words exchanged between John and Philomena as she has fallen back into a semi-conscious state.

Philomena manages to wake enough to eat and drink sporadically.

John continues his duties of caring for her wounds and cleaning her after she has messed herself.

Kevin continues to sit in his chair at the back of the room, usually sleeping.

One morning Philomena wakes up feeling much stronger from her prolonged rest and recuperation.

She is surprised how well she feels

She notices that John is not sitting in his chair and is absent from the room.

Looking around the bedroom she sees framed photographs on the walls These photographs are too far away for her to see in detail

Intrigued Philomena struggles up off the bed to get a closer look at the photographs. Philomena moves slowly across the carpet of the room. Philomena's willingness for more knowledge pushes her on and nearer to the photos.

As she approaches the photographs they soon start to come into focus.

To her horror her eyes reveal a terrible secret which has been kept from her.

Philomena sees John is pictured in these photos as a British soldier standing proudly along with his British army colleagues in full battle dress.

To her shock she realises that she is in the company and care of her worst enemy, a British army soldier.

Philomena simultaneously has an overwhelming sense of anger and vulnerability.

She wants to react and move but the pain and injury prevents her from walking properly.

Philomena manages to get to the window only to see John carrying a body out of the boot of a car and into the cottage.

The body is of a naked man, its face is covered with a black bag and appears to be dead. This makes Philomena really scared which heightens her sense of urgency to escape. Philomena is stuck rigid as she considers what to do. She has no sense of time as she quickly tries to conserve a plan of action.

Suddenly, John enters the room carrying a tray with soup

John sees the bed is empty. As the bedroom door closes behind him Philomena is standing behind the door with an old-style bed pane in her hand. She sends the bed pane crashing down onto the back of John's head. This knocks John to the floor and unconscious.

Philomena looks at John out cold on the carpet.

Dropping the bed pane, Philomena steps over John and tries to walk herself out of the room. Philomena finds it difficult to walk.

Philomena struggles with her injuries and in particular her broken leg. Her will to escape is pushing her. However, as she gets to the bottom of the hallway, Philomena capitulates and lays on the floor unable to continue.

Philomena's injuries are too serious for her to move, she is helpless and lays on the floor crying.

After a few minutes laying on the floor. Philomena can hear john groaning from back in the bedroom as he regains consciousness.

John stumbles out of the bedroom and as he gathers his bearings, he sees Philomena laying on the floor crying.

John walks over to Philomena. Philomena has her arm covering her face while she sobs in tears.

Philomena realises John is approaching her. Philomena lashes out at him shouting, 'Fuck off, you English Bastard. Keep away from me, soldier boy.'

John realises Philomena has uncovered the truth. John says nothing but instead tries to help her up.

Philomena slaps him in the face multiple times uncontrollably.

John does not move to defend himself, he just says nothing and tries to pick her up.

Philomena spits in John's face and slaps him.

John stops to wipe the saliva from his face.

Philomena, laying on the floor in more pain from her wounds because of her exertions.

She looks at John hatefully. She lays on the floor in tears

John without warning grabs Philomena up and puts her over his shoulder. This creates obvious pain from Philomena's broken leg and injuries.

Philomena says, 'Put me down, you bastard.'

Philomena tries to hit John, but this has little effect on John.

Philomena screams in objection as John marches back down the hallway with her over his shoulder.

John enters the bedroom and drops Philomena, unceremoniously onto the bed.

Philomena shouts and screams at him saying, 'You fucking English murderer.'

John sits down in his usual bedside chair saying nothing.

John makes a big sigh as he looks intently at Philomena, who stares back at him with stubborn eyes.

John shakes his head and sits looking at Philomena.

Philomena is quiet now panting heavily after her ranting. The pain and upheaval of her assertion has tired her out. Philomena is struggling to stay awake still muttering obscenities under her breathe.

Philomena soon falls asleep. John continues to look at Philomena now she is asleep. John ponders his thoughts on the latest turn of events. John looks at the photography of him and his army colleagues on the wall. John realises how Philomena came to discover his past.

John is startled by Kevin who is sitting in the chair behind him, reading a superman comic.

Kevin says, 'Well, she is trouble. She is a real firecracker.'

Kevin smiles and continues saying, 'She is very fiery, your new girlfriend. Rather you than me mate. Good luck with that one.'

Kevin then closes his eyes and goes back to his own thoughts reading his comic. John now also falls asleep.

John is dreaming of his childhood. It is a happy place full of sunshine. John is dreaming he is back as a five years old child. John is in the park playing football with his dad.

John dreams he is smiling, absorbed in a warm magical light.

John is back in his childhood memories. John feels the sun on his face and smells the freshly cut grass of the park as he plays. In his dream John feels a sense of complete love as a child with his parents.

John kicks the ball to his dad who kicks it back.

Johns' mum lovingly watches John as he plays with his father.

John's mum speaks to him saying,' I love you son, I love you so much'

In the dream John is like a voyeur. An adult of himself watching over this beautiful memory of himself from his childhood.

As his dream continues, John sees himself as a child holding his mum and dads' hands. In the dream John and his parents begin to walk away. The dream starts to fade.

John is calling saying, 'Come back, come back.'

But in Johns dream all three including him as a child fade away.

John feels happy and privileged at seeing his parents again. Simultaneously John is sad at knowing it is all a dream. John misses his parents.

John wakes up back in his chair in the bedroom. It is morning and Philomena is calling to John.

Philomena has woken up to the realisation that John has handcuffed her left hand to the bedpost.

Philomena tugs her handcuffed hand, desperate to release it. The handcuff is secured tightly. Philomena has one free hand and one handcuffed.

Philomena looks around angrily to see john sitting in the chair asleep.

Philomena shouts over saying, 'Wake up soldier boy, wake up and take the handcuffs off me. You got no right to chain me up like this, you Bastard'

John has his eyes closed as if still asleep and calmly says, 'Language please.'

This infuriates Philomena who shouts, 'I'll give you bad language, you fucking British Bastard'

John, opening his eyes, says, I am not British actually. I am more Irish than British.'

Philomena, belligerently surprised, says, 'What are you fucking talking about?'

John says, 'I am both Irish and British. Both my parents are Irish. They are born and bred in the republic of Ireland. My mother was born in Dublin. My father was born in county Carlow. So, technically you are incorrect.

I was born in England. South East London born and bred. So, actually, I am Irish and English. I am proud of both nationalities.

Philomena says,' Well then, you are a traitor.'

John says, 'No, I am London Irish.'

John smiles and continues saying, 'Also known as a geezer.'

Philomena says, 'You think you're funny you Bastard. But you didn't look so funny laying on the floor, unconscious after I'd hit you over the head.'

John ignores her comments and says, 'So what have you been doing for the Irish Republican Army? To be interrogated and supposedly killed by the Ulster Defence Army?'

Philomena says angrily,' I am not part of the IRA, my brother is part of it. They interrogated me to try and get my brother's whereabouts from me. They want to capture and kill him but I would never betray my brother, so they killed me or think they have. '

John, intrigued, says,' So, you do not want a united Ireland?'

Philomena says, 'Of course. I do but I am a pacifist and believe that the only way to really achieve a free united Ireland will be peacefully and politically' Philomena continues,' I want your lot out of Ireland forever, but we play into the British Government's hands by using violence as it gives them an excuse to justify themselves being here. Violence leads to violence but intelligent peaceful pressure will unify Ireland. We will win our Country back'

John says,' Well, Good Luck with that, as all I see is violence. I cannot see how that will ever stop between both extreme elements the IRA and UDA, so I guess you will be waiting a long time'

Philomena says, 'You are a murderer, I saw you carrying in a body from a car outside, your evil how can you live with yourself.'

John says, 'I stopped living a long-time ago but that's a different story. I am not a murderer, I just take out the trash. Trash being your IRA mates who have been interrogated by the Ulster Deence association.' The same IRA that killed my mates.

Philomena interrupts says, 'You are the trash, you are a psychopath and a weirdo.'

John smiles saying,' Well, this psychopath saved your life when you were on death's door. This weirdo has cleaned you up when you have messed yourself unconscious.'

Philomena says, 'Was I one of those bodies you carried in ?'

John in a hesitant voice says, 'Yes.'

Philomena says, 'So how do you dispose of the bodies?'

John seems uncomfortable with Philomena's question but then relaxes and says, 'Well, if you really want to know, I chop them up and feed them to my pigs outside?'

Philomena says, 'What the fuck? You chop the bodies up and feed them to your pigs?'

John says, 'Yep. They call me the Pig feeder.'

Philomena, 'You are a Fucking Psychopath and a weirdo.'

John laughs saying, 'Well your lucky I did not chop you up'

Philomena is silent feeling afraid of her new reality

John seeing Philomena looks scared so changes the subject and says, 'You don't look like a typical Irish woman.'

Philomena has dark eyes and had long black shoulder length hair before John cut it all off. She has olive skin and is about 5 foot 4 inches.

Philomena, surprised at the comment, says, What do you mean?'

John says,' You look more Spanish or Italian with your dark features. The typical Irish look is more like ginger or red hair with pale skin. You have dark eyes and you did have long dark hair before I unfortunately had to cut it off.'

Philomena says, 'Yes, you cut my hair off?'

John says, 'I had no choice, I had to get to your head wounds to stitch them or they would have become infected and life threatening. If it helps, I think short hair suits you.

Philomena dismisses the compliment saying, 'Yeah, whatever.'

Philomena continues saying, 'My family originated from northern Spain in the Basque region. A little seaside town called San Sebastian. I do have some distant relatives who still live there. I have not been back to see them for many years. I last went when I was young. My brother has been back and has many contacts and friends in Spain. Many of them are members of ETA, the outlawed Spanish separatist group. ETA means Euskadi Ta Askatasuna translated into English and reads Basque homeland freedom. My brother uses his contacts to liaisons with ETA and the IRA. ETA and the IRA have close ties with each other. They are both looking for independence in their country.'

John says, 'Well, no wonder they wanted your brother, if he is connected to ETA. Another extreme group of murderers like the IRA and the UDA. They are all mad.'

John, changing the subject, says, 'Anyway, it is time for food.'

John gets up from the armchair and goes out of the room. John is gone for some time. Philomena still pulls at her handcuffed hand to no avail. John returns with a bowl of soup and some bread for Philomena, on a tray.

John sits down on the side of the bed next to Philomena. With a spoon, John goes to feed Philomena her food.

John tries to feed her, but she turns her face away

Eventually Philomena takes some food in her mouth only to use it as a weapon and spit it back into john's face.

Patiently, John puts the soup bowl down on the side table saying, 'I will leave it for you to help herself.' John wipes his face with a tissue and throws it like a basketball into the bin.

John then leaves the room.

Philomena reaches for the bowl of soup but struggles to lift it because she is so weak.

Philomena in the end drops the bowl of soup back onto the table unable to use it.

Philomena now realises how vulnerable she is, and that John is in fact, her carer.

This brings a stark reality to her, that she is in a new situation. She realises that her main aim is to survive.

Philomena is very much aware that her opinion of John must be secondary, if she wants to survive. She must forget that John is her enemy and put aside her differences, if she wants to live. As human beings in life, we all need each other at some point, regardless of our differences.

The basic rule in life is to survive and live your life. Ultimately, you must let go of hatred and revenge towards your enemy and co-exist with them.

This epiphany is difficult for Philomena to come to terms with, but she knows she must if she wants to survive.

Chapter 8

Reconciliation – Athmhuintearas

It is late morning and Philomena is laying in the bed still handcuffed by one hand. Philomena is restless and irritable, stuck in bed unable to move courtesy of her handcuff. Unable to contain her frustration she starts shouting and screaming at the top of her voice. This progresses into her banging her body up and down on the bed and pulling at her handcuff.

The noise is loud and is enough to summon John into the room. As John enters the room this gives rise to even louder screaming aimed at John. Johns' ears struggle to filter this mayhem of noise. John grabs Philomena in a surprise fit of anger. John holds her still and shouts at her saying, 'What do you want me to do?' There is silence from Philomena.

The fact Philomena has got a reaction from John startles her which makes her stop in her tracks.

John sits down next to Philomena on the side of the bed. John now in a calm voice continues saying, 'You should be dead, and I saved you.'

Philomena then shouts back at John saying, 'I don't need your help, you are my enemy, you are a British soldier and have killed my people and my country.'

John says, 'My mates were killed by you and your fucking IRA Scum, so don't go there.'

John continues saying, 'You should be dead. I had to keep you alive and now I'm stuck with you until you are well enough to go your own way.'

Philomena says, 'Let me go now.'

John, defiant, says, 'No, because if I let you go, the UDA will find out you're alive. They will not stop until they have killed you. If I take you to your IRA Colleagues, they will kill me and Kevin.'

Philomena says, 'If you release me, what do you care if the UDA find out and kill me?'

John points at Philomena saying, 'You and your fucking friends in the IRA may not think a life is worth anything but I do.'

John continues saying, 'A long time ago I made a promise to someone never to be the cause of anyone's death. I'm not going to be responsible for yours.'

Philomena says, 'Don't be so dramatic. Just let me go, I won't get killed.'

Philomena pauses, then says, 'Well, what are you going to do with me?'

John says, 'I don't bloody know.'

Philomena and John are both silent.

Philomena breaks the awkward silence saying,' Why are you helping the wombles?'

John says, 'What do you mean the wombles?'

Philomena says, 'The UDA, I mean.'

John says, 'Why do you call them the wombles?'

Philomena says, 'Where have you been? Don't you know?'

John says, 'No.'

Philomena replies saying, 'We call those UDA Bastards wombles, like the furry characters from the kids tv programme called The Wombles in the 1970s.

John says, 'I don't understand.'

Philomena says, 'Because of the fur trimmed Parka jackets they all wear. They look like the furry animals from the tv programme. It's like a sort of uniform to them.'

Philomena continues saying, 'Do you not know anything?'

John stays quiet and does not reply.

Philomena in a more passive tone continues to say, 'What are you doing here?'

John says, 'I help dispose of their dead for them.'

Philomena says, 'What do you mean?'

John says, 'I take their dead and put them to rest.'

Philomena, angrily says, 'Don't fool me. You mean you dispose of the bodies of people they murder. Are you delusional?

Philomena continues saying, 'You chop them up and feed them to fucking pigs. You are not putting them to rest. Your recycling them as fucking food for pigs.'

John stays silent.

Philomena says, 'You're an animal'

They are both quiet.

John says, 'You are not well enough to go anywhere yet. Once you have healed you will have to go far away from here. Like America or Europe, someplace like that.' John looking moody says, 'You can go to the moon for all I care once your well enough you're not my responsibility then anymore.' John gathers his composure and says,' You can go where you like but until that point you are staying here with me, until you are well enough.''

There is silence again

Philomena in a lighter tone then says, 'You say your parents are Irish, what part of Ireland?'

John pleasantly surprised at the congenial conversation replies saying, 'My mum was born in Dublin. She moved down to County Carlow in the south east of the republic of Ireland when she was a baby. A little town called Bagenalstown.'

Philomena says, 'Yes, I know it well, you mean Muine bheag.'

John says, 'What ?'

Philomena says, ' Its proper Gaelic name is called Muine bheag.'

John, ignoring Philomena, continues saying, 'My Dad was from Borris, a small village also in County Carlow, Ireland. After they were married, they both emigrated in the 1960s to England like a lot of Irish.

John reminisces saying, 'I remember when they would look for lodgings in London. I remember seeing the sign in the windows of the lodging houses saying, 'No Dogs, No Blacks, No Irish. I remember the discrimination and harassment they received in England. I remember seeing my dad and mum being jeered at and insulted by strangers because they hear their Irish accent. It was very upsetting to hear as a child. I was born in Lewisham in South east London and grew up in Eltham. South East London Born and breed. There is an easy atmosphere as the two are both reminiscing about their childhood.

Philomena says, 'I remember growing up in Belfast during the troubles. I remember people who were Protestants, spitting at my mum and me in the street as we walked past. Just because we were catholic. As a child growing up in Northern Ireland. I remember seeing the British soldiers swearing at my father for being catholic, trying to provoke him.. I remember then seeing my dad beaten by British soldiers when he answered them back.'

Philomena stares into space reliving her memories, 'My dad was a good man, he was a republican but did not believe the Irish Republican Army was the answer to unifying Ireland. My dad knew that Ireland will only be reunified together as one when its people come together in peace. His faith taught him of love not war regardless of their religious beliefs. I will never forget seeing his head swollen up like a Melon after the soldier had attacked him.

John says, 'Me or my mate would never have beaten or mocked anyone. We were proper soldiers.'

Philomena looks sceptical at John and says nothing, politely ignoring johns' comment.

Philomena continues her sense of nostalgia saying, 'My mother died when I was young so after my dad died from his drinking, my brother was the only family I had.'

John listening intently interjects saying, 'My mum died when I was young too and I found my dad dead at a young age. The only family I had after that was the army'

Philomena suddenly feels her neck as if searching for something. She then starts looking in the bed and around the room in panic.

John, looking concerned, says, 'What is wrong?'

She replies in haste saying, 'My father's rosary beads, I have always had them around my neck since he died but they are missing. Where are they?'

Philomena starts to cry uncontrollably as she tries to look for the rosary beads. She feels pain from her injuries which limits her capacity to search for her father's Rosary Beads.

Finally, she stops her search and cries inconsolably, realising her father's rosary beads are gone.

Philomena drops her head down in sorrow as she continues to cry.

John says to Philomena, 'They would have been taken when you were interrogated, they were not on you when you were delivered to me.'

John feels ashamed and guilty after he finishes his sentence.

John realises that the bodies he has been taking consignment for all this time were real people with real lives. John has woken up to the realisation that these bodies were not just pieces of meat to be chopped up and fed to the pigs. The bodies he has chopped up were human beings deserving of the basic human right of a civil burial. They had lives and families and should not have been eaten by pigs after death. They have no grave to be visited or memorial stone to be prayed to. What John has been doing was wrong and Philomena has opened his eyes to that fact.

John has a moment of clarity and knows he must change the life that he has been living.

Philomena is seated upright in the bed, looking down in sadness and continuously crying.

John thinks for a moment, then without speaking, stands up and approaches Philomena seated on the bed. John then pulls out from around his neck his own rosary beads and crucifix. John takes it off over his head and he puts it over Philomena's head and around her neck. John says, 'This was my mother's. I always have it with me. It is not the same as your dads rosary beads but similar. At least it will feel like your fathers one is still there around your neck.

Philomena is speechless but before she can speak, john has walked out the room. John not really knowing what to say himself. In John's mind the gesture speaks for itself.

Philomena, in tears, stunned by the sentiment of kindness shown to her by john. Philomena, still in shock, is alone in the room with the memories of her father. She yearns for her late father and the unconditional love he gave her.

John is sitting by the table in the kitchen. John is consumed with guilt for being the pig feeder even though the bodies are dead when he gets them. John realises they were people with lives and families.

As John realises this epiphany, he is aware of the kitchen table surface under his hand. The same table that has put so many dead bodies for processing. John is silent in solitude with his thoughts.

Philomena is sitting up in bed. She has stopped crying and is calm now. Philomena is shocked by John's kind actions towards her.

Even more importantly she is shocked by the feelings she realises she has for John. Philomena has an unexpected attraction towards john.

Philomena cannot suppress these feelings even when she tries.

Her attraction for John goes as far as even affection for her previous enemy.

Philomena is tired and tearful from her upset. She falls quickly asleep.

The night is upon them. John resumes his night watch over Philomena, in his usual chair. Kevin, as per usual, takes up position in his chair behind john, at the back of the room. As always Kevin has fallen asleep and continues to snore through the night.

Kevin's snoring does not affect John or Philomena while they sleep.

In the night during the darkness John hears Philomena talking to herself. Philomena, still asleep, is saying, 'Please stop, please stop.'

Philomena's sleep talking develops into groans and then sporadic shouting. Philomena body tenses and relaxes. Her body spasms like she is in convulsions, as if possessed by the devil.

John watches, not sure what to do. It is obvious she is reliving a nightmare. John reaches out his hand and touches her forehead. She does not notice as she is in a deep sleep.

John notices Philomena is sweating and she is cold and clammy.

Philomena gets more violent in her movement and is now shaking. She murmurs random words which are broken with screams and shouts.

This prompts John to retrieve a key from his trouser pocket and unlock the handcuff on her wrist. John places this down on the bedside table.

John lays on the bed and holds Philomena, hugging her around the shoulders and wiping her brow. John caresses Philomena's head and her short hair. Philomena opens her eyes and looks directly at John, saying, 'Help it go away.'

John says, 'Help what go away Philomena?'

Philomena says, 'The nightmare.'

John says, 'It is gone, and you are safe, I am here for you.'

Philomena becomes calm and her feverish shaking has stopped. It is as if John's calming voice has purged her of her fear. Philomena is now relaxed and looking in johns' eyes.

Philomena whispers softly to John, saying, 'Inside, I want you inside me.

John says, 'No, you don't want me inside you.'

Philomena says, 'Yes John, I want you to hold me and I want to feel you inside me. I need to feel love.'

John is holding Philomena and their faces are so close they could kiss. John says, 'You are delirious, you do not mean this.'

Philomena says, 'I do mean it john. I want you to make love to me, now.' Philomena leans forward and kisses John on the lips gently. They pause for a second looking into each other's eyes. Without speaking they engage in a deep passionate kiss.

John pulls the bed covers off and gets inside. John gets on top of Philomena under the bed covers. The two embrace and continue kissing. Philomena relinquishes from kissing and says, 'Hold me john. Don't let me go. I want to feel safe forever. I never want to be scared again.'

John holds her saying, 'It is ok now Philomena. No one will hurt you, I promise'. John's words make Philomena feel better.

Philomena opens her legs from under John and says, 'I want you inside me. John is aroused and Philomena can feel John's penis which is erect and hard. Both of them are feeling attracted to each other and are increasingly horny to have sex. Philomena pulls her night dress up, being completely naked underneath. philomena then opens her legs wide enough so that John can enter her. John takes off his shirt and removes his trousers and pants. John throws them on the floor.

John now can smell Philomena's skin and feel the warmth of her body as he lays between her legs. They are both skin to skin. John manoeuvres his body, so his hard cock is now resting on top of Philomena's pussy. They are rubbing up against each other. John's cock is throbbing and he can feel Philomena's vagina is wet and juicy. John says, 'Are you sure about this?'

Philomena replies, 'Yes, I am sure, put it in'. John is exhilarated and using his hand guides his penis into Philomena's vagina. Philomena tips her pelvis up slightly to help John's cock go deeper inside. Philomena says, 'Augh!'

John stops and says, 'Are you ok?'

Philomena says, 'Yes, it's been a while since I have had sex and you feel big inside.' John touches Philomena's leg and is reminded of her plaster cast. John says, 'Your injured leg is still healing, maybe we should stop?'

Philomena says strongly, 'No way. I want you to fuck my brains out.' Philomena grabs johns arse and says, 'Fuck me.' John without speaking starts fucking Philomena. Philomena starts to moan and groan and John pants and grunts with pleasure. Philomena whispers to John saying, 'Kiss my neck.' John precipitates kissing her passionately on her neck, as he fucks her hard. Philomena continues to groan with enjoyment. The bed is shaking with the movement of the two of them. They both are in the throes of passion, hot and sweating. John catches his breath and says, 'I am going to come.'

Philomena, exhilarated by this, says, 'Yes, spunk inside me, fill my pussy up with sperm. Forget the pig feeder, tonight you're the pussy feeder and my pussy needs feeding. Fill it up with your cream.' Philomena, filled with excitement, shouts, 'Come on John! Fuck me harder.' John, indulging in Philomena's demands, bangs his cock into Philomena with more power.

Philomena scratches johns back as john fucks her as hard as he can. John says, 'I am coming' Philomena says, 'I am coming too, keep fucking me hard, you bastard.' Philomena, like a possessed banshee, then bites John's chest and nipples repeatedly. This act makes John ejaculate, he stiffens as he unloads his sperm into Philomena's pussy.

Philomena screams and groans as she simultaneously climaxes in orgasm. This results in rhythmic involuntary muscular contractions. Philomena feels the sperm inside her and this comforts her desire for love. John and Philomena are now motionless. They are still in the same sexual position. Both of them have their eyes closed and seem to be enjoying the feeling they have just had. John is the first to open his eyes and rolls off Philomena. Philomena has lowered her legs down flat on the bed now, from the spread eagle position. Philomena with eyes still shut is smiling and rubbing her clitoris, playing with her pussy.

Philomena opens her eyes and looks at her hands which have sexual fluid on them. Philomena takes pleasure from this sight. John and Philomena are both on their backs looking at the ceiling in thought. There is an awkward silence as they both comprehend what has just taken place. Without speaking, John touches Philomena's hand. Philomena smiles then holds John's hand. Philomena turning to her side pulls John next to her. The two of them lay on the bed holding each other. John is behind Philomena. In the foetal position they both are comfortable and content. They soon fall asleep together.

Philomena wakes up in the morning to notice that John is gone from her bed. John is back in his chair and more importantly, Philomena's hand is free from the handcuff. Philomena is surprised at this and looks at John.

John says, 'You are free to go.'

Philomena is lost for words and cannot believe these latest turn of events.

John, seeing her shock, says, 'You are correct Philomena. It is not right to keep you here. If you're well enough, you can go free. I won't stop you. It is your choice.'

John continues, saying, 'We are all human beings, and it is your God given right to choose what to do.'

Philomena gathers her thoughts then says, 'No, I will stay a bit longer to help with my recovery and to help you.'

John, bemused, says, 'What do you mean, help me?' Philomena says, 'To let go of your past and move on.' John says, 'It is too late for me.'

Philomena says, 'John, what are you doing here? you are a young man, with the rest of your life to live.'

John, angry and confused, says, 'I don't want to live. I do not want a new life. I am happy living this life.'

Philomena says, 'You are not living, you are dying here.'

John says, 'Well, then I will die here. I am already dead, just walking dead.'

Philomena says, 'Well, If you're dead then so am I. I too, have that pain and feeling of nothingness that kills you inside. That pain that makes you feel like nothing is worth living for. That feeling of sorrow and loss.'

John, ignoring Philomena, says, 'Go now and see your brother and be free.'

Philomena says, 'None of us are truly free. My brother is consumed with hatred. My brother is killing himself and others with his hatred.'

John says, 'Then go and save him.'

Philomena says, 'He is beyond saving but you are not. So, I'll stay here and we will slowly die together if need be.'

John says, 'Why can you not save him?'

Philomena continues saying, 'Because my brother is lost to revenge and hating, but you are not. You are just lost, John. You are just a lost soul that just needs to find the path back to redemption.'

John is surprised by Philomena's decision to stay but secretly comforted by it. John says, 'How do you suppose I find my path to redemption then ?'

Philomena says, 'Through reconciliation.'

John says, 'Reconciliation with who? the IRA?'

Philomena says, 'No, reconciliation with yourself.'

John looks at Philomena, reflecting on her comment but says nothing. Instead, John turns to his old record player and puts on a vinyl record. Classical music comes out from this old record player but very low as if you can hardly hear it. John sits back in his chair. John closes his eyes and listens to the music.

Some time has passed and the record player is still playing classical music. Philomena is sitting up in bed in deep thought. Philomena seems bothered in some way.

John stands up from the chair and turns the record player off. John moves towards Philomena saying, 'I need to treat your wounds.'

Even though she is now free, Philomena says, 'Don't come near me.'

John says, 'I need to check your wounds and change your bandages.'

Philomena feels emotional and vulnerable after what has happened between them in the night. Philomena says, 'I don't need your help.'

John contemplates on the fact they have slept together.

John says, 'Don't be so stubborn. If I don't do it, you could get infections.'

Philomena resolutely shouts, 'No, this is all wrong. I am confused with the way I feel for you and yet I cannot help it.'

Philomena says, 'Why are you doing this, why are you helping me?'

Philomena continues saying, 'What we have just done, it is all surreal. You are a British soldier and I am a Catholic. How can this be happening, but at the same time I want it to happen.'

Philomena continues saying, 'I should hate you, as you are my enemy, but I do not feel that towards you. I cannot help feeling attracted to you.' Confused with her feeling towards John Philomena starts crying.

John is silent. John wants to say how he feels about Philomena but finds it difficult to express his feelings to her. John wants to tell her he feels the same way and has feelings for her. Struggling to relay his feelings to Philomena he breaks the silence by saying, 'My mum and dad were from the Republic of Ireland and Catholics like your family.'

They emigrated to England in the 1960. As we discussed before, I explained that growing up I remember the discrimination that they faced. The abuse they received just for being Irish and no one cared.'

No dogs, no blacks, no Irish were the signs in the windows of the lodging houses. That is what my parents had to put up with, when they first moved to Britain. They first settled in Kilburn in North west London then they moved to Lewisham, where I was born. Finally, we settled in Eltham, South east London where I grew up..

When I was a child, I was always an outsider in some ways because I had Irish parents. I always supported Ireland at football and rugby or any competition between England and Ireland.

All the other kids supported England, so I paid the price for being different as a kid. The verbal abuse and fights were relentless because I had a different allegiance for Ireland. I looked the same as them and had a London accent but I had a different viewpoint than them.

But equally, when I would visit Ireland as a child with my Father, I would always stand out in the village. Coming from

London with a London accent. I attracted a lot of unwanted attention from the villagers, who disliked the British.

Again, I had to deal with the discrimination from the Irish with them taunting me and spitting at me, because they heard my London accent. As soon as I opened my mouth and spoke, I was a target. Again, I faced abuse because I stood out as different.

John continues saying, 'So, you may think it wrong to have feelings for me because you say, I am your enemy, but what you see is not what you get. I learned from an early age that it is ok to be different. It is ok to be yourself and to be proud of who you are. I am only one generation back from being like you. I am not your enemy. I see people through my own eyes, not through other people's eyes. I take as I find, and I make my own judgement on people.'

Philomena is listening to what John has to say. Philomena is curious and says, 'Ok then John, Tell me more about yourself?'

John continues saying, 'Ok, I grew up in a tough southeast London area. Most of my friends were either criminals or they had joined the army. So, I joined the army like my mates to have an opportunity to get away from my area and get a life. I didn't want to end up like some of my mates, either dead or in prison. So, I joined the army, not to fight you or Catholics but to get out of my toxic environment and get a new life. So, I might be your enemy, but I am also your friend at the moment trying to help you.'

Philomena says, 'But why do you want to help me? Why do you care if I live or die?'

John thinks for a moment then says, 'I made a promise to myself never to let another human life be wasted again.'

John pauses then continues, 'I was part of a counterintelligence group that allowed an IRA cell to slip through our fingers and detonate a bomb at the cenotaph, on Remembrance Day in Enniskillen. I was there after the bombing and found a young girl in the aftermath, she died in front of me. I promised myself that day I would never be responsible for the death of another human being. It is my vow as penance and guilt, to that young girl who had her life taken away and wasted so needlessly.'

John continues saying, 'On her last breath, I made a promise to myself that I would never be responsible for any more loss of life. No matter who they are or what the consequences are, I will never take a life ever again.'

Philomena, in a moment of enlightenment says, 'So, that is why, you saved me. It is your guilt.'

John says, 'I am not going to be responsible for your death.'

Philomena says, 'Is that why you scream in the night?'

John says, 'What do you mean?'

Philomena says, 'You hear me screaming in the night, but I also hear you screaming in the night John.'

Philomena continues to say, 'Is it the guilt and shame of your actions?'

John says, 'Yes, I feel ashamed 'John looks down feeling guilty. John looks at Philomena saying, 'Sadly, in this war of two opposing ideologies, people do not realise that we are all the same. We have more similarities than differences.'

John continues saying, 'For instance, The Catholics and Protestant religion both have rosary beads. Rosary is Latin for rosarium meaning the rose garden. The Catholic Rosary beads consist of 59 beads and the Protestant Rosary beads or Anglican beads are 33 beads. A difference of only 26 beads prevents them being the same. That is the only difference between both rosary beads. The only difference is the number of beads. They even worship the same God. These two sides are killing each other over their ideological differences when they are basically the same. How crazy is that? Foe or Friend it is all subjective.

John says, 'We need to ignore the labels that society wants to put on us and see each other as human beings. If we did that the world would be a much happier and safer place.'

John continues saying, 'At the Remembrance Day Massacre, I saw a beautiful young girl dying in front of me. It didn't matter what religion she believed in. When you, Philomena, had been delivered to me and I found you alive but dying. I did not see you as a catholic but as another human being needing my help.'

John looks at Philomena saying, 'So, if you are confused about your feelings for me because you think I am your enemy. Don't be.'

John says, 'I am not your enemy and never will be.'

Philomena is silent then asks, 'Tell me more about what you did as a soldier and what happened at the Enniskillen bombing?'

John explains saying, 'I was head of a four-man team, they were like brothers to me. We were SAS but were operating in counterintelligence. We were seconded into the Force Research Unit. A counterintelligence organisation operating both in Northern Ireland and across the border in the republic. Our task was to seek out IRA cells on Terrorist operations and to relay intelligence back to our superiors. Our superiors would then act on our intelligence. Then, they would make the decision to either order us to apprehend the IRA operatives for interrogation or if needed neutralise them.

Philomena, listening intently, interjects saying, 'Neutralise being another word for kill?'

John says, 'Yes.'

If the threat to life was imminent, we would usually be expected to eliminate the Terrorist cell. We were a successor from the infamous Military Reaction Force in the 1970s and succeeded by the Special Reconnaissance Force aka 14 Intelligence company in the 1980s.

There was me, Kevin, Jocky and Tom. Tom was my second in command. We were a tight unit. We joined together, went through selection together and fought together for many years like brothers.

In the late summer of 1987, a new IRA cell surfaced, and we began to track them. We found out that a 140 pound bomb had been made in Ballinamore, County Leitrim. An IRA terrorist cell of 30 people were planning to detonate it in Enniskillen.

The IRA Cell worked in teams. We were tracking the lead team with a young woman in charge of the IRA operation. By late autumn we discovered there was an imminent attack planned on the 8th November 1987, at the Cenotaph in Enniskillen. As per procedure, I sent a request to my superiors to detain or eliminate the IRA cell planning to perpetrate this atrocity.

However, I was told to stand down by my British army superiors. We knew the whereabouts of this IRA cell but we ordered not to physically detain them. Concerned for the safety of the public, I immediately filed a formal complaint to my superiors. I officially requested permission to eliminate the IRA cell as an immediate threat to the lives of the public. We were told by our superiors that in no circumstance should we engage or interfere with this IRA Cell.

Myself and my team were threatened with court-martial by my superiors unless we stood down. So consequently, we stood down allowing them to go free. Subsequently, after this action, the attack happened. The IRA cell planted the bomb in the town church reading room which was next to the cenotaph. November 8th, 1987 should have been no different than any other Remembrance day. Bystanders had gathered on a pavement, protected from the rain by the Catholic Church building called the Reading Rooms. An IRA bomb planted inside exploded, collapsing the gable wall of the building on top of the bystanders.

I always remember the Cenotaph itself, which had a memorial statue built in Belmore Street after the first World War. The figure of a bronze statue of a soldier, head bowed, on a plinth. Engraved below are the names of local men who died in World war one. Protestant family names such as Johnston and Thompson intermingled with Catholic surnames like McCaffrey, Maguire and McManus.

I was at the Cenotaph that day and tried to help after the explosion. I could see the statue of the soldier on the war memorial through the mist of smoke and the steam from the detonation. The Memorial statue had the words saying, 'Our glorious dead' on the bottom of the memorial stone. How apt as bodies lay dead around their memorial. A War memorial that remembers the soldiers that fought in both world wars. Catholic and Protestant soldiers who fought together for freedom against tyranny. What would these soldiers think now?

As I look around this carnage from hell. It was surreal to see the signs of normal day life, the carpet shop, the pub and the chemist. All set as the background to a scene from Dante's inferno.

I found a young girl under the rumble. She asked me why she had to die. I had no answer. I watched her father hold her hand until she died. I knew that I could have prevented her death and the death of all the innocent people on that day. I have never forgiven myself for not acting and doing the right thing. I should have killed those IRA murderers, before they detonated their bomb. I watched that young innocent girl die. I promised myself, I will never stand by and let another human being die again.

John, in sombre tone, continues saying, 'There would have been many more murdered on that day by the same IRA cell, as they had planted a second bomb. After the Enniskillen blast, the IRA notified a radio station, saying they had abandoned a 150-pound bomb in Tullyhommon, 20 miles away, as it had failed to detonate. That morning, a Remembrance Sunday parade, including many members of the Boys' and Girls' Brigades had unwittingly gathered near the Tullyhommon bomb. Soldiers and Royal Ulster Constabulary officers had also been there. The IRA had tried to trigger the bomb when soldiers were standing next to it, but it failed to explode. It was later defused by a bomb disposal unit.

At the time, the British and Irish governments were struggling to negotiate an Extradition Act. This Act would make it easier to extradite IRA suspects from the Republic to the UK. The Bombing helped force this act easily through Parliament, by putting pressure on both sides to agree to it.'

John continues saying, 'The Enniskillen Bombing was our secret. We knew that the British Government had allowed IRA terrorists to remain free to perpetrate the bombing of innocent people. The powers that be, knew we knew this and that was a problem for them.

To silence and tidy up loose ends our superior commanding officers sent me and my team on a mission. It was an ambush for the IRA to kill us. This had been orchestrated by the powers that be to eliminate us, and silence the secret of Enniskillen.

They sent us to a suspected bomb making factory in an isolated cottage. This was on the borders of the republic of Ireland and the north. Our commanding officer told us that there would be little resistance and an easy job.

How wrong he was.

We were set up as the IRA were lying in wait for us. The IRA knew we were coming. They had been warned in advance by our own side. The IRA had set up an ambush around the perimeter of the woods leading into the cottage. The trap had been set and we were not expected to survive. But we were made of stronger stuff. We fought our way out of the ambush and out of the woods

With the IRA in pursuit, we all nearly made it but Jocky and Kevin took a grenade hit. Jocky had been killed and my best mate Kevin had been seriously injured having his legs blown off.

After surviving the ambush Tom used his connections in the UDA. Through the grapevine word got back from the powers that be, that if we vanished and kept quiet we would be left alone. So, that is what we did. Eventually, the heat died down and we were left alone. Never again to speak about the Remembrance Day bombing and the truth behind what really happened.

Tom and I escaped uninjured. Kevin and I were medically discharged, Kevin with his amputee paraplegic injuries and me with my mental health issues. Tom was medically fine and went to work for the Ulster Defence Association.

Me and Kevin went into hiding.

Through Tom the UDA offered me a job disposing of the IRA operatives that the UDA interrogate and neutralise.'

Philomena interrupts saying,' You mean that the UDA torture and murder, like they tried to do to me.'

John says, 'I am not proud of what I have done but I did not killed these people. I only disposed of them'

Philomena does not respond and continues to listen

John continues, They set me up in this isolated UDA safe house. So, here I am, in this cottage.

Philomena questions John asking, 'Who tipped the IRA off?'

John says, 'Who do you think?'

Philomena, astonished, says, 'What do you mean? Your own side, your government and senior military commanders conspired to have you eliminated by the IRA?'

John says, 'Yes'

Philomena, 'But why and how?'

John, 'Why?'

Philomena, 'Yes, why?'

John replies saying, 'Because we knew too much.'

Philomena is silent in astonishment at John's revelation.

John says, 'Basically, through our covert surveillance we knew that we had intel that an IRA cell were about to explode a bomb at the Enniskillen Remembrance Day ceremony and we highlighted this to our senior command.'

John continues saying, 'Instead of stopping it, our commanding superiors told us to stand down and let the IRA go free. As a result the IRA committed an atrocity on innocent people.'

'The powers that be allowed the IRA bombing take place purely for political gain to turn public opinion, especially the American public opinion against the IRA.'

Philomena is shocked and says, 'That is terrible.'

John says, 'The whole thing was allowed to happen and it was so blatantly orchestrated.'

Philomena says, 'What do you mean?'

John says, ' The night before the remembrance day parade the buildings should have been searched by sniffer dogs to detect any bombs but this was not carried out. This is military protocol and should always happen. However, coincidently this one time it was not done. Later, we found out that a suspect was seen, the night before at the church building with a suspicious package. This suspect was known to witnesses as a local man. Even though this was reported at the time to the police. The suspect was never brought in for questioning.

The church yard to the building that exploded, always had its church gates open. They are never locked but according to locals, coincidently the gates were locked shut the night before the bombing. The IRA planted the bomb in the reading room of the church, access would be through the church gates into the church yard. I have lived long enough to know that in this life, there are no coincidences. The events leading up to the bombing at Enniskillen were suspicious. The IRA had an easy time of it, to plan and carry out their attack.

Philomena says, 'It is unbelievable that a government would allow the murder of innocent people.'

John says, 'If it meant that civilians had to die to turn the public opinion against the IRA, then so be it.'

John continues saying, 'The British Government might argue that after the atrocity happened it was a turning point in the troubles. The IRA realised they had gone too far and killing innocent victims did not look good for them. It had a negative effect for them when it came to getting support from America. American public opinion became less sympathetic after the bombing because of the needless loss of innocent life. After the Enniskillen bombing the IRA started looking for a peaceful negotiation to end the troubles.'

John says, 'Some might say that allowing the bombing to happen saved more life in the long run. But I disagree, it is not acceptable to sacrifice even one innocent life, to potentially save more lives later down the line'.

Philomena is in disbelief at hearing the secret of Enniskillen.

John continues saying, 'Our superiors tipped off the IRA. The lines are blurred in this war. The Government talk to the IRA as much as the UDA if it suits them. The UDA and the IRA speak to each other when it suits them.'

John's voice takes an anger tone saying, 'After our own superiors tried to eliminate me and my team. I had no allegiance to my government or the army. After we were ambushed by the IRA after being tipped off by my own side. I sent an anonymous letter to the Taoiseach in Ireland and the Irish minister for Foreign Affairs.

In the letter, I said that British intelligence knew that the IRA had planned to kill innocent people at the Remembrance Day Massacre in Enniskillen.'

I stated that was a British soldier in charge of capturing IRA operatives. I explained that I had tracked the lead IRA team that were planning to detonate a bomb at the cenotaph in Enniskillen on that Day. We had these terrorists in our sights and were ready to capture or kill them.'

John continues saying, 'I stated that the powers that be, ordered me and my team to stand down and not engage the IRA cell and let them go free. In my opinion, the establishment wanted the IRA to succeed in their mission to kill innocent people at the cenotaph that day. The bombing happened and the truth was covered up. An assassination attempt was made on myself and my team to silence this secret forever.'

John continues saying, 'So, I sent an anonymous letter to the Irish Government and the Taoiseach of Ireland. I did this in a desperate attempt to reveal the truth about what really happened at the Remembrance Day Bombings.

Philomena listening intently says, 'So what happened when they read this letter?'

John despondent said, 'Nothing happened. Both governments ignored the letter and kept it secret to cover it up.'

John is silent then says, 'It was then I realised that I could never win against these people, they are too powerful.'

Philomena says, 'So what did you do next?'

John says, 'Kevin was allowed to live with me, as part of a deal with the UDA.

John pauses as if he has felt something painful inside him.

John then continues saying, 'However, whilst living here in this cottage, Kevin struggled mentally. Kevin had difficulty coming to terms with his former British army betrayal and his disability. Kevin battled with alcohol addiction. I think Kevin could have come to terms with losing his legs if it had been from fighting the good fight, against his enemy.

It was the betrayal which gave him his prosthetic legs. Kevin never got over that fact, the army and government betrayed him. The fact was his own side allowed the enemy, the Irish Republican Army to commit such an atrocity on civilians. Additionally, the British Army betrayed their own soldiers and left him and his comrades to be ambushed by the IRA. This betrayal was too much for Kevin to accept and let go. Unfortunately, one day this cumulated with me finding Kevin hanging in the cottage after committing suicide.'

John looks down, closes his eyes to control his emotions. John continues saying, 'After I found Kevin dead. I mentally deteriorated into insanity. I began to develop a ritual of hanging some of the dead bodies. I would hang them up for disposal in a makeshift hanging hut. This gave me some morbid satisfaction and revenge to see my former enemies hanging. This felt like a perverse sense of justice, after finding my mate hanging'

Philomena is silent, not knowing what to say.

John continues saying, 'I would periodically hang the bodies and leave them to rot and decay. There was no practical reason to do this ritual, only that it gave me some satisfaction. Most of the time, I would prepare the bodies and just feed them directly to the pigs without performing my ritual. My behaviour was unpredictable and disturbed.

John says, 'After some time, I began to see my mate Kevin as if alive. Eventually, I would talk to Kevin, as if he was a ghost. In my mind, Kevin is alive and back in the cottage with me.'

John trying to change the subject, feeling insecure at his admission says, 'I need to look at your wounds and change your bandages'

Philomena pauses in thought and contemplation. Philomena looks at John with different eyes, she smiles at John saying, 'Come on then, have a look at me. So I can get better and get out of here.'

Philomena smiles again at John.

John, looking at Philomena, is surprised at her willingness to cooperate. Without speaking John begins his usual routine of checking her wounds and changing her bandages.

There is a silence between them but a comfortable silence as John helps treat Philomena.

John says,' Right, your wounds are healing fine, before you know it you will be ready to get back to the real world.' Philomena contemplates on the idea of returning to the reality of her life.

Philomena has feelings of sentimentality. In a tone of nostalgia Philomena says, 'When I was a kid, I loved painting and drawing. You'd always find me with a brush in my hand painting.' John asks, 'What did you paint?'

Philomena says, 'What didn't I paint. I just loved painting everything and anything. It was my passion.'

John asks, 'So, did you do anything with your painting?' Philomena says, 'No, when my dad died I gave up. I just didn't have the spirit to paint. I felt too sad, like someone had switched the light off in my life. I was only left with darkness and seriousness.

Philomena continues saying, 'My thoughts were just how to survive and live. There was no more room in my life for painting. Philomena pauses then continues saying, 'What about you?'

John says, 'What did I love doing as a child?'

Philomena says, 'Yes, what was your passion?'

John thinks for a moment, then with hesitation says, 'I just loved poetry and music for as long as I can remember.'

Philomena laughs out loud and says, 'You like poetry? Are you joking with me?'

John says, 'Yes, you can laugh but just because I am a soldier does not mean I am a savage. Yes, I like poetry.'

Philomena, still laughing, says, 'Well, that is a new one on me. The big rough-tee, tough-tee soldier likes poems.' She laughs even more loudly.

John is unsure how to react. John goes from a serious look on his face to one of amusement, then laughter. Joining in with Philomena's joke.

John says, 'Alright that is enough. Yes, believe it or not, I did love poetry and music when I was young.'

John continues saying, 'As I got older into my teenage years, I was too busy keeping out of trouble.'

John continues saying. 'Living in London after my dad died was tough, I was alone. I virtually lived on the streets and had to fight to survive. I grew up with my mate, Kevin. We were like brothers, so we both decided to join the army. This was our way to escape the tough existence on the streets of south east London.'

John thinking, pauses then says, 'But ultimately, we escaped one horror into just another different horror, when we were sent over to Northern Ireland.'

John pauses for a few seconds and seems to look away, out of the window with a glazed look on his face. It is after this conversation with Philomena that John begins soul searching his emotions and feelings.

John realises he no longer wants to be the Pig Feeder.

John feels ashamed of what he has been doing, disposing of dead IRA Operatives, by feeding them to pigs.

Philomena and John spend the rest of the day relaxing and the evening passes uneventfully.

The next morning is John's weekly drive out to the nearest village for supplies. John also wants to telephone his Ulster Defence Association contact to quit as the pig feeder.

John pops his head around the door of the bedroom to Philomena and says, ' I am going to the village for supplies, do you need anything?'

Philomena says, 'Yes, I fancy a drink.'

John says, 'Whiskey?'

Philomena says, 'Perfect.'

John nods and leaves. John has an old beaten-up range rover.

He drives through the country lanes, travelling about fifteen minutes to the nearest village. The village is very basic, one pub, one shop, one bank. John parks outside the only pay phone in the village. It is early morning and no one is around, the mist of the morning is still clearing. It is a clear frosty autumn day in Ireland. John enters the pay phone box.

John pulls a scrap of paper out of his pocket. There is a phone number on it. John picks up the receiver and dials the number. John waits, then a man on the end of the line says, 'Hello.'

John says, 'Is that Patrick?'

Patrick says, 'You mean Paddy?'

John says, 'Yes, I mean Paddy.'

Paddy says, 'Yes, this is Paddy, who is this?'

John says, 'It is the Pig feeder.'

Paddy says 'Ok, What do you want?'

John says, 'I am ringing to tell you that I am no longer the Pig Feeder. I quit. I will leave the cottage in the next few weeks. I will let you know when I am gone.'

There is no acknowledgement from Paddy on the other end of the receiver.

Paddy then says, 'No.'

John says, 'What do you mean, no?'

Paddy says, 'It is not as simple as quitting. You are in too deep. You cannot quit.'

John says, 'I can do what I like and I want to quit. So, it's over.'

Paddy says, 'No, no ,no, you cannot tell the UDA you are leaving them.'

John says, 'You are correct, I cannot tell them. You can.'

Paddy in an angry voice says, 'You do not know who you are messing with.'

John says, 'I could not give a fuck who or what you or your boss thinks. I am not the Pig Feeder anymore. I quit. So deal with it.'

There is silence from Paddy.

Paddy in a calmer voice says, 'Ok, well I warned you. I hope you know what you are doing. There will be serious consequences for you. You cannot fuck off the UDA without repercussions.'

John says, 'It is not your concern. Leave that for me to deal with. You just make sure you make it clear to your superiors. I am no longer the Pig Feeder.'

Paddy continues saying, 'It was you that came to us suggesting you offer your services, disposing of our victims by feeding them to Pigs. Now, you just want to walk away but you know too much. It is not as easy as just quitting.'

The telephone conversation concludes with an ominous threat from the UDA operative saying, 'Let me give you one chance, one friendly warning, which is, do not upset the status quo for everyone involved, especially for you, John.'

John saying, 'I am sorry, but I'm adamant, I'm finished helping you.'

Paddy says, 'I will need to inform my boss which will take the situation to a more serious and dangerous conclusion for you John.'

John says, 'You do that.'

Paddy now says, 'OK, I will pass the message on.'

John says, 'Thank you.'

Paddy says, 'You're a dead man walking.'

John says, 'Tell me something I don't know.'

Paddy then hangs up without another word.

John puts the receiver down and pauses in thought for a moment. The thought that he is no longer the Pig Feeder is a relief to him, even though there may be danger ahead.

John then gets his weekly supplies as well as some extra.

Chapter 9

Butcher of Belfast - Buisteir Bheal Feirste

There is darkness.

A weak, nervous voice is muttering very quietly saying, 'Though I walk through the valley of the shadow of death, I will fear no evil, for thou art with me, thy rod and thy staff, they comfort me.'

A tear runs down a bloodied and bruised cheek.

The voice whispering in desperation continues saying, 'Thy rod and thy staff, they comfort me.'

There is still darkness.

But then there is light. A door opens to shine the light on a man.

This man is slumped in a chair. We can only see him from behind. The man is tied to this chair.

Two men enter the room and prop the slumped man upright in the chair. The two men are big and tall. They both have shaved heads and clean shaven faces. Dressed similarly, in parka jackets with shirts underneath.

As the two men prop the man up, we now realise the man is in a romper room.

The man tied to the chair is now visible from the front. A slim, wiry, middle aged, white man. He sits forlorn. battered and bruised. This restrained man has been severely beaten, his body and spirit looks broken.

This wretched soul is a prisoner, and the two men are his interrogators.

One of the interrogators holds the man's head as the other picks up a steel mechanical device from a table.

The interrogator holding the surgical looking instrument asks the prisoner to open his mouth. This is to no avail as the prisoner refuses.

This results in consecutive punches from one of the interrogators into the prisoner's rib cage.

The punching works and the prisoner capitulates and complies by opening his mouth. Once the prisoner's mouth is open, the other interrogator forces the metal, mechanical device into the prisoner's mouth. The prisoner groans and gags. The steel device is so tightly packed into the man's mouth that the metal scraps on the man's teeth. This gives the same painful sensation, like when fingernails are scratched down a blackboard. The tooth enamel squeezes as the metal rubs against it. Once sufficiently inside the prisoner's mouth. The mechanism is twisted and tweaked. Various parts are turned by the interrogator. This results in winding the prisoner's mouth involuntarily open, to a wide-open position.

The prisoner continues to gag on the metal object in his mouth. The interrogator then gets an additional separate metal plate and start to work it onto the prisoner's tongue. The metal plate holds the prisoner's tongue in a rigid position. The prisoner is obviously in pain, he grunts noises of anguish.

Once this is done, the two interrogators step back away from the man, who is still tied to the chair. The interrogators are quiet and motionless, as if waiting for someone.

Suddenly, a noise is heard from another room, there are footsteps near the door. The door opens and a large framed man, stands in the doorway, like a silhouette.

The man looks in his early 30s. He has a shaved head and a stocky neck, like a bulldog. The man is a commanding figure. Six foot, two inches tall. A well-built, big man. He looks like a cross between a bodybuilder and a sumo wrestler, muscley but fat with it. Wearing a parka jacket zipped up to his neck. Blue jeans and smart black lace up shoes.

He enters and stops in front of the man tied to the chair.

With a gritty deep voice, in a strong Northern Irish accent, the man says, 'Despair is the key that opens the door to know thyself, and in so, know thy God.'

The man continues saying, 'Gentlemen, welcome to today's tutorial on denial torture. I hope you have been studying you notes on practical applications of torture.'

The man continues saying, 'You have not met me before. I am your area commander and I am known as Bob.'

Bob stares at the two men saying, 'Gentleman, you may assume that my name is unassuming and possibly portrays that I am a gentle character. However, make no mistake, my nickname stands for Butcher of Belfast. For when it comes to torture and butchery of human bodies, I have forgotten more than you will ever know.

Torturing and the art of pain persuasion is my speciality.

You could say it is my passion in life. I like to think that it is my calling from God. My God given talent. So listen up and you will learn something. There is a reason God gave you two ears and only one mouth, so be quiet and listen. You will learn something.

The area commander, also known as Bob, was an orphan in the 1960s. Born in 1965, Bob's parents were murdered by the Provisional Irish republican army in 1971 at the beginning of the troubles. His father was a police officer in the Royal Ulster Constabulary.

His father was killed in 1971 in an IRA explosion when his police station was bombed. His father uncovered the IRA plot to blow up the police station. However, his father was too late to prevent it, being killed himself in the blast. Bobs mother never recovered from losing her husband and committed suicide a month later. The IRA murdered his father and indirectly Bob's mother.

After his father's murder and his mother's subsequent suicide. Bob went to live with his grandparents. Bob was six years old when it happened. Unfortunately, life still had more hardship for Bob. His grandparents died in short succession, one after each other. Bob found himself an orphan.

Bob was put in an orphanage but in a predominantly republican area.

Bob was bullied, mercilessly because he was known as the Protestant child. This abuse was constant and severe. Bob would become accustomed to fighting every day and receiving multiple injuries. Being the only protestant, he was hopelessly outnumbered. Bob paid the price in pain and blood for his religious beliefs.

Bob became hardened and dehumanised to pain and suffering. After experiencing all this evil hatred, fuelled by religion. When Bob got older he decided he wanted to be a priest in the Protestant religion. Committed to his religious vocation, he was ordained as a Protestant priest in his early 20s.

However, after seeing numerous sectarian murders and presiding over the funerals, Bob began to have a change of heart. The flash point that changed Bob's direction in life was the

Remembrance Day Massacre in Enniskillen. This litany of innocent deaths by the hand of his arch enemy, the IRA, affected him.

Bob viewed that the only way to serve God was to systematically rid the world of these evil devils. Bob became dark in his soul, feeling that the only way is to kill all the IRA, ruthlessly. Bob saw it as his mission from God. Bob found his calling in life, killing the IRA. He turned against the priest hood, instead taking up a vocation of violence. Bob renounced his religion for the religion of revenge. To end the IRA killings and sectarian campaigns. He dedicated himself to a lifelong mission to run all the Catholics out of Northern Ireland. He wanted to force all the IRA from Belfast. If he could, he would force the IRA right down through the republic and drive them all into the sea at Rosslare.

Bob joined the UDA and quickly went up the ranks with a very methodical, cold, clinical way of operating. Firstly, he was a UDA operative then progressed through various positions to that of the area commander. Bob is a very ambitious man and wants to progress further up the high command of the organisation.

He is known as Bob standing for the Butcher of Belfast.

Bob was part of the infamous Butchers of Belfast, who sadistically kidnapped innocent Catholics off the street. Once captured these unsuspecting souls were furiously tortured and murdered. They then butchered their bodies, chopping them up into mincemeat. Allegedly, they then perversely made meat pies from their remains and sold them back to the Catholics.

This was done in a morbid sense of humour. Thus, the gang were given the name of Butchers of Belfast as a badge of honour for their ruthless aggression against their foes.

Bob looks intently at his pupils which immediately grabs their attention.

Bob says, 'I am here to teach you how to interrogate a prisoner, using the old art of denture torture or teeth twisting.

This type of torture has been around for hundreds of years. Eight hundred years ago in Pakistan. The first drill was used on teeth, which was obviously hand operated as electricity had not been invented yet. The first pliers were used in the 1300s taken from the local blacksmiths foundry and used to pull teeth. Even as far back as around 500 BC. Aristotle and Hippocrates wrote about the use of forceps as a means of extracting teeth.

So, welcome to this ancient skill. I am here to teach you the technical ways to get the best results from this. Gentlemen, I see that you have already fitted the mechanical device called the mouth gag. Used by surgeons in operation. This is needed to restrain the mouth and jaw open, fixed and rigid to operate. This device is an essential piece of apparatus for performing torture in the mouth area.

Using the surgical Denhardt mouth gag, retractor and tongue depressor, which can also have a tongue plate. Again, I see that you have been doing your homework and have fitted the tongue plate that holds the tongue in place. This is so it does not hinder the access to the teeth and gums. This mouth gag and retractor along with the tongue depressor was introduced in 1887 by Doctor Charles E. Denhard in New York. He described his device as a modification of O'Dwyer's Gag device. Doctor Denhard invented these as he felt it was too easily dislodged during surgery. Just as in torturing as in surgery, we do not want the recipient mouth to move, so this is perfect for holding it tightly in place.

I hope you are taking note, gentlemen. Some trivia for you both. The first mouth gag was invented in the late 1500 AD. Mr. Lorenz Heister, a military surgeon who first described his apparatus as a screw-like device. It was used to open the patient's mouth in the treatment of trismus. trismus is another word for lockjaw or bilateral restriction in the mouth opening.

As the lecture continues the men ignore the man restrained in the chair. The prisoner tied up and uncomfortably restrained, groans and mutters. Bob, oblivious to the prisoner's pain, says, 'That is some general knowledge, for the pub quiz, next time you are down the pub.'

Bob in deep thought continues with his lecture saying, 'Alternatively, you can use a bite block or rubber block which is a wedge that can be fitted into the mouth.'

Bob points to the apparatus in the prisoner's mouth saying, 'It has a quick release mechanism, this suits when your torture requires two-way conversation with the prisoner. The mouth gag we are using today is more rigid so not as quickly removable than a bite block. Depending on the requirements for your torture, you must factor in which apparatus you use to restraint the mouth. Mouth gag or bite block?'

Bob continues saying, 'So, we have covered the first stage of dental torture the restraining of the mouth. These are the tools we can use to create a sterile environment for us to torture. These tools secure the mouth and tongue ready for the business of torturing.'

Bob moves close to the prisoner and puts his hand on the prisoner's jaw saying.' Now, we move onto the areas to apply the pain. We predominantly use the tooth for pain but another area to consider when torturing your prisoner is the gums.' Bob uses his fingers to pull up the prisoners lips to show the prisoners gums. Bob says, 'The gums also known as the gingiva is the soft Pinky casing for the teeth. An epithelial tissue that surrounds the teeth. The technical term is a mucous membrane that keeps the mouth clean and protects it from germs and injury.'

The prisoner hopeless in his helplessness is motionless and quiet like a captured animal playing dead.

Bob says, 'The technical term for removing or cutting of the gums is an Apicoectomy. An apicoectomy is a common dental procedure where gum tissue and the end of the root of the tooth is removed and cut away. While at the same time the top of the tooth is left in place. It is often called a root-end resection because it works on the end or tip of your root called the apex. This procedure will cause excruciating agony and pain. It is a useful option to apply when torturing. The tooth's most painful parts are the nerve endings and the root canal. These are protected by enamel. You need to drill down deep into the tooth, clearing away all the enamel to expose the nerve endings.'

Bob says, 'For more effectiveness you can use a normal household hand drill with a masonry drill bit. It is advisable to buy a drill bit set then you can choose the right size drill bit depending on the size of the tooth. Always start with a masonry drill bit, as it will drill easiest into the tooth.'

Bob points to the wall saying, 'Gentlemen, if you look at the wall, there is a poster that has the cross-section of a tooth. All the different parts of the tooth are labelled. It is self-explanatory. The "root" is the bottom part of the tooth, and the top part is called the "crown" There is more to teeth than meets the eye. If you start torturing your prisoner without knowing what you're doing. you can bite off more than you can chew, excuse the pun.'

Bob continues saying, 'I want you to know more about teeth, so you'll have a greater understanding. For when you use dental torture as one of your interrogation techniques. We're going to talk about the tooth from the crown to the root.

The Crown is the top of the tooth and is made up of enamel. This enamel is the toughest outer layer of the tooth that protects the rest of the tooth from decay. Right below the enamel is the dentin. The dentin is a little softer than the enamel

Dentin has tiny tubes called dentinal tubes that run through it. When the enamel wears through and the dentin is exposed to heat and cold, the tubes carry those sensations to the softer parts of the teeth, causing sensitivity and pain. Underneath the dentin lies the cementum.

Bob says, 'Cementum is about the same hardness as bone tissue. It covers the surface of the root and connects the tooth to the bone. Periodontal ligaments attach to the cementum and the jawbone, anchoring the tooth in place and giving it stability. Next is the root of the teeth.

Bob continues saying, 'The root is the pulp or nerves in the centre of the tooth and provides nutrition to the tooth. It is made of soft tissues which have nerve endings housed inside. There are two kinds of pulp, coronal pulp, which sits under the cementum, and the radicular pulp, which is the part of the nerve that runs down through the root canal all the way to the bottom of the tooth. This is where the periodontal ligaments anchor it to the bone. The radicular pulp once aggravated will deliver the most pain to the recipient.

At the end of the root canal, radicular pulp basically merges into the periapical tissue which is full of blood vessels and nerves. This runs between the tooth and the jaw, connecting with the periodontal ligaments along the way.

This area is the holy grail of pain for the recipient, once you penetrate this area of the mouth, maximum pain is achieved. The entire root of the tooth is covered by the gums (or gingiva), a soft tissue that surrounds the jawbone as well and provides protection for all the sensitive nerve endings housed in the root.

Bob looks at the two students who are slightly shell shocked by all the information they are being bombarded with, by their teacher of torture.

Bob says, I know this is a lot of information to process. However, you need to be completely aware of the workings of the mouth, so as to understand the most pain you can create. Are you still up with me gentlemen?' The two men nod in agreement.

Bob says,' I will continue then.'

Bob walks away from the prisoner and smiling at his two students saying, 'Now, a bit of trivia for you both. Did you know that teeth are the hardest substance in the body.'

The two heavily framed students continue to listen without speaking.

Bob says, 'Many assume that bones are the hardest substance in the body, but that's not the case. It is teeth! Teeth are composed of over 96% of minerals, and harder than bones. So, your best option is your household hand drill as mentioned previously or a hammer and chisel if you have no drill'

Bob looks more seriously at his students saying, 'Before we get started, I want to talk about health and safety. You need to protect yourself from injury when torturing.'

Bob continues saying, 'An adult human has a biting force up to 200lbs. This is an incredible amount of power! Believe it or not, the human biting force is similar to that of a pit bull, which comes in at 235lbs.'

Bob says, 'So, always think about health and safety, make sure your mouth gag or bite block is secure. Always double check that the mouth is held rigidly tight. Locking the jaw open before you start putting your hands in their mouths. If the prisoner's mouth bites down on your fingers or thumbs you are in danger of losing them. Especially, if the prisoner is in excruciating pain and the restraints fail. You could have your fingers or thumbs bitten off.

So always check your health and safety housekeeping before you begin your torturing. And make sure the prisoner's mouth is nice and secure before you start inflicting pain.

Bob continues saying, 'They could have a muscle spasm with the pain and chomp down on your hands, if the mouth is not secured tightly open.'

Bob pulls some ear plugs from his pocket and says, 'I want to cover the subject of ear defenders to protect your ears from the screaming.' Bob continues saying, 'I hope you have both read the memo circulated about ear defenders. Whilst torturing you are advised now to protect your hearing, from the screaming of prisoners. This is after a survey was carried out on experienced torturers. The survey highlighted significant hearing loss after a long career of torturing.

Over years of torturing, they had developed tinnitus and hearing loss. Unfortunately, this will affect them later in life when they retire. So, under our new health and safety regulations you must use ear protectors or ear plugs when you torture. Especially, during prolonged torturing sessions.'

Bob looking at his students says, 'Understood?'

The two student interrogators say,' Yes, understood.'

Bob says, 'Good stuff, so let me see your ear plugs in before we start.'

The two burly men take their ear plugs out and insert them in their ears.

Bob says, 'Our safety mantra is, Safe place before torture face.'

Bob grabs the prisoner who has been silent all this time. Bob is gentle with his grip on the prisoner as if putty in his hands.

Bob says, 'Right gentleman, firstly our prisoner has already been processed and information gained from him. The prisoner is here purely for training purposes. We will not apply the pain persuasion technique for extracting information. This session is purely centred on pain application. Generating the maximum amount of pain possible in the teeth and gums using the techniques we have discussed today. So, don't be shy, I want to see you really get hands on. Take the opportunity to get comfortable with experimenting on your prisoner to get the best results.'

Bob picks up a handheld drill and turns it on to test it. The drill is loud and noisy. The prisoner now starts making noise and wriggling in the chair afraid of the drill. The prisoner's screams are muffles and thwarted by the steel mechanica. apparatus inside his mouth.

Bob is oblivious to the scared prisoner. Bob grabs the first student and puts the students hands onto the prisoners saying,' Get stuck in, you need to get right in there.' The student is unsure and nervous. Taking the drill the student puts it inside the prisoners mouth and drills into a tooth. the prisoner screams intently and moves around. Bob says, 'That it, press harder.'

The student is unconfident and scared. Bob, seeing this, is annoyed and says, 'No, not like that.' Bob takes the drill from the student and says, 'You really need to apply some pressure like this' Bob takes the drill from the student. Bob demonstrates, grabbing the tortured man's face and forcing the drill into his mouth and hard down into a tooth. The man screams in agony to the application for BOB. Bob forces the drill further down hard onto the prisoner's tooth. This makes a noise of teeth breaking. The prisoners' screams. Shards of tooth enamel fly out of the prisoner's mouth. Blood spurt out of the man's mouth and onto Bob. This does not bother Bob.

Bob brings the drill out of the prisoner's mouth and hands it back to the student saying, 'Do it like that. Try another tooth.'

This time the student pressed much harder inside the prisoner's mouth to the intensified screaming. Bob sees this and smiles saying, 'That is more like it, good well done.' Bob looks at the other student waiting his turn and says, 'Right your turn.'

This student takes the drill and with much relish drills straight into the prisoner's mouth breaking a tooth. Blood shoots out of the prisoner's mouth again. This time as the drill has slipped off the tooth into the prisoners gums, slashing and cutting it open. The prisoner is in so much pain that he is going in and out of consciousness.

Bob says, 'Ok, that is enough, step back from the prisoner.'

The last student moves back with the drill still in his hand. Bob takes the drill from him and places it down on the table.

Still with his mouth restrained in the open position.

The prisoner is still conscious but silent, exhausted from his ordeal.

Bob, dehumanised from feeling any emotion for the prisoner, continues with his lesson. Bob says, 'Gentlemen, now that the tooth of our prisoner is exposed, having drilled away the enamel and the dentin. We can get more access to the root of the tooth and maximise our pain ten times. Once the root is exposed any pressure using a needle or any heat will enact extreme pain to the recipient.'

Bob continues saying, 'If the objective of the torture is to extract information, then extreme pain is needed from the beginning. Most human beings have a low threshold to pain when tortured. So, immediate extreme pain will quickly give us the information we need. For the purpose of saving yourself time, immediate, extreme pain is advisable. When you have a stubborn prisoner who will not give in, then apply gradual pain over an indefinite time period, will give you the result you need.'

Bob says, 'If you perform a prolonged application of constant pain, this will normally break the more difficult prisoner.

However, you must bear in mind the consequences of torturing a prisoner over a prolonged period of hours. You run the risk of the prisoner dying or being rendered unconscious. This will defeat the object of the goal, if it is to extract information.

For this reason you may need to have a break from the torture to give the prisoner a rest. Too much extreme, constant pain may kill the prisoner or render them unconscious. This is not what we want at this stage of the torture.'

Bob continues saying,' Once the information is gained then you can inflict as much pain as desired but until then you must be disciplined and clinical. Conversely, once information has been extracted you can torture your prisoner for as long as you want or just execute them. That is your prerogative to choose.'

As Bob is speaking, the two students simultaneously notice that there is a piece of fluff on the end of Bob's nose, which Bob is blissfully unaware of.

The two men nervously look at each other. They are undecided whether to stop Bob in full flow of his lecture, to point out that he has some bum fluff on his nose. Or whether just let Bob carry on speaking with this fluffy appendage on his hooter. Such is the fear Bob commands, that the two men are scared to tell Bob concerned about the reaction it may provoke from Bob. Would Bob feel that the men were making fun of him? Bob's seems like a mad man, not to be messed with. So, the two hapless students decide not to tell Bob and ignore the fluff. But ignoring the fluff is impossible. They can do nothing else but focus on the fluff. No matter how hard they try to focus on Bob's lecture, that tiny little bit of fluff on Bob's nose looms larger and larger in their minds.

Metaphorically speaking, that fluff is now as big as a white elephant in the room. Getting bigger and bigger until the men are oblivious to Bob's lecture. The men are hypnotically transfixed on Bob's nose and the fluff.

Then suddenly, Bob notices the two men staring at his nose. Bemused, Bob then realises himself and sees the fluff on the end of his nose. Bob stops talking and looks at the two students. The fluff fiasco is now out in the open. There is silence and the two students sweat with fear at what Bob's reaction will be.

Bob raises his hand and swipes his nose, chopping the fluff off in one foul swoop. The fluff innocently floats away into the air. The silence is palpable and awkward. Bob considers his options then says, 'Are you committed gentlemen ?

Bob continues saying, 'I need committed hard men to undertake the job of torture and interrogation. I need to know gentlemen, are you committed ?

The two men obediently shout, 'Yes Sir.' In a calm voice Bob says, ' Let me continue then.'

Bob continues saying, 'An interrogator has no room for emotion, You must be clear headed and cold hearted. The sole aim is the extraction of information from the prisoner. You need to be hard, gentlemen. Life is hard, after all, it kills you!'

Bob continues saying, 'So, you must extinguish any emotions and be emotionally cold.

Bob takes a cigarette from his jacket. He lights it with a lighter out of his pocket. Bob then removes his parka jacket placing it on a hook on the wall. Bob reveals he is wearing a white shirt and black slim tie. His shirt looks white and immaculately pressed, with all the creases in the right places.

Bob takes a long drag of the cigarette and inhales it all in. Bob pauses for a moment to enjoy the cigarette then continues his lecture.

Bob says, 'Now that the nerve endings and the root canal are exposed. We have options to choose, either a sharp object into the nerve or applying heat to the area. One speciality of mine is to use a lit cigarette into the exposed tooth. Depending on the size of the tooth cavity you may want to use a slimmer cigarette like a roll up. You can roll the cigarette up to the desired size to insert into the open tooth, burning the exposed nerves.

Bob gets close next to the prisoner and taking a puff of the cigarette and blows it into the prisoner's face. The prisoner squints his eyes and squirms in the chair, helplessly.

Bob continues saying, 'The cigarette technique will maximise the agony to your prisoner. Bear in mind that once the heat has burned the nerve ending away the prisoner will not feel the pain. So, it is advisable to then repeat the technique on another tooth, to continue the pain. Remember that you can additionally use the ash from the cigarette into the exposed tooth. Ash will fill the tooth cavity and create extreme heat on the open nerve resulting in severe pain and agony'.

Bob cigarette, seem nervously close to the prisoner's face as the prisoner looks terrified of being burned with it.

Bob says, 'It will smoulder inside the cavity and burn through the nerve endings into the root canal. The cigarette technique will cause extreme pain from the outset. Remember to be careful that the cigarette technique does not cause the client to pass out. It is a failure for an interrogator if your prisoner is rendered unconscious during torture. It cancels out any pain they can feel, and they can not divulge any information while unconscious. Highlight this in your notebook. When there are no nerve ends to send a signal to the brain to tell that it's in pain. It is important you must then start on a different tooth and repeat the processes.'

Bob looks at the prisoner and puts his hand on the prisoner's shoulder as if he is going to demonstrate the cigarette technique on the prisoner. The prisoners' eyes bulge out in horror at his impending torture. But Bob then turns slightly away from the prisoner, it looks like the prisoner has had a reprieve. Suddenly, Bob turns back and swiftly and accurately places the cigarette directly onto the prisoner's tongue. Bob puts pressure on the cigarette, and it burns into the prisoner's tongue. The restrained prisoner whales like a banshee in pain and jumps up in the chair to no avail. As Bob pushes the cigarette down you can smell the scent of burning tissue amongst the muffled screaming.

Bob says directly to the students, 'As we discussed in your previous tutorial on tongue torture last week. You can alternatively use cigarette burns on the tongue. Especially, as the tongue is nicely held in place by the tongue plate.

Bob continues saying, 'Cigarette burns on the tongue are still high on the pain chart.' As Bob talks, he holds the cigarette on the prisoner's tongue to the point that the prisoner is exhausted from screaming. Bob then releases the cigarette and takes a long suck on the cigarette. Bob blows the cigarette smoke back into the prisoner's face.

The prisoner lowers his head down. Bob lifts the prisoner's head up to check he is still conscious. The prisoners' eyes are open and staring into space.

The fact the prisoner is not unconscious pleases Bob.

Bob says, 'This concludes our tutorial today on the art of denial torture. I want you to write up your notes for me to mark assess. They need to be handed in by tomorrow, please. I now have an urgent meeting.'

Bob looks at the tortured man slumped back in the chair.

The prisoner has his face tilted up, and his eyes are now closed. Bob reaches into his jacket and reveals a piston. Bob is standing in front of the prisoner. Looking at the tortured prisoner, Bob makes the sign of the cross, with his free hand. Simultaneously, Bob's other hand holds the piston directly to the prisoner's forehead. Bob speaks in a solemn tone saying, 'In the name of the father, and the son and the holy spirit, Go in peace to love and serve the Lord. Your trials and tribulations are over now. Peace be with you.' Echoes of Bob's priesthood sermons come to mind. These sacred texts are quickly punctuated, by Bob unceremoniously shooting the prisoner point blank in the head. The force of the bullet sends the man backwards onto the floor and still tied to the chair. Blood oozes out onto the floor from under the prisoner's head.

Bob, unphased at his actions, looks at his two oversized students saying, 'I hope you have both done all your homework and preparation for our tutorial next week. The art of fingernail pulling or as I like to say, pain pedicures. We will concentrate particularly on nail extraction.

The two students seeing the murdered prisoner on the floor, nod nervously to Bob. They are intimidated but at the same time mesmerized at the Butcher of Belfast.

I'll be taking questions and answers before the tutorial so ensure you have studied the information I have given you.

Bob then puts his jacket on and straightens his tie. Bob washes his hands in a bowl of water and dries them with a towel. Bob notices blood on his shirt but ignores it.

Bob turns to his students and says, 'I leave you with this thought.'

Bob pausing for a moment then says, 'Pain to a person is like rain to a plant. They need it to grow.'

Bob stares hard at both his students saying, 'To do this job you must be hard.'

Pausing again Bob says, 'So be hard gentlemen and most of all enjoy the rain.'

As Bob is leaving the room he turns back to the students saying, 'Good evening gentlemen, I leave you to clean up the mess and take the trash out.' The two men nod at Bob, but Bob has already left the room.

Bob is now in another room of the building. The building is an unknown terrace house in the unionist area of Ulster. This standard two up, two down is no different in appearance, than any other house in the street. However, this particular house is Bob's headquarters. Heavily fortified inside with numerous UDA operatives on guard. This house is prive to all the command-and-control decisions in that area for the UDA. This house holds the secrets of much evil perpetrated inside and outside. Whether IRA or UDA, these houses of horror are dotted all over the streets of Northern Ireland.

Paddy, the UDA contact for John, who was arguing with John, on the phone previously, arrives outside the house in a car. Paddy exits the car and knocks on the front door looking around nervously waiting to be let in.

Paddy is wearing a parka jacket and jeans and is small in stature. He is one of Bob's foot soldiers, a lower-level UDA operative. As a foot soldier Paddy is the contact for John and also runs low level operations and makes errands for Bob. The front door opens, and paddy enters the house.

We are now in a room in the house. The room is dimly lit. A large writing desk dominates the room. Bob is now seated behind it. Additionally, there is a slim tall man sitting in an armchair to the side of this desk.

Bob's foot soldier, Paddy knocks on the door of this room. The foot soldier is beckoned in by Bob saying, 'Enter.'

He respectful enters quietly shutting the door behind him.

He sits in a chair positioned in front of the writing desk as if to be interviewed.

Paddy is reluctant to inform Bob that John is refusing to dispose of the UDA dead bodies. Paddy, nervously says, 'Bob, I am here to report that a problem has arisen with the Pig feeder'.

Bob says, 'What problem?'

Paddy says, 'He has informed me that he is quitting and is no longer being the pig feeder for us.'

Bob says, 'Have you asked why he is quitting?

Paddy says, 'Yes, I have asked him and he will only say that he has had enough of being the Pig feeder. He wants to quit, so he is quitting.'

Bob says, 'Oh he does, does he'

Bob continues saying, 'Have you tried to make him reconsider his decision?

Paddy says, 'Yes, but he is adamant he has quit.'

Bob says, 'Have you made him aware of the consequences if he quits.

Paddy says, 'Yes, I told him that there will be serious consequences for him and that he will be dealt with severely. Paddy continues saying, 'But he still says he has quit and he is severing all his ties with the UDA and moving out of the cottage.'

This information angers Bob who stands up and kicks his chair away. However, the tall slim man still seated does not react to this and stays motionless, just listening.

Bob, still standing, picks up the chair and hurls it across the room at Paddy. Paddy, who is still seated in front of the desk, ducks to avoid it as it flies over his head.

Bob orders paddy saying, 'You need to send someone down to convince the Pig Feeder to change his mind. If he refuses again then I will deal with him personally.'

Bob says, 'This ex-SAS British soldier needs to know who he is dealing with' Bob continues saying,' We need to make him an offer he can't refuse.'

Paddy repeatedly, nods in agreement as he is petrified of Bob.

Bob looks at Paddy saying, 'This soldier has one last chance. Tell the old man to make a delivery to him. If this so-called Pig feeder refuses, he has signed his own death warrant.'

Paddy nods again. Browbeaten Paddy leaves the room, exiting backwards still facing Bob in respect.

Bob, still angry, shouts at the Paddy saying, 'Shut the fucking door on your way out.' Paddy closes the door behind him and disappears..

Bob turns and looks towards the slim man still seated to Bob's side. This man is slim and tall, he is also wearing a parka jacket with smartly pressed jeans and black shoes. This man has been watching patiently and silently like a panther observing its prey. He rolls an apple around in his hand repeatedly.

Bob, still shaking with anger but more calm now, points at the man saying, 'Whispers, I may need you to take a trip for me with the boys?'

The slim man answers to the name of Whispers. He looks at Bob and says nothing, just smiles. Whispers then peels the apple with a knife and slowly eats a chunk.

His face is stone cold apart from his teeth chewing the sliced apple.

Whispers is Bob's right-hand man for the UDA.

Tall, thin and wiry framed man. Whispers has no outstanding features. Whispers is like a grey man, A person that does not stand out in a crowd. Whispers can blend into the background and go unnoticed. Whisper's appearance suits a man in his profession.

Whispers has a reputation of a nasty, ruthless operative who oversees all interrogations and executions. A cleaner of mess. A solver of problems. Whispers makes people disappear and helps Bob's operations work smoothly.

Called whispers due to his whispering voice.

His voice was a result of his larynx being virtually severe in a knife attack years ago. Ironically, this was not a sectarian incident but a fight in a pub, due to an altercation with three men over drug dealing. These men were not locals and did not realise that whispers was managing the pub drugs deals, as part of the UDA protection rackets. They assumed that due to whispers being outnumbered three to one, they had good odds on telling him to go fuck himself. So, they challenged whispers, when he confronted them about dealing drugs in the pub.

Unfortunately, for them they misjudged whispers and the situation. Whispers did not look too kindly on the men trying to take control of his territory. An ensuing fight between Whispers and the three men took place. Even though Whispers was outnumbered three to one, he held his own with them. One of the men pulled a knife on whispers and he had his throat cut from ear to ear. However, this did not stop whispers, it even angered him more. Legend has it that despite whispers bleeding out from his throat with life threatening injuries. Whispers managed to completely fuck up all three men with his bare hands. At the end, two of the men ended up with life changing injuries and one ended up in the morgue.

The subsequent police investigation decided it was a case of self-defence for whispers and no murder charge was brought against whispers. It may also be the case that the police were mainly in the pockets of the UDA, and were paid off.

Whispers survived but his voice was never the same, only managing to whisper from that day forward.

So, whispers became his name.

Chapter 10

The Lovers - Na leannain

It is evening in the cottage and already dark and cold outside, on this winter's night. .

Philomena, looking at John, says, 'Can I ask you something?'

John says, 'Sure'.

Philomena says. 'Would you wash my hair for me? I have tried to wash it properly, but it is difficult to do it myself because of my injuries.

John says. 'Of course, I will do it now, if you like.'

Philomena says, 'Yes please.'

John says. 'Come into the bathroom and I will wash it.'

Philomena is using a walking stick that she found in the wardrobe in the bedroom. It must have been left behind from the people that previously lived in the cottage. Philomena sits on a chair in the bathroom and leans her head backwards into the sink. Philomena's hair is very short from earlier in her recovery. John needed to shave her head to heal her injuries. John puts shampoo on his hands and rubs it into her scalp.

John touches Philomena's wounds and checks them to see how they are healing. John gently runs his fingers through her short hair, slowly and sensuously. Philomena exhales in relief at feeling her hair being washed. Philomena says, 'It feels so nice to have someone wash my hair.' John continues to caress Philomena's head and moves his hands lower to massage the back of her neck, this pleases Philomena. Philomena has her eyes closed enjoying the sensation of her head and neck caressed. John then pours water over her head, washing the shampoo suds from her hair. John says,' Is that ok?'

Philomena opens her eyes and looks at John saying, 'Yes, that was lovely.' Philomena smiles at John, who nods at her in acknowledgement.

John dries her head and neck until it is dry enough for Philomena to sit upright. John kneels down in front of Philomena and continues drying her hair. As John stops rubbing her hair, they both find themselves at eye level. They look yearningly at each other. Philomena leans forward and kisses John on the cheek saying. 'Thank you, John.'

John smiles and says, 'Your welcome.' For a split second they both have the same thought, to kiss each other on the lips. However, the moment passes as quickly as it arose. The feelings are strong between them. The awkward moment is broken by John putting the towel away saying, 'All dry.'

They then exit the bathroom together. John is holding Philomena by the arm as she still finds it difficult to walk.

Philomena gets back into bed and John makes Philomena some food. Soon after she has eaten, she falls asleep.

Philomena is finding her recovery tiring. John sits in the bedside chair watching over Philomena. The pair of them are secretly in love and there is a sense of bonding emerging between them.

There is a car blowing its horn outside. John springs up, walks to the front window and looks out. John sees the familiar sight of the old man in his car. It has begun to rain outside and the evening is closing in. John opens the front door which signals the old man to exit the car. The old man approaches the boot of his vehicle, he opens the boot as usual for John to remove his deadly delivery of bodies. John approaches and stands next to the car. John looks into the boot to see dead bodies lying over each other. The corpses waiting to be carried inside for the pigs to eat.

John looks at the old man and says, 'It's over, I have quit. I am no longer the pig feeder. The old man says nothing but stares into Johns eyes with a deep focus as if examining john's inner soul. After a few seconds quizzing John's eyes for the truth. The old man without speaking walks back to his car.

John, thinking it is over and turns to walk back to the cottage. In the corner of John's eye, he catches the old man returning to John with a brown paper package in his hands. John says nothing as the old man hands the package to john.

John looks at the old man with confusion. John knows that there is money in the package but only if he takes the bodies, which he has already refused. The old man knows this but still wants John to have the money, knowing he will need it.

John thinks for a split second then takes the brown paper package. John smiles at the old man and says, 'Thank you.' The old man smiles back which seems to crack all the skin on his face. The old man then turns to go. John says, 'Your name?'

The old man looks back at john. John repeats his question saying, 'What is your name? All these years and I don't even know your name.' Then, the old man looks at John with sparkling blue eyes and says in a dark croaky voice, 'Dayda.' 'My name is Dayda.'

Before John has a chance to continue talking, the old man has gone in his car.

John returns into the cottage and back to Philomena. The night passes with Philomena tossing and turning as she dreams.

Philomena wakes up from her dreaming.

John is asleep in the chair, she laughs and says, 'Great guardian angel you are'.

John wakes up and says, 'What's wrong?'

Philomena says, 'I was dreaming of my dad, and it was lovely, then I woke up.'

John says, 'Were you close to your dad?

Philomena says, 'Yes, very close. Especially after my mum died.'

Philomena continues saying, 'My dad drank himself to death after my grandfather was murdered by the British government. The black and tans wanted his son, which was my dad. My grandad would not betray his son. So the black and tans threatened to kill my grandad if he did not say where his son was. My dad was a campaigner for a united Ireland. He did not believe in doing it by force but by a peaceful political movement.'

Philomena, trying to contain her anger, continues saying, 'They executed my Grandad on his own front doorstep in-front of his family because he would not give up his son to them.

Philomena says, 'The Black and Tans murdered my grandfather because he would not betray his son.'

John says, 'Who or what are the Black and Tans?'

Philomena, 'Don't they teach you history in the army ?

John says nothing, just shrugs his shoulders..

Philomena continues saying, 'Most of them were former British soldiers from the First World War. In the 1920s The British Government recruited extra men into the Royal Irish Constabulary as reinforcements against the Irish Republican Army fighting for a free Ireland.'

Philomena continues saying, 'The British Government enlisted about 10,000 former British soldiers that served during the First

World War. They were tasked to reinforce the Royal Irish Constabulary and fight to destroy the Irish Republican Army.

Philomena continues saying, 'This group of ex British soldiers were known as the Black and Tans for the colour of their uniform. These bastards were known for their cold-blooded brutality.

John interjects says, 'I can understand that because if they had come back from the First World War, they probably were mentally dehumanised, fucked up and mad from the horrors of the war.'

Philomena says, 'That may be the case, but it was no excuse to behave the way they did.' They were notorious for their cruelty towards the Irish. They murdered my grandfather without justification. In turn my father would never forgive himself for being the cause of my grandfather's murder. My father drank himself to death with the guilt of my grandfather's murder. My grandfather gave his life to protect his son from the British army and the British government. After my dad's death I vowed to get justice from the people who were responsible for the murder of my grandfather and in turn my father. The British government will answer for the killing of my dad and grandad. They have their blood on their hands.'

Philomena is close to tears as she says, 'It is our country, not Britain's. It is our land, our homes and our loved ones who have been killed, just for wanting their country back.'

She says, 'My grandad refused to yield to their intimidation and ultimately paid the supreme sacrifice for his son. He was murdered in cold blood outside his front door for loving and protecting his son. My dad never would forgive himself for being responsible for the death of his dad, my grandad.' Philomena pauses again trying not to cry.

Philomena wiping her eyes says. 'My dad's drinking was a way of dealing with his guilt for his father's murder. My father drank himself to death.'

Philomena continues saying, 'In my father's mind he would act like his dad had not died. I remember when I was younger seeing my dad talking to my dead grandfather. For years my father did this, so I understand what you are doing John. You are not mad or crazy. You are just human'.

John, shocked, says, 'What are you talking about?'

Philomena says, 'I know you talk to a ghost, is it your mate who killed himself?'

John makes a sharp intake of breath with anxiety and then exhales. John is uncomfortable with discussing such a sensitive issue.

Before John can reply Philomena says, 'It's ok John. I understand. You're not mad, you're just grieving for your loss.'

John cannot speak, shocked by Philomena's words. Philomena takes John's hand and says, 'If talking helps then it's ok to talk to someone who has died. If they are in your heart and mind then they are not dead. So it's ok to talk to them. Our loved ones who have died are always with us. They never leave us, they never die, they just are somewhere else and waiting for us.'

John is unable to speak, overwhelmed with the loss of his friend but also full of emotion towards Philomena for understanding him.

Philomena looks around the room to pick out a slip of paper on the mantelpiece. Something she has noticed previously and now feels it is the right time to bring up with John. It is a funeral service card and on the front is a photo of a soldier and his name. It says, 'In remembrance of Kevin Patrick Thomas.' Inside is the order of service and prayers.

Philomena reads it. John sees Philomena reading the service card. John quickly approaches Philomena and takes the card out from Philomena's hand.

John with uneasy, says, 'Why are you reading that for'

Philomena is unphased saying, 'Is this the order of service card for your friend that lived here with you ?'

John says nothing at first and puts the funeral card back on the mantelpiece. John pauses, then in a subdued voice says, 'Yes.'

Philomena retrieves the card from the mantelpiece. Philomena with the funeral card in her hand, looks at the front and reads the man's name out, saying, ' Kevin Patrick Thomas.'

There is no reply from John

Philomena says, 'It's ok if you want to talk to me about it.'

John pauses then says, 'Kevin was my best friend. We grew up together and we joined the army together. We did everything together.'

Philomena is silent, not sure what to say in an awkward way. This is something new for Philomena and she is out of her comfort zone. It is hard for her to show sympathy for a dead British soldier. Up until now for her, a British soldier had always been her enemy. But she does feel sadness for John's sorrow and loss.

Instinctively she says, 'I'm sorry for your loss.'

John pauses again and exhales, then says, 'You are right. He is not dead, he is in my head and my heart.'

John in a hopeful tone says, 'I talk to him every day.'

Philomena says, 'Is that who I hear you talking to?'

John says, 'Yes, Ghost or just a figment of my imagination. He is real, he is still here with me.'

Philomena says, 'It is ok, like I said, my father would always speak to my grandfather. My dad would talk to him, as if he was standing right next to him. I did wonder if my dad really would see him as a ghost, but I will never know now, as they are both dead.'

Philomena smiles at John and puts the funeral card respectfully back down onto the mantelpiece. John smiles at Philomena but says nothing. John's mind is elsewhere.

Ignoring Philomena, John snaps out of his daydreaming and says, 'I have got you a little something.'

From behind his chair, John reveals a plastic bag. John gives it to Philomena, laying the bag on the bed. John says, 'I thought of you, while I was getting supplies in the village.'

Philomena is surprised by this. Upon opening the bag, she notices a cluster of pencils and paint brushes with an array of paints. The gift is also accompanied with some blank paper to draw and canvas to paint. Philomena is nearly brought to tears with gratitude at this surprise gesture of kindness. John smiles approvingly at Philomena who is overjoyed at his gift. Philomena touches the paint brushes with fond nostalgia.

John continues saying, 'You should never stop being a child at heart. Never forget your passions. If we all kept the child inside us, the world would be a better place. So, I hope you start painting again. I got you them to get you started.'

Philomena startled by John's gift says, 'I don't know what to say.' John, smiling at Philomena, says, 'That makes a change.'

Philomena joking smiles back saying, 'You better watch it with the sarcasm, or I will hit you with that bed pane again.'

Philomena is speechless.

Some time has passed and it is now night-time. Philomena is asleep and having nightmares. Philomena stirs as she is recalling her torture and subsequent attempted murder at the hands of the UDA. She is sweating and restless. Philomena, still asleep starts crying, intertwined with screams and groans.

John is awake and watching Philomena as she goes through this ordeal. John tries to comfort her by saying, 'Philomena it's ok, it's ok.' John gets a damp cloth and mops her brow to help calm her down. But this does not help and Philomena is getting increasingly distressed. John, desperate to comfort Philomena, puts his arms around her and holds her.

This show of affection from John wakes Philomena up out of her nightmare. Philomena, seeing John holding her, breaks down and cries uncontrollably. John says nothing just holds Philomena as she weeps.

Philomena cries in John's arms for a while. Philomena then lays back down in the bed. Resting after her traumatic episode.

After a few hours Philomena wakes from her sleep.

Philomena looks around to notice the room silent without John

As she lays in bed the door opens and John walks in with a glass of water.

John, noticing Philomena is awake, says, 'That is timing, I have a glass of water for you.' John places the glass of water on the bedside table and sits next to the bed in his chair.

John says, 'Your nightmares are bad. Do you know why you have them?'

Philomena says, 'It is too painful for me to talk about it'

John looks at Philomena intensely saying, 'I think I know what it is.'

Philomena, curious, says, 'How would you know?'

John says, 'Because I have nightmares too and I wake up sweating and screaming in the night.'

Philomena says, 'I know I've seen you.'

John looks at Philomena with surprise and embarrassment saying, ' I didn't realise you saw me.'

Philomena says, 'Of course, I saw you. I might be incapacitated but I'm not blind or deaf.'

John says, 'Is your nightmare from what happened when you were held captive by the Ulster Defence Association?'

Philomena says, 'Yes.'

Philomena looks away in shame then says, 'Those bastards, what they did to me. They treated me like I was not a human being'

Philomena continues, 'They tortured me and abused me in one of their romper rooms, finally murdering me or so they thought.'

John says, 'I knew of these romper rooms through our counter intelligence. I have never spoken to anyone that has actually been in one. What were these romper rooms ?'

Philomena says, 'They were killing rooms, set up for torture, interrogation and murder. A room would be prepared and their victims would be captured and brought there. Once in a romper room, unspeakable depraved acts of evil were carried out on the

victims. Once killed they liked to leave the dead bodies in humiliating degrading ways. For example, slicing the throat off and leaving the head propped up by a stick or leaving the body in various deformed contortions. Arms and legs facing the wrong way. One unlucky couple were caught and the woman was repeatedly gang raped in front her partner. They were both viciously tortured and murdered. They had their genitals cut off and stuck in each other's mouths. It is Pure evil. These romper rooms were kept out of the media and not published to the public.

It was called the romper room after an American children's television series, which was shown in Northern Ireland in the 1960s. That is how sick these people are. In the children's programme the kids would romp around doing what they liked. I suppose these bastards think they can do what they like, without any repercussions. They perpetuate depraved, evil acts without an ounce of guilt towards the human beings they inflict it on.'

John says, 'Why did they have you in one of these romper rooms?'

Philomena continued saying, 'They wanted me to tell them where my brother was but I would never betray my brother, so they tortured and tried to kill me. John says, 'History repeating itself.'

Philomena says, 'What do you mean?'

John continues saying, 'Just like your grandfather would not betray your father, out of love for him, you did the same for your brother.'

Philomena says, These bastards thought I must be an IRA operative because my brother is in the IRA but I'm not.'

Philomena stops to get her composure then continues saying, 'Yes of course, I hate the UDA, the British army and the British Government. Just because of that, it doesn't mean I kill for freedom, like my brother. I do not believe killing people will give us a free, United Ireland. In fact, it plays into our enemies' hands.'

John says, 'From your injuries when you first arrived, I had a good understanding of who your interrogator was. Our counterintelligence knew her as the Crucifier. It was a notoriety she revelled in. Her trademark torture technique was to crucify her victims to the floor. I believe it was the crucifier that tortured you due to the wounds to your hands and feet. You also had puncture wounds in your side and on your head. Classic signs of her evil handy work.'

Philomena is visibly shocked by John's revelation. Philomena, full of anger at the thought of her ordeal, goes to speak but quells her anger.

She pauses for thought then says, 'There will be a free United Ireland one day. It will be achieved through justice and Love. Love of our country, north and south and love of each other. When we realise, we are all Irish people together on this island of Ireland.

It will be through a political and social movement that we will ultimately win the freedom of Ireland. Once they realise murdering will not work. Once they get tired of opposing each other with death and destruction. Only then will society change and move away from ignorance towards enlightenment. A future that is happy, with prospects for our children on both sides. Violence and turmoil will never achieve anything, only more misery and sorrow. Killing will not change things, just lead to more killing and more excuses to keep Ireland in chains.

John listens, as Philomena continues saying, 'I believe that once we all come together as Irish people, despite our differences, we will rightfully take back our country from Britain. It will not be now but in the future when the murderers on both sides are dead and long gone. When the hatred and ideology has exhausted itself and runs its course. Once this generation has gone, we will start on the right road to win our peace and our country back. It will happen together as Irish people living together in one Ireland. Light will always consume the darkness. Good will always overwhelm evil in the end. It is and will always be the way of things.'

Philomena says, 'It is not those that inflict the most pain but those that can endure the most suffering that will win.'

Philomena continues saying, 'Hatred and ignorance will fade with time. It is the next generations of Ireland who will emerge victoriously into a peaceful, loving Ireland. A younger generation of people who just want to live in peace and have a good quality of life for themselves and their children. The future generations of Irish will be forward thinking and enlightened.

John says, 'Your words are very deep and philosophical.'

Philomena looks at John saying, 'There are good and bad people on both sides. I pray for every soul lost in the troubles for they all mattered to someone. A father, a brother, a mother, a son or daughter.'

John says, 'It seems that both sides had their own female Femme fatale. The UDA had the crucifier and the IRA had Queen Bee. The bitch that was the head of the IRA terrorist cell that blew up the cenotaph at Enniskillen. That bitch escaped justice too, like the crucifier, I heard she went to America and married an American general.'

Philomena says, 'It is time to forgive and remember. It's time to have compassion and empathy. One Ireland means one love for all, regardless of our difference.

John is stunned by Philomena's speech

Philomena continues saying, 'We can have different opinions, without needing to kill each other because of them.'

John says, 'Well, I don't know whether to applaud or cry. I may not be the right person to judge but it makes sense to me. However, you have one problem.'

Philomena says, 'What?'

John says, 'Hatred.'

Philomena says, 'What do you mean?'

John says, 'The hatred that has been caused by all the killing. Hatred naturally leads to more bitterness and revenge, that naturally leads back to more hatred. That is the problem. It is a vicious circle of retaliation and killing.' Through hatred comes killing and that will stop your suggested, peaceful revolution.'

Philomena says, 'The only way to take that hatred away is forgiveness and if not forgiveness then at least acceptance.

John says, 'Acceptance of what?'

Acceptance that hatred and revenge will never solve the injustice or bring back the dead. The dead have been murdered through hatred or revenge. It will only perpetuate more of the same. It will not solve the problem. It will not heal the sorrow or the loss. Only forgiveness and acceptance is the answer. This is achieved through the spirit of love. Love for each other. Love for yourself. Love for your country.'

John says, 'The UDA and IRA would say that they are fighting each other for the love of their country.'

Philomena says, 'Rubbish, that is an excuse to attach a moral reason to justify an evil act. They just want to kill another human being. These murders, these serial killers, these bullies on both sides. These earthly devils have kidnapped the concept of love for your country. They murder, rape and bully in the name of their country. It is a trick that governments throughout history have used to get normal people to commit abnormal acts of evil upon each other.

This concept is hidden behind the patronage of a country, to excuse the real reason, which is to make it acceptable for people to kill other human beings. Even if Ireland had been completely unified in 1920, these people would always have been murderers and bullies. Because that is in their character. There are millions of other people who love their country but they would never kill another human being because of it.

If you truly love your country, you will peacefully unify it. If you love your Ireland, then you will be accepting of everyone, regardless of their opinions or differences. These people are your own countrymen and women. Do not kill each other but have empathy for each other.'

Philomena pauses, then says, 'Love is the only truth.'

Philomena looks at John who is in quiet contemplation at Philomena's comments.

John says, 'That all sounds great in an ideal world but it is not an ideal world. Sometimes people fight for their country because they are being invaded as in World War Two from an evil enemy. The Nazis wanted to enslave countries. In Northern Ireland, I killed people not because I like killing but because I was protecting my army mates. To say that everyone who fights for their country must want to kill and hurt people is not right. Sometimes there is no other choice but to fight and to kill.'

Philomena says, 'There is always a choice. There is always another way. It won't make it right and it won't be fair but it's the only way for lasting peace. So, the next generation of young soldiers won't end up like you, suffering from madness. We need to prevent the next generations from being like you or my brother. Driven by hatred towards death and destruction for everyone.

Hatred is an emotion, and we need to stop acting on our emotions. We need to cut our emotions off and see what needs to be done to have peace. We need to respond not react. To act on emotions is a reaction, but to act on common sense is to respond. We need to respond to solve the problems in Northern Ireland, not just react with our emotions.

John says, 'I refer to my previous comment, In an ideal world but this world is not ideal. It is easier said than done to have love and peace for everyone. That's difficult for people who have had their loved ones murdered or soldiers who have seen their mates blown up. I think your intentions are true but you are deluded. We are not in an ideal world. In an ideal world democracy would really mean something. Instead, it is a concept prostituted out to governments to excuse their depraved behaviour on its people and other countries.'

John continues saying, 'It is a cruel world. Democracy is like a parliamentary prostitute paid for by politicians to be used and abuse for their own gratification. Government should be the custodians of the truth but instead they choose to twist it and distort it.

The Truth is abused for power and greed. Truth is bought by the highest bidder, like a possession to be owned. When convenient, truth is taken out and paraded around to the world. When it suits, truth is hidden away in darkness to mislead. The only truth is that truth is not free. We must fight to free it and protect it from governments and dictators who want to own it and control it.'

John exhales in desperation then says, 'Love is the only Truth. You are right Philomena but hatred blinds us from the truth. The governments will always want division amongst people. That is how they can manipulate everyone for their plans of how they want the future.'

Philomena says, 'We need to save our future children from that fate. We need to take back our freedom, so our children can control their future for themselves. We need to be bigger people. We need to be the great ones. We need to use our hearts and minds for a greater future. Regardless of our religious beliefs. We want the future Irish generations to look back and say, that we were the generation of reasoning and enlightenment.

John says, 'It must get so bad that people will want a peaceful solution more than unending conflict.'

John continues saying, 'Maybe once our damaged generations are long gone, the next generations will do the right thing for Ireland.'

Philomena says, 'Well, we did it.'

John says, 'What do you mean?'

Philomena says, 'We looked past our prejudices of each other and saw each other as human beings and not enemies.'

Philomena ponders her thoughts in silence then looking straight into johns' eyes says, 'Love will overcome anything.'

John is quiet but smiles.

Philomena continues saying, 'People have more similarities than they do differences.'

John says, 'I guess we have come a long way since you hit me over the head with a bed pane.'

They start laughing together. Their laughter concludes their conversation and they settle down for the evening. The night passes uneventfully with Philomena resting and John watching over her.

ACT III

Chapter 11

The Visit - An Chuairt

Christmas Eve 1993

The night has given birth to the morning. The sun bursts through the curtains like a newborn baby, screaming loudly into the bedroom. Philomena has been asleep but the piercing sunlight wakes her up. Now awake, Philomena hears music in the distance. Philomena semi mobile with some difficulty gets out of bed. Philomena puts on a bathrobe and with a walking stick she opens the bedroom door into the hallway. Philomena hears the music becoming clearer.

Philomena pauses to listen and to her surprise, it seems like Christmas music is playing. Her curiosity carries her along towards the noise. It leads her down to the bottom of the hallway, to the doorway of the living room. Philomena peers around to see a big Christmas tree in the corner of the room. The room is lit up with various colours and tinsel. The open fireplace is burning bright and crackles with laughter.

This scene is reminiscent of a classic Christmas card picture. Philomena is surprised but also smiles with pleasure as she admires this scene. John walks out from the kitchen with a box full of Christmas decorations.

As John sees Philomena, he stops in his tracks with caution. Philomena smiles at him like a happy child.

Philomena says, 'Christmas Tree?'

John replies saying, 'Well, it is December and tomorrow is Christmas Day, so I thought I would decorate the place.'

Philomena presumed that Christmas is not something that John would be interested in celebrating. Philomena realises that there is more to John than she thought. John seems like a little boy excited at the prospect of Christmas Day.

Philomena is feeling sentimental and remembers memories of Christmas when she was young with her family.

Philomena smiles saying, 'It is fantastic. It looks lovely.'

John says, 'Great,' leaving the room for more decorations.

As John places the decorations around the room, he knocks his mates' funeral card onto the floor. John picks it up and for a moment is lost thinking of his mate, who he spent many Christmases with.

Philomena, noticing John lamenting his best friend's demise, approaches John. She touches his face tenderly with her hands. Looking into John's eyes. Philomena says, 'It's ok, I am with you now. You're not alone, I won't leave you.'

Philomena takes John's hand and slowly leads him out the front room and down the hallway. She walks slowly as she still struggles with her injuries. She looks back at John as she walks towards the bedroom. They both enter the bedroom, John is led by Philomena.

Philomena whispers to John saying, 'Lay on the bed.' John lays back onto the bed. Philomena smiling at john unbuttons and unzips John's trousers. She pulls his trousers and pants down, revealing john naked from the waist down. Philomena plays with John's penis until it is hard and erect.

Philomena then lifts up her skirt to reveal she has no knickers on. John is excited at seeing this. Philomena straddles John and guides John's cock into her pussy. Philomena feels her plaster cast is slightly uncomfortable as she straddles John. She ignores this discomfort over her urge to have sex with john. Philomena leans forward and lovingly kisses John, who kisses her back with deep passion. Philomena then rides John, gently grinding on his penis. John shows his pleasure and slaps Philomena's arse. John rubs Philomena's breasts which are now protruding from out of her dress. John kisses and caresses her nipples until they become hard.

Philomena then pulls up her dress over her head and throws it onto the floor, exposing her naked body. John continues kissing and sucking Philomena's tits. Philomena proceeds to move her pelvis harder up and down on John's dick. Suddenly John cannot contain himself and orgasms, ejaculating everything inside of Philomena. The sight of seeing John cum excites Philomena and she orgasms as well. They both are motionless, enjoying the euphoric feeling, Philomena, still on top of John, lays down on John's chest. They both hold each other lovingly.

John rubs Philomena's head and caresses her hair until Philomena falls asleep. John falls asleep not long after. Outside the window, the wind blows the leaves around like an Irish jig, on this frosty cold Christmas eve night.

Christmas Day 1993

The day has come and it is Christmas morning. Philomena and John are in bed together. Philomena moves under the bed covers and starts kissing and licking john bollocks. John, still asleep, starts to awaken due to the sensation of having his balls kissed. Philomena then moves on to suck down on his cock. Swallowing the head of John's penis in her mouth.

Philomena deepthroating John's cock, gags slightly as she does so. Philomena moving her mouth all the way down to the base of his penis. John is fully awake now and holds Philomena's head as she moves in a pivoting movement up and down john's cock. John grabs Philomena's hair and pulls it with delight.

Philomena senses John is getting extremely excited. Noticing this excitement she takes her mouth off John's penis. Still under the bed covers, she moves up to the top of the bed. She then appears from out of the bed sheets to see John smiling at her.

Philomena says, 'I want you to masturbate over me, as I play with myself. John sits up and watches Philomena as she pulls the bed covers off the bed. Philomena lays on her back with her legs apart. With one hand on her pussy she starts to masturbate herself. Philomena plays with her clitoris as John watches intently. John wanks himself off as Philomena then puts her fingers up inside her vagina and finger fucks herself. Philomena fingers herself while John, playing with his penis, starts to stiffen with excitement. John says, 'I am going to cum.

Philomena breathing fast and heavy says, 'I want you to spunk all over my tits.'

John without speaking straddles Philomena at the waist ready to orgasm over her breasts. Philomena, still fingering her pussy, says, 'Spit on me.'

John, surprised by her request, says, 'Do what?'

Philomena says, 'I want you to spit on me. It turns me on, spitting on me. Quickly, as I'm going to orgasm. I want you to spit on me, come on! do it.'

John then starts spitting over Philomena's body as he masturbates. Philomena close to orgasm shouts, 'Spit on my face, you bastard, come on.'

Philomena smiles as she shouts her demands to John, saying, 'Come on, soldier boy!'

John, who is starting to orgasm himself, spits repeatedly at Philomena's face, John exhales in release as he ejaculates, John's throbbing penis spurting sperm all over Philomena's tits. Philomena, feeling the sperm falling on her breast screams saying, 'Yes,' with excitement.

Philomena rubs her hands over her tits, rubbing the spunk into her skin, Philomena then groans and screams with ecstasy as she orgasms. John's saliva still on her face from spitting on her. Philomena sits upright on the bed, leaning towards John, she kisses him passionately on the lips. They both embrace with pleasure and sexual satisfaction. Philomena looks at John and with a cheeky smile saying,' Merry Christmas soldier boy. John smiles, saying, ' Merry Christmas.'

John and Philomena get out of bed and enter the front room of the cottage. John switches on the lights on the Christmas tree. Philomena sits in the armchair admiring the decorations. John goes into the kitchen and after some time emerges with a tray of teas and biscuits. John sits in the armchair adjacent to Philomena and they both relax, drinking tea and eating biscuits. Chocolate digestive biscuits, of course.

Philomena says, 'I have a little something for you.' With the excited anticipation of a child, Philomena gives John a hand painted portrait of his comrade, Kevin. Philomena has utilised her paints and canvas to create a portrait of Kevin. She has painted the image taken from the picture on the funeral card.

John is visibly shocked and cannot speak. He is dumbfounded at this kind and thoughtful gesture.

John says, 'That is amazing. Thank you.' John continues saying, 'I didn't know what to get you, so I got you this.' John reveals a bottle of whiskey.

Philomena smiles at John saying, 'Perfect, you do the honours'.

John, smiling in agreement, puts two glasses on the table and opens the whiskey bottle, filling up the glasses. They both take a drink which creates a relaxed vibe. They sit back in their chairs, enjoying the moment. John puts on a vinyl record of Christmas hymns.

The two of them seem to drift off into their own worlds. John and Philomena making the most of the relaxing atmosphere and the whiskey. They are in a festive mood. John is in deep thought and says. 'There is something I want to read to you.'

Philomena says, 'What?'

John says, 'Promise you won't laugh'.

Philomena says, 'What are you talking about?'

John says, 'Just promise me, you won't laugh'.

Philomena says, 'John, what are you talking about ?'

John says, 'Just promise'.

Philomena says, 'Ok, I promise I won't laugh'.

John says, 'I have written a poem'.

Philomena burst out laughing.

John in annoyance says, 'You promised not to laugh.'

Philomena gathering her composure says, 'Sorry, it just surprised me, that is all.'

Still smirking Philomena says, 'Are you going to read it to me?'

John nervously says, 'I had planned to. but if you're going to make fun of me, then I will leave it.'

Philomena now serious, realising how important reading his poem is to John says, 'John, I promise I will never make fun off your poetry ever again, now just read it to me,'

John opens his notebook and says, 'Ok, this is my poem called a soldier's life.'

Composing himself john begins reading his poem, saying,'

A Soldier's Life

'Don't look and judge me and our lord above thee
For I have dealt in death and taken breathe
Forgive me for what I have done
the battles lost, it's never won

For I have seen the blood and smelt the death
and now I know I cannot rest

Even though I worked against my foe
there is something now I know

No matter who the opposition,
we all must bear the same position
for when it comes to life or death
we all must take our dying breath

A soldier's life for me
to escape my atrocity
of living in the slums of Britain
I saw the wall the writing written
So, I found myself in foreign lands
and raised my gun to other man's

Not knowing now, who I can tell
My struggle now is private hell
The lonely nights, sweats, pains consume me,
my guilt and rage I feel entomb me

If only I could turn back time.
Rewrite the story that was mine
Instead of fighting, I'd walk away,
to hear my enemy I'd say
No soldiering for me today
A soldier, my opposition,
they share with me the same position
Left with a broken life condition

A mind in torment both we share,
and twisted thoughts we could compare
Soldier, soldier same as me,
blinded but we just can't see.
No different, only as the streets
and pavements that we used to meet

So now I lay awake at night
my devils play with great delight

My private petrifying fight
Not knowing was I wrong or right

Faces unknown and also knew,
Friends or foe what can I do
Nothing can change my history,
and rescue me from purgatory
No Redemption for my contention
My guilt, my shame, my pride, my loss,
these tortured memories my cost

Fate or folly please find a plan,
to give me back the upper hand
My enemy is now my mind,
takes me away from all mankind

For wisdom is wasted on the old,
my younger self could not be told
That war is just an endless folly,
of pointless death with ever volley
Now the fight for me has gone,
no time to try and right the wrong

Put me to death and let me rest
Erase this shame upon my breast
They arrive, the angels now I see
and wipe my guilty brow for me

I go to rest, ceasefire for me
a soldier's life no more to be
Please God I go to take my leave
into your hands my soul receive'

The End

John puts his notebook down and sits in quiet contemplation.

Philomena is speechless. She ponders on John's private thoughts and feelings expressed in his poem.

Philomena says, 'You are a sensitive man, you are a kind soul and you are a good man John.'

John does not speak, instead changes the subject saying, 'We need to look at your wounds.'

John goes out of the room to get fresh bandages.

After a few minutes John returns back into the bedroom.

John starts unwrapping the bandage on Philomena's arm. John caresses her arm lovingly, to the point of being sensual. As John does so, Philomena looks lovingly at John who reciprocates smiling back.

John says, 'I need to take the plaster cast off your leg.' John touches Philomena's plaster cast saying, 'I need to get it wet, so it's easier for me to get it off.' John continues saying, 'If you get in the bath and soak your leg. I can then cut it off, as the water will soak into every little crack and crevice making you moist. I can gently ease it out and take it off.' Philomena has an increased sense of innocence and excitement at the prospect of John's actions.

Philomena says, 'Ok, will you help me to get in the bath?'

John replies with eagerness saying, 'Yes, of course.' John runs the bath water for Philomena. Stirring the water with his hand to get the temperature just right. John gets it warm and soapy. As John does this, something makes him turn his head to the doorway of the bathroom. Philomena is standing in the entrance in a bathrobe. She looks at John intently simultaneously untying the robe as she walks in. Her bathrobe drops to the floor revealing Philomena's naked body, apart from her plaster cast on her leg.

John has feelings of sexual excitement and yearning for Philomena. Philomena smiles with amusement at seeing John aroused at her naked body. Philomena says nothing but holds her hand out for John to help her enter the bath. John holds Philomena's hand as she slowly slips into the warm water. Easing herself gently into the bath. Philomena stares at John as she slides into the warm soapy water.

Philomena lays in the bath up to her shoulders in water. Philomena plunges her head under the water, coming back up running her fingers, sensually, through her short black hair.

John is trying his best to stay focused on the job of removing the plaster cast from Philomena's leg. John puts his hand into the bath water and raises Philomena's leg up out of the water. With a pair of scissors in his hand, John starts cutting the plaster cast. Philomena looks on approvingly, as John cuts the plaster cast off with measuring degrees of ease. Philomena has her eyes fixed on John's hands all the time.

Finally, John cuts the plaster cast the whole way up, to the top of Philomena thigh. John puts the scissor down by the side of the bath. With both hands John prizes the plaster cast away from Philomena's leg. John lifts the cast out of the bath and onto the floor. John picks out some loose plaster floating in the water.

As John is doing this, Philomena gently touches John's hand. John looks at her and says nothing. Philomena is also silent and smiling at john. Holding John's hand she guides it down under the water between her legs to where her vagina is. As John feels her pussy they both smile at each other with excitement. From under the water Philomena moves John's hands up and down on her vagina.

John is visibly aroused and shocked by Philomena's actions, as she continues pleasuring herself with John's hand. Philomena is enjoying this and starts to show her enjoyment. Philomena is breathing heavily as she arches her back slightly stiffening her pelvis onto John's hand. John then penetrates her with his fingers. They both are increasingly sexually aroused as Philomena helps John finger her pussy. John's breathing has quickened and is enthused with his attraction towards Philomena. John has been kneeling next to the bath but now John stands up, still pleasuring Philomena from under the water.

As John stands up Philomena can see that he has an erection through his shorts. It is strong and hard and it makes a big bulge in the cloth of his shorts. Philomena takes her other hand out of the water. Philomena rubs John's cock and then slips her hand under his shorts and plays with his penis They are now joined in their sexual pleasure.

Suddenly, Philomena sits up and with both hands pulls John's shorts down. Philomena leans forward out of the bath and puts her mouth around John's hard cock. Philomena looks up at John as she proceeds to suck down hard on John's dick. Philomena then slides her mouth from off john's cock and his cock flops out of her mouth. Philomena puts her hand around the stem of John's penis then starts masturbating John, in a rhythmic motion. John groans with excitement as Philomena wanks him off, at a fanatical pace. Still in the bath, Philomena rubs her vagina with her other hand. Philomena is simultaneously, masturbating herself, while masturbating john. John is taking his time to enjoy this. John kicks his shorts off and then climbs into the bath causing the water to splash everywhere. Philomena welcomes John, smiling at him seductively. John now in the throes of passion holds Philomena by the ankles and opens her legs apart. John then lies between Philomena legs.

Their bodies are now entwined. John penetrates Philomena's vagina. John starts fucking Philomena. The bath water spilling over onto the floor as John's arse rises up and down, as they have sex in the bath. John stops in full flow kissing Philomena on the neck.

John whispers saying, 'I want to take you to the bedroom,'

Philomena says, 'Take me and fuck me hard.' With this John stands out of the bath and lifts Philomena out. Philomena is impressed by John's strength and she wraps her legs around John's waist. John walks out of the bathroom and down the hallway, carrying Philomena.

John carries her into the bedroom. They are both dripping wet, this intensifies the frenzy of their sexual desires for each other.

Philomena is still straddled john. Her arms are around John's neck and her legs around his waist. John stumbles through the bedroom door and throws Philomena onto the bed. Philomena is naked and John is naked from the waist down. Philomena grabs John's shirt and rips it off causing the buttons to burst off. John opens Philomena's legs, as he does so he moves his face down onto her pussy. John licks and sucks all around Philomena's vagina.

John finds her clitoris with his tongue and licks it softly. John then bites her clitoris gently not enough to hurt but enough to send a tingle up the spine of her whole body.

John then slowly moves up towards Philomena's face, kissing her body as he ascends. As John does this, Philomena raises her legs in a crouched position beckoning John to penetrate her. In a state of euphoria and immediacy, Philomena shouts, 'Fuck me hard John.' On hearing this, John penetrates Philomena. Philomena arches her back and lets out an exhale of breath as she accepts John into her. Both their bodies now twisted and entwined with each other. John starts to fuck Philomena hard.

Amid Philomena shouts and screaming, John grunts and groans. There is an orchestral orgasm of noises from both of them, as they have uninhibited sex. The release of sexual tension between them is tremendous. The taboo of love between a soldier and a catholic woman, like an exorcism is now expelled between them. This orchestral orgasmic performance builds to its crescendo as John is ready to ejaculate. John bites Philomena on the side of the neck as he ejaculates. John's body stiffens as he spunks inside Philomena.

As John ejaculates into Philomena, this spurs Philomena into orgasm. She bites John's chest and sinks her nails into John's arse cheeks. Philomena makes a high pitch scream, climaxing along with john. Philomena kisses John and bites John's lower lip as she finishes her orgasm. The pair both sigh and relax into each other's embrace. John is still inside Philomena, lying between her legs. Their bodies stay locked entangled as they both enjoy the moment of ecstasy.

There is silence then John says, 'Well, I think your leg is healed now.'

They both burst out laughing and kiss each other in a loving clinch. John moves out from between Philomena legs. They both lay back on the bed looking up at the ceiling. They smile to themselves at the unmentioned forbidden love that has finally come to fruition.

They spend the night together asleep in bed curled up tight. In love with each other.

Boxing Day 1993

It is early morning on Boxing Day. John wakes up to see Philomena straddling him. Philomena is naked and is staring at him with a cheeky smile on her face. John goes to move and realises that John realises he is handcuffed. In fact, Philomena has used the original handcuff john used on her to handcuff both his hands to the bedpost.

John, amused, says, 'What is happening?. Philomena says, 'Payback'.

John, slightly nervous, says, ' What do you mean?.

Philomena smiling says, 'Payback for handcuffing me for days to that fucking bed.'

John is worried now, not sure how to take what Philomena is saying. John is thinking to himself, is Philomena joking or has everything been fake? Does Philomena really hate him? Has she been waiting all this time for a chance to get revenge?

Philomena now with a serious look on her face says, ' It is time for you to pay for your sins'. John is definitely worried now saying, 'Are you fucking joking me?

Philomena says, 'No, this is no joke, soldier boy.'

John says, 'I thought we loved each other. Philomena laughing says, 'Love or no love, it's time to pay.' John pulls at his handcuffs says, 'What the fuck are you talking about?'

Philomena says, 'Your payback for keeping me locked up like a prisoner.' Philomena stops smiling and looks angrily into John's face saying, 'Now I am in control and I am going to make you pay.' John, realising this is not a joke, hopelessly starts pulling at his handcuffs again saying , 'Let me go.'

Philomena shouts at John saying, 'I am going to take my revenge on you, soldier boy.' Philomena, ominously puts her hands around John's throat.

Philomena says, 'It's time for me to.' Philomena pauses and stares hard at john saying, 'Fuck your brains out.'

John stops in his tracks saying, 'What?'

Philomena smirks at john saying, 'I am going to ride you like a rocking horse, Death by fucking.' Philomena bursts out laughing saying, 'I had you there, soldier boy.'

John's face shows a big sigh of relief. John realises Philomena is joking with him.

Philomena, laughing uncontrollably, says, 'Forget being the pig feeder, you are going to be the pussy feeder and my pussy needs feeding.' Philomena, who is still grasping John's throat, releases her grip and kisses him on the lips. Philomena who is still straddled on top of John, grinds her pussy on John's groin saying, 'Fill my pussy up with your fresh cream soldier boy or should I say the pussy feeder.'

Philomena can't control her laughter as she relives seeing John's face, when she was fooling him. Philomena says, 'I had you there.'

John realising Philomena was joking the whole time laughs in relief. John is laying naked on the bed still handcuffed to the bedpost.

Philomena slips under the bed covers. Philomena kisses John's body, moving downwards until she reaches John's balls. John's penis is hard and erect. Philomena smiles, looking at John's erect cock. Philomena admiring John's hard cock says, 'Hello, morning Glory.' Philomena proceeds to kiss then suck his dick.

Philomena then pushes the bed covers off and squat down on John's erection. Philomena works it into her pussy. Philomena pants as she grinds herself down on John's penis. Philomena starts bouncing up and down on John, violently. Philomena says, 'I told you, I was going to ride you hard. They both convulse as they fuck each other. John is groaning and Philomena is moaning. John is still handcuffed to the bed, and this causes the bed to rock and roll violently.

John and Philomena culminate to a crescendo of sex as they orgasm together. Philomena screams with pleasure. John is exhausted with Philomena's rampant sex. John says, 'I thought you were going to rip my dick off, you bounced so hard on me.'

Philomena, still panting but getting her breath back says, 'I'm not finished with you yet. You still must pay for your sins. I want you to suck all the love juice out of my pussy.'

John smiles saying, 'Whatever it takes to pay you back for handcuffing you'. They both laugh in unison with amusement.

John is still handcuffed as Philomena moves up the bed. Philomena puts her open thighs around John's face.

Philomena says, 'I am going to sit on your face, so suck my pussy dry.' Philomena sits on John's face. John proceeds to suck on Philomena's vagina, sucking down on it hard. Philomena groans with pleasure. John continues sucking and kissing her fanny. John pushes himself further underneath Philomena's pussy to her bum and licks her arsehole. This sends a shiver of excitement up Philomena's spine. John can feel Philomena gushing onto his face as Philomena orgasms on John's face. John chomps down on Philomena's vagina, sucking all her juice up, to Philomena's delight. Still in their same positions, Philomena looks down at John, saying, 'Well, you definitely paid for your sins.' John smiles at Philomena saying, 'I enjoyed paying for my sins. I need to sin more often.'

Philomena uncuffs John from the bedpost. John and Philomena start kissing passionately. They hold each other and relax in bed saying nothing.

The silence is disturbed by a knock at the door. The knocking is constant and loud. John looks out the window and sees a car parked outside the cottage. John, not recognising the vehicle, gets out of bed and puts on his pants and trousers.

John whispers to Philomena, 'You stay here and keep out of sight' John, moves silently out of the bedroom down the hallway and into the kitchen. John carefully opens a kitchen draw and takes a knife out. The knocking continues to disturb the silence. John walks towards the front door. John is holding the kitchen knife in his hand in readiness to attack any intruder.

John tentatively opens the front door to reveal that on the doorstep is a man. A well-built tall man. The man has his back to John as he stands in the doorway.

The man turns around and smiles at john. On seeing the man's face John immediately smiles. John warmly says, 'Tom, what are you doing here?'

Thomas McNulty or Tom to his mates is John's old army mate. Tom formed part of the four-man team that John led. The same team that discovered the IRA terrorist cell that blew up the cenotaph at Enniskillen on Remembrance Day.

Tom was John's second in command. John was a more than capable man, highly intelligent and ruthless, if needed. Tom is tall, dark and handsome. A well-spoken man, he originally grew up in a wealthy family. Tom's father was a banker in London. From an early age it was destined that Tom would pursue a career in the military. Coming from his position of privilege, it was presumed that Tom would go to Sandhurst. However, the family's situation took a different turn, after father was sacked for improper practices in the banking industry..

Tom found himself living in Streatham, Southeast London, as his family struggled to live, having no income. His father got a low paid job, unable to work in the banking industry after his name had been unfairly tarnished. His father always said he was made a scapegoat for the bank, who were embezzling money. Undeterred, Tom joined the rank-and-file army core and met John at basic training. Tom is a survivor and a clever hustler who can live on his wits. Tom is now working for the UDA as an interim between them and the British Army. After the ambush Tom left the Army and now works freelance with the UDA. Part mercenary and part negotiator, but always independent of any organisation.

Tom, still standing in the doorway says, 'Hi John. I was in the neighbourhood, so I thought I would drop in'

John says, 'How are you mate?

Tom says, 'All the best for seeing you mate, can I come in?'

John says, 'Yes, of course, what brings you around this area?'

Tom says, 'I am on some business.'

Tom continues, 'I have not seen you since the regiments last reunion a few years ago'

John says, 'I know I have been meaning to come more frequently. I have been busy here at the cottage. I am quitting as the pig feeder and leaving here soon, so will have more time to come to the next reunion.'

John continues says, 'Come in Tom. Do you want a drink?'

Tom walks into the kitchen saying, 'No, I am ok.'

John says, 'Take a seat.'

Tom pulls out a chair from the kitchen table and sits down.

Tom says, 'Well, that actually is why I am here. I need to talk to you about your decision to stop helping the UDA dispose of their dead.'

John, surprised at Tom's comment, says, 'I just want out Tom.'

Tom says sympathetically, 'I know mate but it's not as easy as that.'

John says stubbornly, 'It looks easy enough for me Tom. I have quit and that is that.'

Tom looks disappointed with johns' views. Tom nervously scratches the surface of the kitchen table with his fingernails. Tom says, 'We are aware you have someone living here mate. We can only assume it is one of your deliveries that was not dead, as we know you are a recluse and don't know anyone.

Tom continues saying, 'So, I need to check that you are not hiding someone.'

John says, 'Mate there's no one here and who's we Tom?'

Tom looks down awkwardly from John's question. John continues saying, 'You mean you and the UDA'

Tom says, 'How long have we known each other mate?. I know there is someone here,'

Tom continues saying, 'Come on John, it is me you are talking to. We bled together on many battlefields. We both saved each other's lives numerous times. I got your back mate. We know someone is here. The old man saw her when he was last here. When you refused to take his delivery.'

Tom continues saying, 'It is better you tell me what's going on rather than you having to explain it to the UDA men. I had to pull in some favour in the UDA for me to make this visit rather than one of the UDA enforcers.

John ponders for a minute then relaxes saying, 'Ok, Yes there is a woman here.'

John continues saying, 'The UDA had not killed her and when delivered here for disposal she was barely alive, so I nursed her back to life.'

Tom interrupts asking, 'So why didn't you tell the UDA?'

John says, 'Because it would be like me signing her death warrant. They would have just killed her. I am not having her murder on my conscience. I have enough blood on my hands already Tom.'

Tom in a sombre tone says, 'We all do brother.'

John says, 'She is living here until she is well enough to leave. Then she is not my responsibility.'

Tom is quiet for a moment contemplating what John has told him. Tom's analytical mind runs through in his head various repercussions of what has happened. He breaks his silent saying, 'John, you need to turn her over to the UDA'

John says, 'What, turn her over so she can be killed?'

Tom says, 'Whatever mate, it's not your concern.'

John says, 'No mate, I took a vow never to take a life again. To give her over to the UDA would be a death warrant for her.'

Tom says, 'What do you care about an IRA woman, after everything we have seen and experienced from the IRA?'

John says, 'Despite what we have seen from the IRA. I won't let her die because life is not about conflict, Tom. It is about working out any problems peacefully with reconciliation.'

John continues saying, 'I have seen too much death and what has it achieved? Absolutely nothing.'

Tom says, 'Tell that to all our mates killed by those IRA Bastards. No mate, I'm saying this for your own good. If you don't give her up, they will come and kill her and you too.'

Tom, getting emotional, says, 'I am not going to let that happen to you John.'

Tom stands up saying, 'If you will not tell me where she is, I will just have to find her myself mate'

John stands up and grabs Tom's arm saying, 'No Tom, I'm not giving her up.'

Tom angry and frustrated says, 'What the Fuck is wrong with you?' Why are you so adamant to risk your life for this woman?'

John says, 'because I took a vow.'

Tom says,' Fuck the vow. This is your life at risk mate. I need to take her back with me to the UDA.

John increasingly angry says, 'No Tom, you're not taking her, I will not let you'

Tom says, 'Why the fuck are you doing this John?'

John, becoming more and more agitated, replies, 'I took a vow never to take part in any more killings.'

John still holding Toms arm strengthens his grip on Tom

Tom noticing this says, 'What is wrong with you John? Are you fucking mad ? Why are you doing this ?'

John shouts, 'Because' then suddenly stops and refrains from continuing.

Tom shouts at John saying, 'Because what ?'

John resets himself then says in a calm voice, 'Because I love her.'

Tom amazed and in shock by Johns comments says, 'What the fuck are you talking about? Are you kidding me?' You love her, an IRA operative!'

John proudly says, 'Yes, I Love her. I love Philomena, not an IRA Operative. Her name is Philomena'

Tom says, 'She finally has a name, Philomena is her name. Fuck me john, have you lost your mind ?' Tom continues saying, 'I'm not letting you do this to yourself.'

Tom pulls his arm out of John's grip and reveals a handgun from his jacket.

Tom says, 'I am sorry John, but this is the only way to save your life. If I do not kill the woman, the UDA will kill you both.

Tom, with a sense of urgency, moves towards the door looking for Philomena.

John without hesitation jumps on top of Tom's back. Tom reacts instinctively, elbowing John in the side of the face. John feels the blow but shakes it off. Still on Tom's back. John puts his arms in a locking position around Toms' neck and locks on with both arms

John tightens his grip around Tom's neck. Enough for Tom to stumble backwards, slamming John into the kitchen table. This action sends them both over the table backwards onto the kitchen floor. John still has a neck lock. Tom has lost his gun in the fighting and with john still on his back struggles to release himself.

Tom tries punching John. Due to the awkward position Tom finds it difficult to land a punch from behind. Tom in a strained voice says, 'Don't do this John.'

Tom tries to reach for his ankle, but he misses. He manages to stretch enough this time to reach his ankle. Tom reveals he has a small knife tied around his ankle. Tom pulls it from its holster and stabs John in his arm.

This action immediately results in John relinquishing his neck lock on Tom.

Tom then reacts immediately from being released out of the neck lock.

Tom turns on top of John, punching John repeatedly in the face several times in quick succession.

Philomena appears at the doorway to the kitchen to see what is happening.

Tom then starts to strangle John with both hands. Tom straddles over John, using his legs to pin John's arms down. John tried to stop Tom but to no avail.

Tom tightens his grip around John's neck as John begins to lose consciousness. John's face strains under the pressure. John begins to succumb to the strangulation.

Suddenly, there is a big bang and a thud.

John feels his neck free from the weight of strangulation. John gasping to breath, sees Philomena standing in the doorway with a gun in her hand. Philomena is frozen in shock.

John looks to his side and sees Tom slumped, face down, motionless on the floor. There is blood oozing out onto the floor, in an increasingly large pool of blood.

John leans over pulling Tom onto his back.

As John does this, Tom groans and opens his eyes.

Tom is clearly unwell from the gunshot wound and shows lack of responsiveness. Tom is passing in and out of consciousness.

Philomena shouts, 'Is he ok? I thought he was going to kill you.'

John says, 'He is injured.'

Tom starts trying to talk. Murmuring at first but then he becomes coherent and his speech more comprehensible. Tom opens his eyes saying, 'John are you there?'

John says, 'I'm right here Tom.'

It's as if Tom is struggling to see but his eyes are open

Tom continues saying, 'Fuck me, the bitch shot me.'

John says, 'Bloody hell Tom, I'm sorry. Are you ok!'

Tom says, 'No mate, I'm dying.'

John looks down at the gunshot wound in Tom's side, to see he is bleeding heavily.

There is silence.

John looks to Philomena who still has the gun in her hand. Philomena is in shock but resolute at defending John. Philomena says, 'I'm sorry I thought he was going to kill you john.'

Tom looks at Philomena and laughs saying, 'Kill john? You must be joking. I would never kill my mate. We were just having a friendly disagreement. John is like my brother. I have saved his life many times, isn't that right john?'

John with watery eyes says, 'Yes mate many times.'

John lowers his head in sadness at the thought of his army mate, now laying mortally wounded on the kitchen floor.

Tom says, 'We are soldiers and brothers in arms.' Bled together in many grounds, in many towns'

Tom continues saying, 'I would never kill john. I was just going to strangle him unconscious so I could get to you Philomena'

John, holding back from crying, says, 'I am sorry Tom, I just can't let you take Philomena. I am so sorry Tom. Let's get you to a doctor.'

Tom says, 'We both know that is not an option mate. I am dying. We both know that John.'

Tom looking at his wound says, 'I am bleeding out mate, I haven't got long.'

Tom grabs John by the arm and pulls him closer saying, 'Listen to me very clearly John. I had to convince the UDA to allow me to come and speak to you first. They just wanted to send a death squad down straight away and kill you both.

Tom winches with pain but continues saying. 'Because of my connections with the UDA, I convinced them. They granted me the chance to peacefully come and persuade you to give the girl up. That is not happening now, so you need to get away from here. The UDA said if I did not convince you and clean up the mess. They will deal with it. The UDA gave me until tomorrow morning to let them know I had sorted things out. If they don't hear from me by tomorrow morning, they will send a death squad to kill you and the woman. They will come the following day at dawn, so you have 48 hours to escape.'

John adamantly says I'm not running. Philomena is in no fit state to run anywhere.'

Tom is feeling the pain in his side as he bleeds out. John is putting pressure on his wound.

Tom looks ominously at John saying, 'You must prepare for the coming battle. I have a rifle and spare handgun in my car with ammunition.'

Tom is still holding John's arm but now let's go and leans further back flat on the floor. Tom looks at John saying, 'You need to use guerrilla tactics and bring the war to them. They will come at dawn. One team normally five or six with light armour, no grenades or rocket launchers. Nothing serious, just rifles and pistols.'

John is trying not to cry as he knows his friend is dying and there is nothing he can do.

Tom's face creases in pain holding the side of his body as he continues saying, 'I am dying john. I'm glad I'm dying mate. I go to be with Jocky and Kevin. Tom continues saying, 'I have been dead ever since we allowed those IRA Bastards to blow up the cenotaph and kill innocent civilians. I stopped living after that, only just existing. To die is peace. This is closure to die mate. I'm not scared to die, I embrace it.'

John is trying not to cry, unable to speak.

Tom then with a sense of urgency says, 'John I want you to promise me one thing ?'

John says, 'What is it Tom? '

Tom says, 'That you won't feed me to those fucking pigs.' Tom laughs which makes john smile briefly through his anguish.

John says, 'Don't be fucking stupid. I'd never do that and anyway you are going to live. We need to get you up.' John goes to move Tom from the floor.

Tom grabs johns arm tightly saying, 'Fuck off john, this is it. I'm dying mate. Let me be. You must promise me you will carry on.'

Tom squeezes John's arm saying, 'You must survive. You must live. If you love that woman like you say you do, then you and that woman must survive. Get out of here and live your life to the fullest.'

John says, 'I don't know how to live. I don't know if I can do it.'

Tom says, 'Do it for me and all your mates who never got the chance to live. Our mates who were cut down in their prime in Northern Ireland. Live for them.'

Tom then seems to lay back looking up at the ceiling saying, 'I'm tired John, I'm so tired mate. Hold my hand john, I need you to help me do this.'

Tom looks over at Philomena saying, 'I hope you are worth it.'

John holds Toms hand

Tom whispers to himself saying, 'God have mercy on me'

Tom looks at John then looks down. Squeezing John's hand Tom lets out a deep long breath of air. At the end of this breath, Tom's body relaxes then stops motionless.

Tom is dead.

John, still holding Tom's hand, cries uncontrollably.

A few moments pass then Philomena puts her hands on john saying, 'He's gone John. You must let him go.'

Philomena reaches over and with her hand closes Tom's eyelids. Philomena reaches down and helps to prise Tom's hand out from johns.

Taking a blanket from the kitchen. Philomena covers Tom's face and body with it.

John and Philomena are rigid to the spot in silence and in shock. Looking at the covered body on the kitchen floor both in disbelief. John is only broken from his shock in the knowledge he must prepare for war.

Now, Tom is dead, and the UDA Death Squad will be on their way, to tie up their loose ends, killing John and Philomena.

John and Philomena look at each other, resolutely aware of the oncoming fight before them.

John says,' We have work to do'.

Kevin comes into the kitchen to the scene of Tom's Murder. Tom was one of Kevin's army colleagues and a friend. Kevin in disbelief stares at Tom's lifeless body on the kitchen floor

Kevin shouts, 'What the fuck has happened?'

John says, 'Tom wanted to kill Philomena. I had to stop him and things got out of control.'

Kevin says. 'What do you mean things got out of control? Tom is dead. Who killed him?'

John says, 'I killed him in the heat of the moment?'

Kevin says, 'Don't fool me john. Whether it was you or Philomena who pulled the trigger is irrelevant. Tom's blood is on Philomena's hands for turning your head and heart. You have betrayed your mates for a woman.'

John says, 'Philomena is not just any woman. She is the love of my life, my soulmate.'

Kevin says, 'Then it is your hands that are covered by Tom's blood. You have murdered your friend.'

Kevin continues saying, 'I may be a ghost, or I may be a figment of your imagination like your girlfriend says. But, whatever I am, I don't betray my army mates. You're out of order John and your girlfriend. I want no more part of this and you.

Kevin comes up close to John's face and says, 'Where is your loyalty John ?'

Kevin continues saying, 'We are all brothers in arms you, me and Tom. Tom is dead now thanks to you. I may as well be dead now too.'

John says, 'I love you Kevin like my brother and Tom too, but I also love Philomena.'

Kevin says, 'You have made your choice John. I'm out of here'

Kevin walks out of the kitchen and the cottage and disappears.

John has his eyes closed and is silent as he processes in his mind his new reality. A world without Kevin by his side but a world with love in it, with Philomena..

John opens his eyes and looks at Philomena saying, 'We need to prepare.' Philomena nods resolutely at john.

John gets the rifle and gun from Tom's car. Philomena carries the ammunition into the cottage.

John chiffons the petrol from tom's car using a pipe, sucking on it then running it into a petrol can. John starts making petrol bombs, filling empty glass bottles with petrol. John picks up a bottle of washing up liquid and squeezes some into the glass bottles filled with petrol. Philomena sees John doing this and with curiosity says, 'Why are you putting washing up liquid into the bottles of petrol?'

John says, 'When on patrol, the kids would make up their own petrol bombs to throw at us. They learned that if you mix washing up liquid with petrol. The petrol bomb becomes like a napalm bomb and sticks to anyone it hits. I will never forget seeing the damage it does to human skin and hair, when it comes in contact with it.'

John stares into space with a disturbed look in his eyes, reliving the horrific sights he has seen.

Philomena says, 'Wow, I didn't know that.' John says, 'Yes, there were things I didn't know, before I came to your country,'

Philomena says, 'What do you mean?'

John says, 'Well, for example, I thought being tarred and feathered was something that happened to people in the medieval times. I was wrong because when I arrived in Northern Ireland, I saw people tarred and feathered in the streets of Belfast.

John continues saying, 'I was shocked that this happened in this day and age. Tied to a lamp post and hot tar poured over them or a concrete block dropped from a height on them. Don't forget the feathers at the end for decoration and humiliation.'

Philomena says, 'The horrors that have been resurrected during the troubles are unbelievable, So much evilness.'

John nods saying, 'When will people learn, violence is not the answer.' John says this as he finishes making his petrol bombs.

John goes into the butchering room to get some knives and utensils, which he uses to prepare the dead bodies. John then goes into his bedroom and reaches behind the wardrobe. He retrieved a bow and arrow.

Philomena to her amusement sees John with a bow and arrow. Philomena starts laughing saying, 'Now, it is getting weird. Do you think you are Robin Hood? I suppose that will make me Maid Marion.'

John laughs saying, 'Whatever turns you on, but I was regional champion two years running, in 1988 and 1989. So, yes. I'll be Robin Hood and you can be Maid Marion. If it helps us to survive, I will do whatever it takes.'

Chapter 12

The Battle - An Cath

28th December 1993

Dawn has arrived and the birds are singing. The morning mist floats through the fields, enveloping the isolated cottage. John and Philomena are waiting for the arrival of the UDA death squad.

John watching out the window reminisces saying, 'When I was a young boy, I would go to Ireland once a year from London with my dad. We would get the train from Euston train station to Holyhead. It was a long journey. Once at Holyhead, we would start the arduous journey on the Sealink ferry across the Irish sea to Rosslare. I remember it was always a night-time sea crossing and the Irish sea was so dark and stormy. As a young kid, I recall it was a scary experience.'

'I was always seasick. In fact, I remember everyone was seasick on those rough holiday trips. Once in Ireland, I would stay with my lovely little granny. She lived in the south east of Ireland. She always would say that in the 1920s, during the Irish uprising, her uncle was on the run from the British army and hid a rifle in the back garden. I always would search for that rifle when I was over on holiday, but I never found it. I loved those holidays with my father. Me and my dad would walk everywhere as we had no car. We would walk through the Irish countryside to the nearest village of Bagenalstown. Sometimes, we would hitch hike and a car would always stop and give me and my dad a lift into the town. It didn't matter whether we were protestant or catholic, those people were just being kind. My dad would chat to them during the short journey, my dad loved talking to people.

I always remember one early morning. My dad and I decided to walk into a nearby village called Leighlinbridge. It was a fresh misty morning, very much like today. As we walked, I remember seeing a hill in the distance. The sun was rising behind this hill as the dawn was breaking. A beautiful golden sunrise was silhouetted against the hill.

On the top of that hill, I noticed a sheep giving birth to a baby lamb. I was amazed, as I watched the birth of this new life. It was amazing to witness the birth of a life. I was so enthralled and privileged to see a life created. I realised then as I do now, that is, how beautiful and valuable life is. It is a magical thing when you see the gift of life. Every life is a miracle.'

John continues saying, 'As I wait for assassins to arrive, hoping to kill us. I wonder when did human beings get so lost? That we treat life as if it is worthless. We, as a species, seem to disrespect and denigrate the sanctity of a life. Life is the most spiritual event on Earth and yet, it is valued so cheaply. When will human beings stop killing each other ?'

John looks at Philomena who looks back without an answer.

Suddenly, a distant sound appears in the damp fresh air. It is a murmuring, which slowly turns into the sound of a vehicle approaching.

The noise is now very present in the calm of the countryside melancholy. A silver car appears moving at high speed through the country lanes. It is driving fast and starts to slow. The vehicle continues a steady reduction in speed until it arrives, stopping at the gate of the field leading to John's cottage.

The car is packed with passengers, and they all exit the vehicle. The driver remains in the car with the engine running. The men are all wearing balaclavas, physically well built. Two of the men are very tall.

There are five assassins who make up the UDA death squad.

The men are brandishing guns and have a sense of intent to get somewhere. They open the gate and start walking down the track in the field towards the cottage. The men spread out strategically to close in on their prey as they hunt for John and Philomena.

As they get closer to the cottage something makes a whistling sound. One of the men drops to the ground with an arrow in his face. This act of aggression makes the men drop to the ground to take cover.

Four assassins left.

The assassins open fire on the cottage with a barrage of bullets. This destroys the front door and shatters the glass in the windows of the cottage.

The assassins hear a noise from directly behind them, like a movement in the undergrowth. A bottle comes hurling out from the bushes to the side of the assassins. The bottle hits one of the men.

As it does so, it bursts into flames sending the man screaming from the fire that has engulfed him. The assassin drops and rolls on the ground, trying to extinguish the flames on him. The screaming fades to groans as the man lays on the ground in agony. The man is now extinguished but incapacitated.

Three assassins left.

The other men unload a torrent of ammunition into the bushes, where the petrol bomb had been thrown. There are three men still active. These assassins run at the cottage to overrun the inhabitants of the cottage. One assassin goes through the entrance of the cottage while another assassin backs him up from behind.

As the first unwelcome visitor disappears inside the cottage, He is forcibly propelled backwards out of the entrance. This assassin falls backward onto his colleague behind him. The pair of assassins fall backwards onto the ground.

Frantically, the first man repelled from the cottage lays on the ground in agony. Blood is spurting from the man's neck as he clutches onto his throat. The assassin is unable to stop the torrent of blood gushing out of his neck. The man is unable to speak due to his severed thorax and artery. The man rolls around uncontrollably only managing to spit and gurgle as the blood froths from his mouth. The assassin struggles helplessly. Eventually, his body is motionless leaving only the movement of the blood, still pulsing from his neck. The blood oozes into the wet grassy earth.

The dead assassin's colleague is still on the ground staggering to get up, momentarily knocked unconscious. He stands up regaining his senses and looks around seeing his colleague dead on the grass. Nervously, the assassin backs away from the entrance of the cottage and rejoins his remaining colleague.

Two assassins left

The last two assassins are watching from the periphery of the cottage. They spot Philomena running out from the back of the cottage. Philomena has her head covered with a red scarf.

Seeing Philomena escaping, one of the assassins signals this to his colleague. They both acknowledge this and one of the assassins gives chase across the field after her. The remaining assassin moves cautiously towards the cottage looking for John.

The pursuing assassin shoots at Philomena as he chases her. Philomena runs as fast as she can. Her face is covered by her scarf fluttering in the wind as she runs. The bullets miss her as she makes a run for it. She is running towards an area of trees, a small wooded area. As Philomena gets there, she disappears through a break in the woods. The man approaching the trees aims to run into the same opening, where Philomena disappeared.

As the assassin arrives at the opening, he disappears out of sight. He shouts but cannot be seen. The assassin has fallen down through footing underneath him, into a large hole full of what appears to be water.

The assassin reacts and tries to get his bearings. As he does so, he soon realises he has fallen into a man made hole and a trap. There is an overwhelming smell of petrol. To his terror, the assassin realises that he is floating in a pool of petrol. The man starts to sink as his petrol sodden clothing starts to weigh him down. The more he struggles and tries to pull himself up, the more he sinks.

The hole has been dug in such a way that the assassin cannot pull himself out. He struggles as he tries to stay afloat, he shouts for help as he submerges out of sight. Reappearing again, spitting the petrol out of his mouth. The bitter taste of the petrol makes him choke and wretch. The man looks up to the top of the hole for help. But to the assassin's horror he sees John appear like a silhouette against the sky.

John has a red scarf around his neck, identical to the one that Philomena was wearing, which he pulls off himself. The assassin realises, in fact, that the woman he was chasing was actually a masquerade for Philomena and was actually John. It was John impersonating Philomena. John looks unemotional at the man as he reveals a cigarette lighter from his pocket and lights it.

The entrenched man looks at the flame from the cigarette lighter in panic. Realising what John is intending. The assassin begins shouting and pleading to John saying, 'No, Please wait. Please don't do it.' The man frantically but pointlessly tries to clamber out of the hole but just sinks back into the pool of petroleum.

Without flinching, John drops the cigarette lighter still alight into the hole. It is only a few seconds in reality. But to the assassin watching, the lighter falling through the air, seems like an eternity. The world has stood still in slow motion as the assassin watches the lighter drop into the hole. It has sealed the assassin's fate. Conversely, John watches on as the lighter disappears into the hole, igniting the petrol. There is a whooshing sound from the roar of the flames, engulfing the hole. The assassin lets out screams that would shock the devil himself. John cannot see the man amidst the flames, just the screams coming from the hole in the ground. The hole is like a chimney bellowing out thick black smoke against the background of unearthly howling from the burning man. The smell of cooking flesh permeates the air.

The assassin burns until there is silence. The man is now dead and free of his ordeal.

John is already far from the hole on his way back to the cottage, as he knows Philomena is there. One assassin remains and is still at the cottage. John runs with haste to the cottage.

As John runs, the sky is darkened by the black smoke coming from the hell hole behind him.

One assassin left.

The last assassin is walking quietly through the cottage searching for his kill.

The butchering room is in darkness and Philomena is sitting in a corner hiding.

The assassin hears a noise coming from the butchering room. The assassin raises his rifle zooming in on this. Aiming straight ahead, he enters the butchering room to see a dead body on the table. The surprise of seeing the body startles the assassin, who sends one shot into the body just to check it is dead.

The body is that of John's mate, Tom. John has left Tom's body there as a place of rest.

Philomena is still hiding in the corner of the room. Hidden by the darkness and crouching down behind a chair.

Suddenly, a pair of hands come from the dark and grab Philomena from behind.

A hand muffles her mouth to silence her. John's face appears to the side of her. Philomena's shock turns to relief as she realises it is John.

John signals at Philomena to be quiet. John then guides Philomena behind him to protect her from the assassin.

The butchering room is silent, the assassin is slowly scanning the room with his firearm. John and Philomena are holding their breath in silence not to attract the predator in the room.

The assassin slowly turns around his gun sight in the direction of John and Philomena.

The assassin says, 'Where are my little insects? I am the new pig feeder now. When I am done with you, I'm going to feed you to those fucking pigs outside.'

The assassin glimpses John and immediately goes to shoot.

Suddenly, Kevin appears from behind the assassin saying, 'Boo!.'

The assassin startled by this, instinctively turns his face towards Kevin.

In that split second of the assassin looking around at Kevin's distraction. John reaches out of the darkness and with a metal skewer, sticks it straight up into the assassin's head. The steel point enters the assassin through his chin, then up inside his head. The force of the blow pushes the man's left eyeball out of its socket. It bulges out onto the man's cheek. This protruding eyeball lays there looking in the opposite direction to his other eye.

John holds the skewer in this position as John and the man go face to face. The man groans and tries to scream but is muffled, unable to open his mouth, due to the metal skewer holding it shut.

John comes closer to the assassin's face, the man looks at John in shock, one eye open, the other hanging off his cheek.

John looks into the eye of the assassin and says, 'There is only one Pig feeder.'

John glances past the assassin and captures a glimpse of Kevin. Kevin smiles and winks at John before fading into the darkness.

Without saying a word John reveals the bottle of whiskey he always drinks when preparing his dead bodies. John looks into the assassin's face as he takes a long swig.

John looks at the man until the assassin's unaffected eyeball rolls upwards. With John holding the metal skewer into the assassin's head. John feels the tension leave the assassin's body as life leaves the man. The assassin is dead.

John then pulls the metal skewer from out of the man's head and the body drops to the floor with a thud.

Philomena, seeing the final assassin killed runs and hugs John, relieved that they have survived.

John says, 'We need to get out of here fast.'

They both run out of the cottage through the destroyed front entrance, so as to escape in John's car. But as they reach the car they are stopped in their tracks. Up by the gate, the driver of the UDA car has a machine gun and is raining bullets down on them.

The couple helplessly take cover behind John's car. They now cannot run back to the cottage without getting picked off by the gunman. They seem doomed. The couple shelter behind the car, which they know will eventually not hold back the bullets from hitting them. The windows of the car shatter and the tyres burst out with the multitude of bullets firing down on them.

The pair look at each other with a sense that this is the end. They embrace each other waiting for their fate to unfold.

Suddenly, they hear an explosion up where the gunman is.

They look up and notice another car has arrived. Armed men have exited the vehicle. Without too much opposition they have killed the driver, destroying his car. The UDA gunman is dead.

These new armed men proceed to walk into the field, heading down towards John and Philomena. They are also all big men except for a noticeably smaller man. This smaller man seems to be at the head of this group walking towards the cottage.

The smaller man calls out, shouting, 'Philomena where are you?'

Philomena looks up and calls back saying, 'I am over here Miguel.' as if she has recognised the voice.

John says,' Do you know him?'

Philomena says, 'Of course, I know him. He is my brother'

Philomena's brother and his IRA operatives walk down to meet Philomena and John. John and Philomena are relieved to see them, especially as they have saved their lives.. The men get to the couple and Philomena embraces her brother. John goes to speak to Philomena's brother but before he gets the chance. John is hit from behind with the butt of a rifle which sends him to his knees. The IRA operatives then proceed to restrain John, handcuffing John's hands behind his back.

John protests saying, 'Wait, what are you doing?'

They don't answer but instead pull a black balaclava hood over John's head.

John is unable to see and says, 'You are making a mistake.'

Philomena, is shocked and shouts, 'What are you doing to him? Leave him alone, he is ok.'

The men ignore Philomena.

Philomena looks at her brother saying, 'Stop them, he is with me. He saved my life.'

Philomena's brother says, 'I am sorry Philomena, we can't take any chances. He will be interviewed when we get him to the safe house.'

Philomena says, 'He is not one of them. He is ok. I give you my word.'

Philomena's brother says, 'My dear sister, you have been through a horrific ordeal. You are not in your right mind. He needs to be interviewed.'

Philomena says, 'You mean interrogated.'

Philomena's Brother looks at Philomena and says, 'We know that he is an ex-SAS British Soldier. We know he was helping the UDA to dispose of captured IRA operatives. Once they were tortured and killed by the Ulster Defence Association. this man would dispose of the evidence by feeding their bodies to pigs. Interviewed or interrogated whichever way you want to look at it. This man is our enemy and must be processed as a prisoner.'

Philomena is lost for words. She looks at John on his knees and blind folded saying, 'Don't worry John, it will be ck.'

John says, 'Are you ok Philomena ?' Philomena says, 'Yes, I am ok. I won't leave you John. I am here for you.'

John does not answer but secretly takes comfort from her words.

Two IRA men then pull John up onto his feet and push him forward to walk. John is accompanied up the field by two IRA men with rifles aimed at him. John is put into their car.

Philomena is visibly angry and upset with the situation. Her brother who also brandishes a rifle, walks beside her saying nothing.

Philomena says, 'How did you know we were at this cottage?'

John says, 'Philomena, are you so naive?, to think that we do not know what is happening in the Ulster Defence Association? 'We have spies everywhere.'

Philomena's brother continues saying, 'In turn, we are not foolish enough to think that the UDA do not have spies infiltrated into the IRA.' We knew you were alive. We just needed our informant to tell us where they were keeping you. When the death squad got the go ahead to attack, our informant could then find out the address. It was a close call, we got here as soon as we could, once we got the address'.

Philomena and her brother enter another car that has arrived, which is separate to the one that John is in. Both vehicles drive away together to an IRA safe house.

Chapter 13

Judgement – Breithiunas

There is a typical two up, two down terrace house, in a normal street in the catholic area of Belfast. It is raining and the sky is grey. The city is soaking from the constant rain.

Belfast was declared a city by Queen Victoria in 1888. That same year Jack the Ripper was killing and dissecting women in the streets of London. Belfast is dissected and ripped in half, bleeding and grotesquely disfigured, like a victim of Jack the Ripper. Belfast, the victim of a far more villainous monster than Jack the ripper. The monster of hatred and ignorance.

There is Darkness.

The black hood covering John's face is now pulled off, so John can see the light.

John looks around to see where he is.

Still handcuffed but now seated in a chair. John is in an IRA safe house.

As he sits in a room alone, he can hear the muffled noise of people outside arguing.

The door opens and Philomena and her brother enter the room. Another man enters the room and releases John from his handcuffs, then leaves. Philomena and her brother look agitated and are saying nothing.

There are chairs in the room but no other furniture.

Philomena takes a chair and pulls it over next to John.

Philomena's brother takes a chair and sits further away, opposite both of them.

There is silence.

Philomena's brother breaks the silence by saying, 'My name is Michael or Miguel to my friends.

Michael Martinez is the name of Philomena's Brother. His real name is Miguel, named after one of his great grandfathers from San Sebastian in Spain. This is where Philomena and Miguel's family originates from.

Miguel called himself Michael, the Irish version of Miguel, from a young age. Growing up in Belfast, his Spanish name became the butt of jokes and bullying, so he adopted Michael to blend in.

However, Miguel is proud of his Spanish roots and his family heritage in the region. Many of Miguel's relatives and close friends in Spain are members of ETA.

ETA is a terrorist organisation predominantly in the Basque region of Spain, where Philomena and Miguel's relatives still live.

ETA stands for Euskadi Ta Askatasuna translated into English, meaning "Basque Homeland and Freedom". This terrorist group is an armed Basque nationalist and separatist organisation. Based in the Basque Country in northern Spain.

The group was founded in 1959. Originally a group promoting traditional Basque culture, they transformed into a paramilitary group.

ETA engaged in a violent campaign of bombing, assassinations, and kidnappings throughout Spain, especially in the Southern Basque Country. Its goal was gaining independence for the Basque Country. ETA was the main group within the Basque National Liberation Movement and had prominent participation in the Basque conflict.

As Miguel's friends and relatives are members of ETA. Miguel uses his contacts with ETA, as a contact point for the IRA. The IRA has liaised with ETA over the years, from supplying military hardware to training and intelligence. John sees ETA as the same as the IRA, fighting for the freedom and independence of their own country. One man's freedom fighter is another man's terrorist. Depending on who side they are on. Miguel sees the IRA and ETA as freedom fighters.

Miguel fights for the independence of Northern Ireland.

Miguel says, 'I am Philomena's brother as you already know. You are here as you were helping the UDA dispose of tortured and murdered IRA operatives.

Miguel looks straight at John saying, 'Is that correct?'

John says, 'Yes, you are correct. I am not proud of it, but I cannot deny this fact.'

Miguel says, 'Did you not feel guilty for what you were doing?'

John says, 'At the time no, but since I have been with your sister, I have come to realise that fact. Even though I had not murdered the people I disposed of, I was still complicit in the process. So yes, I do feel guilt.'

John continues saying, 'Can I ask you a question?'

Miguel says, 'Yes.'

John says, 'Have you murdered any British soldiers or UDA operatives?'

Michael says, 'Yes'

John says, 'Do you feel guilty?'

Miguel says, 'No, they are invaders in my country. If they do not want a free united Ireland, then they are my enemy. I kill my enemy, just like you have killed my countrymen, who were fighting for Irish freedom.

John says, 'You are right, I have killed IRA men and unknowingly, innocent civilians too.'

Miguel says, 'Why are you so honest about your deeds in front of your enemy.'

John says, 'You are not my enemy anymore. It is only now that I understand that hatred, revenge and ignorance are all our enemies. These negative emotions are the tools used by politicians to play their games. They manipulate both sides to feed their greed for money and power. Religion is misused like a drug by governments to get good people to do evil deeds. Religious extremists, killing people for no gain but for the power hungry politicians.

John continues saying, 'The really extremist are the politicians and their masters who hide behind them. Behind the scenes they pull the strings of poor misguided souls, who are obsessive in believing in their religion or their cause. Religion has been hijacked and abused through history distorted to manipulate the people to perform unholy acts.'

John continues with his rant, saying, 'In the bigger picture you are not my enemy, no more than I am yours. We are just pawns in a sick and perverted game. Like a drug, people behave addictive and misguided to their ideology. Influence and fact are manufactured.'

John says, 'Religion played against us, to excuse people from thinking that we are all just the same. We are all just human beings. Instead, religion is played against other religions to allow their followers to treat their enemy as if they are not human.'

John pauses to gather his thoughts, then says, 'I resign myself to my fate, as there is no salvation for my soul. It is only at the end do I realise the rules of the game and who are really playing. You and I are just pawns in a game. I am not scared to die, I am dead already. As an old friend recently told me, I embrace death as it gives me peace.'

Philomena says, 'Don't say that John, you are not going to die, I won't let it happen.'

Miguel suddenly stands up and kicks his chair across the room in anger saying, 'Philomena, that is for me and the IRA to decide.'

Philomena says, 'Miguel, you better listen to me. I am your sister and you will not harm a hair on his head.'

Miguel retrieves his chair and sits back down in front of Philomena.

Miguel says, 'I'm sorry sister but there are bigger forces at play here. My IRA superiors are aware of this situation. They want him interrogated and executed.'

Philomena says, 'I don't care. It can not happen.'

Miguel says, 'What do you expect me to do ? Just let him go free?'

Philomena, obstinately, says, 'Yes.'

Miguel says, 'It is impossible.'

Philomena says, 'But I love him.'

Miguel says, 'What reason do I tell my IRA superiors why he must live? because my sister loves him?'

Philomena pauses then says, 'It can not happen, not just because I love him. It can not happen because he is going to be the father of my child.'

John in shock says, 'What?'

Miguel in shock says, 'What?'

Miguel stands up and kicks his chair again across the room in anger.

John says, 'How did this happen?'

Philomena in a light hearted tone says, 'Well, I think you know how it happened.'

John, smiling, says, 'I know how it happened. I mean when were you going to tell me?'

Philomena says, 'Well, with everything that has been happening. I did not know the right time to tell you.'

Philomena continues saying, 'I have been getting morning sickness for the last couple of days. I haven't had my period and I have always been regular as clockwork.'

John excitedly says, 'Are you sure?'

Philomena says, 'John, a woman knows these things. Well, I do anyway.'

John and Philomena smile at each other. Excited and happy, they both hug each other in a long embrace.

This is interrupted by Miguel saying, 'Excuse me.'

John and Philomena are still hugging oblivious to Miguel.

Again, Miguel repeats himself more loudly saying, 'Excuse me!'

John and Philomena stop and look at Miguel.

Miguel says, 'What the fuck has been going on?'

Miguels comment creates a more serious atmosphere as Philomena and John are silent, looking at Miguel.

Miguel says, 'Firstly, I hear my sister has been kidnapped by the UDA. Then, I hear she has been killed by the UDA. Lastly, I find that she is alive and has been fucking a man that was meant to feed her to his pigs!'

Miguel continues saying, 'That is a headfuck in itself but now to find out, I'm going to be uncle to the pig feeder's child!'

Miguel shakes his head in disbelief then continues saying, 'I'm sorry to be a party pooper but I still come back to my question. What shall I say to my IRA superior who want him dead?'

They are all quiet in deep thought.

After consideration Miguel says, 'Let me speak to my superior.'

Miguel looks at John saying, 'If you are willing to help the IRA with disposing of our dead bodies, then maybe I can convince them to spare your life'

John says, 'I am sorry, but I am not the pig feeder anymore. I will not go back to helping the disposal of tortured murdered people, whether catholic or Protestant. I would rather die.'

Miguel says, 'Don't be stupid man, you have my sister and your baby to think of.'

John says, 'I won't, I'm sorry.'

John looks at Philomena. Philomena looks long and hard at John, then says to John, 'I understand.'

Philomena turns to her brother saying, 'If that is his wish, I won't go against it.'

Miguel says angrily, 'You're both a pair of gormless eejits, what am I going to do with you both?'

Miguel goes into deep thought analysing the situation. Miguel then says, 'Well, I will have to speak to my superior and explain that John is my sister's husband.'

John and Philomena in surprise both simultaneously say, 'husband!'

Miguel looks at them both saying, 'Yes husband, it is the only way. If you are married to Philomena and she is my sister and pregnant by you, it may work.

Philomena says, 'Miguel, it must work.'

Miguel says, 'I can only hope I can convince my IRA superior to spare John's life, your husband.'.

Philomena says, 'What if your superior decides not to spare John's life ?'

Miguel says, 'Well, then you will need to make an escape for it, with my help.'

Philomena hugs Miguel in relief saying, 'Thank you brother. I love you so much.'

Philomena kisses Miguel on the cheek.

Miguel says to Philomena, 'The things a big brother will do for his little sister. It is only because you have a baby on the way with him. If it was any other way, I would kill him myself.'

John looks at Miguel and says, 'I know it's not wanted but thank you anyway.'

Miguel without any expression, just nods at John and shouts, 'Guard.' The man who previously uncuffed john, enters the room, he obviously has been guarding outside the door.

Miguel says, 'Take the prisoner to his room.'

Miguel says to Philomena, 'You can stay with your fiancé but the guard stays with him too for now.' Philomena and John smile and say nothing but go with the guard.

John is taken away and Philomena follows. John and Philomena are given separate rooms to sleep for the night.

The morning of the 29th December 1993

Miguel picks up the phone and dials some numbers. Miguel waits for a minute for a voice to answer on the other end.

Miguel says, 'Hi, It is Michael Martinez. I need to speak to Steaknife, it's important.' Miguel uses the English version of his name when speaking to people outside his inner circle of friends.

There is silence on the end of the phone. Eventually, a different voice answers saying, 'Hello Michael, this is Steaknife, what do you want?'

Steaknife is a senior IRA Operative. There is no known reason why he is called stakenife. Some people speculate that he killed three men in a restaurant while eating a steak dinner. Some say it is from the way he would torture his enemies. The original meaning of steak comes from the old Norse, 'steik' meaning roasted on a stick. Perhaps, he impaled his victims on a skewer. No one knows the real reason, only that he is a violent, ruthless man.

Steaknife is completely anonymous and conducts his dealings over the phone. Like a shadow, always behind in the background, unobtainable and illusive.

Miguel continues speaking on the phone, saying, 'We have the man, and my sister is safe. She has informed me that the man saved her life and hid her from the UDA.'

Steaknife speaks in a calm, low, gravelly voice saying, 'That is very honourable, but he has been complicit in helping the UDA dispose of our operatives, both men and women.'

Steaknife continues saying, 'He must be interrogated and neutralised, as we do with all our enemies.'

Miguel pauses then says, 'There is something else.'

Steaknife says, 'What?'

Miguel says, 'My sister is having his baby and they are getting married'

Steaknife laughs but with a haunting laugh, like how you could imagine the devil would laugh.

Steaknife continues saying, 'Am I fucking hearing things right ? What has your sister been doing? Are you telling me, your sister has been fucking the enemy? She has not only been fraternising with the enemy but fucking them?'

Miguel says, 'Be careful with what you are saying. That is my sister your talking about'

Steaknife is silent and makes no reply. Then he says, 'He still needs to die, he is a former SAS British soldier. My superiors are aware of this and have ordered his execution.'

Feeling frustrated Miguel says, 'I understand, but now he is having a baby with my sister. He is family, and I will not kill him.'

In an ice-cold tone Steaknife says, 'Be careful Michael. As I could have you all killed.'

There is silence on both ends of the phone. This last comment has darkened the mood.

Steaknife says, 'Will he help us?'

Miguel says, 'He is adamant he is no longer the pig feeder. He won't help us dispose of dead bodies. Maybe I can convince him to help us in some other way.'

Steaknife says, 'There may be another way he can help us. Leave it with me.'

Miguel says, 'I need your word, we will not execute him. They want safe passage through Europe to Spain.'

Steaknife says, 'He will not be killed by us. I assure you, we will not kill him.'

Steaknife continues saying, 'Keep him there with your sister and stay with them. I will send someone there to take care of it all. I will get word to you when the transport has been arranged for them. I will let you know when I have organised a car to take them to their destination.'

Michael says, 'Thank you, I appreciate it'.

Steaknife says, 'Of course Michael, I understand. I guarantee you, that soon they will have no more problems to worry about. I will personally ensure this is dealt with correctly.'

Miguel, sounding relieved, says. 'Thank you Steaknife.'

Steaknife does not reply, and the phone line goes dead.

Miguel puts the phone down and goes out of the room to give the good news to Philomena and John.

Meanwhile, somewhere in another part of Belfast. Steaknife reflects on his conversation with Miguel. Steaknife then reaches for a separate telephone that sits on his desk. Steaknife rings another number on this phone. Steaknife waits for it to answer then says 'It's me. That problem we have discussed. I have an address for you to go to.'

The voice at the other end whispers, 'I will take care of it.'

Steaknife hangs up the receiver without any further conversation.

Back at the safe house, Philomena and John are awaiting the decision on John's future. Miguel returns into the room where John and Philomena had previously been in the day before. John and Philomena nervously wait for Miguel's news on John's execution.

Miguel says, 'You need to marry my sister, that is the only way you can avoid execution.'

John says, 'Great! I want to marry your sister, regardless of whether it saves my life or not.'

Philomena and John look at each other with relief and also excitement at getting married..

Miguel says, 'There is a local parish church not far from here. I know the priest and he is sympathetic to our cause. I have already spoken to him. He has agreed to marry you both. He will come here tomorrow morning to conduct the wedding ceremony. The Priest will need to come over tonight at some point to see you both. He will need to prepare the paperwork for the wedding.'

John and Philomena nod approvingly. Miguel leaves the room to brief his IRA comrades on what is going to happen.

Twenty minutes have passed. John and Philomena have been seated in the room in the safe house, patiently waiting. They smile and hug each other. They are relieved at John's reprieve and their subsequent marriage.

Miguel returns and says, 'You are free to be together today but you must sleep in separate rooms tonight.'

Philomena says, 'Of course, it's unlucky for the groom to see his prospective wife the night before their wedding.'

Philomena is excited at their imminent marriage and John beams with happiness.

Miguel is still in shock at the turn of events with his sister and John, his former enemy. Miguel says, 'Yes, I suppose so. I need to attend to some business. I will be back later to check on you both. So, keep out of the way of my men and behave yourselves.'

The happy couple, like cheeky children, smile at Miguel as he leaves the safe house.

Chapter 14

The Betrayal - An brath

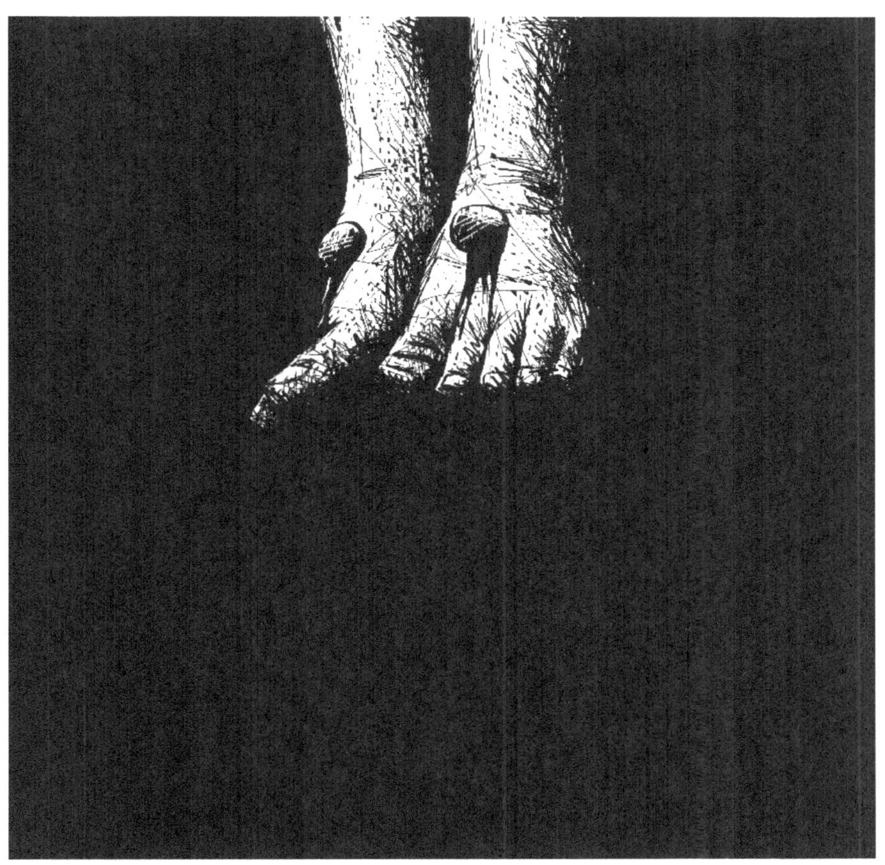

The evening of the 29th December 1993

It is the night before the wedding and John is still awake, sitting in the front room of the safe house. Philomena is upstairs in the bathroom preparing to go to bed. The door opens and a tall, slender man walks in. It is the priest Miguel previously mentioned. Dressed in smart black shoes, trousers and shirt with a white priest's clerical collar. The priest has black wavy hair but the grey running through it shows his age. He looks like he was a handsome man when younger, but age has worn his features. As the man walks in the room, he has an Aura about him. The man seems to carry a sense of wisdom and peace around him, like a halo.

The man smiles at John like Jesus to a child. John is struck by a sense of serenity and feels humble in the presence of this man. John feels like a schoolboy when the teacher walks in the room. A sense of authority and order is present.

The Priest says, 'The wind is fierce outside, sure, it nearly blew me into the ditch, as I walked up the road.'

The priest smiles at John saying, 'Hello my son, my name is Father Murphy, and I am here to marry you and Philomena.

John says, 'Thank you father.' John is now transported back to when he was a child at Sunday school.'

The priest, still smiling, enters further into the room. John realises just how tall the man is. The priest must be at least six foot four inches. The priest towers over John and puts his hand on John's shoulder.

The priest's touch is commanding but comforting to John.

The Priest says, 'Do you want to take your confession while I am here?'

In a calm voice John says, 'No, thank you father, forgiveness will not help me now. I know where I am going when I die, straight to hell for the acts I have committed in my life.'

The Priest says, 'God will be the judge of that John. We all need the spirit of forgiveness towards others but also to forgive ourselves.'

John says, 'I have witnessed many sins against God's commandments. I have also perpetrated some myself, both willingly and unknowingly.'

John struggles to speak but continues saying, 'I allowed many innocent people to be killed and I have knowingly taken lives.'

The Priest says, 'Take a seat John and let me talk to you.'

The two of them sit down. Fater Murphy says, 'It is not for us to decide our judgment. God will judge us all, not you or I, my son.'

Father Murphy continues saying, 'It is not for us to judge ourselves. It is God who truly has the ultimate judgement. Regardless of the troubles we are living in, love will always find a way to unite division and to heal the pain. Love and forgiveness will always lead to unity and peace in the end. Love and forgiveness is the only answer.

John listening says, 'If only it was that simple. I can not erase the sorrow I have orchestrated on others just by confessing to God, Their pain still remains for the loss of their loved ones.'

Father Murphy says, 'We cannot judge ourselves or even each other because we are only human. As human beings we are not perfect but we are all loved by God. All we can do is choose what to do next in our life and which road to go down. We have the freedom of choice. Our past actions are over. It is what we choose to do in the future that will have an impact on us all. If we confess and ask for forgiveness we choose to go into the future with love and forgiveness in our hearts.

When you learn to forgive each other and love one another, indirectly you forgive yourself.

John listens quietly. Father Murphy continues saying, 'Ireland would be a much kinder, loving place, if we all adopted the spirit of forgiveness. Ireland would be a place we can all live together peacefully. The future children of Ireland, will be more loving and tolerant to each other.

Love and forgiveness is the answer my son, not judging and hatred. I believe God still has plans for you John. Just like in the gospels, Matthew 18:12-14 and in Luke 15:3-7. The parable of the good shepherd and the lost sheep. God has not forgotten you. God has not forsaken you.

In fact, he has been with you throughout this whole journey of yours. I believe that for you to be here talking to me right now, tells me that God is not finished with you yet. God's final judgement on you is not yet cast.

Father Murphy places his hand again on John's shoulder saying, 'Take confess with me and ask God for forgiveness and let me marry you both in the true spirit of love and forgiveness from the Lord God, our saviour. The true meaning of life is Love and Peace, my son.'

The Priest continues, 'I can see that you have a heavy burden on your mind. Is that something you'd like to tell me about?'

John says, 'There is nothing really to say, other than the guilt for all the people I have killed in my profession, as a soldier.'

Father Murphy says, 'John, It is always worth talking about it. Please let me know what has been on your mind and lighten your burden by telling me all about it.'

John is hesitant, then opens up saying, 'It is something I can not get out of my mind, something that never leaves me, is the guilt I have for the Enniskillen bombing.' John struggles to continue speaking. Father Murphy says, 'It is ok my son, I am here and I am listening,' John says, 'My guilt for not preventing it and knowingly, allowing the IRA to perpetuate the murder of innocent civilians at the Cenotaph, on the 8th of November 1987, in Enniskillen.

Father Murphy is listening intently and says, 'Please, Go on my son,' John continues saying, 'I was a soldier and part of the

British intelligence at the time. We had gathered intelligence through our surveillance on eight IRA operatives in the area.

They were planning to commit a bombing in Enniskillen. We informed our superiors about this. However, instead of ordering us to apprehend the group. Our commanders ordered us to stand down and not to intervene. They ordered us to basically let the IRA go free and not engage with them. I objected to this decision and argued with my superior officers to detain them or kill them, as they posed an imminent danger to life.'

John starts to get angry saying, 'What is the use in talking, It is over and there is nothing I can do to bring the dead back.'

Father Murphy says, 'John, You are right, nothing will bring the dead back. I am not concerned about the dead, for they are already at peace. I am concerned about you, John. You are alive and need to come to peace with your guilt. Please John finish your story and tell me everything.'

John looks at Father Murphy and continues saying, 'My commanding officers threatened me and my team with a court-martial, if we did not stand down. The one regret I will have for the rest of my life is that I should have made my own decision and stopped the terrorist. Despite the intimidation of court martial, I should have made the right decision. I am a coward. I chose the easier option rather than the right option, even though it was the harder decision. Everyday I think of it with regret.'

John looks downwards in sadness saying, ' I should have disobeyed commanding officers and detained or killed those eight IRA bombers. Instead, they were allowed to freely commit the bombings at the Enniskillen cenotaph. Killing 11 innocent civilians and injuring countless others. I would have killed those eight lives with a clear conscience, as I knew they were going to kill innocent people. I regret that I allowed them to do it. The blood of those innocent victims at Enniskillen is on my hands just as much as the IRA. I will regret that for the rest of my life'

Father Murphy says, 'I hear and understand your guilt my son. As your priest, I can only say that we cannot take back the loss of life. We cannot turn back time but what we can do is understand the meaning of love and forgiveness.

If my memory serves me well, the father of the young girl killed on that day, forgave the killers of his beloved daughter.'

John is silent, listening intently.

Father Murphy continues saying, 'If that father can find it in his heart to forgive the murders, would you not think that he would surely forgive you, for your guilt of allowing the murderers to go free?'

John, close to tears, sad for the loss of the young girl, says nothing but nods solemnly at the priest.

Father Murphy smiles at John and continues saying, 'God loves and forgives us, even when we do wrong. Sometimes we need to forgive and love ourselves as much as we need others to forgive us. As I said, the father of the young girl at Enniskillen publicly forgave her killers. That man's act of ultimate forgiveness to the murderers of his daughter, inspired both sides of the border to peace. If that man has forgiven the bombers of Enniskillen has he not already forgiven you john? John has tears in his eyes but does not openly cry.

Father Murphy continues saying, 'The only way to honour the dead, is to remember them. Did you not tell me that you think about them every day?

John replies saying, 'Yes.'

Father Murphy says, 'Then you already honour the victims every day in your thoughts.' Father Murphy looks John directly in the eyes saying, 'It was not your fault john. It was not your fault, let it go my son, You are already forgiven. Christ died on the cross to save you from the sins of man. You are already forgiven john. Your only obligation in the eyes of God is to live your life with love and forgiveness.'

John cannot contain his emotions and cries uncontrollably as if releasing the floodgates of his anguish. and sorrow..

The Priest is silent in contemplation. Father Murphy says, 'For the hurt we do intentionally and the pain we cause unintentionally. We are all guilty of wrongdoing, we must all find forgiveness in our hearts, if this country of Ireland is ever to reach peace and stability.

We must let go of the past and forgive ourselves, as well as others. I do not have the answer for you John, except that Love is the only truth. From love comes forgiveness. I keep repeating myself but it is the only truth in life. Protestants or Catholics who truly believe and understand the word of God understands this. Just as it's the same cross we pray to and virtually, the same rosary beads we all pray with. We are all the same in life. Whether catholic or protestant, whether black or white. whether British or Irish. We mourn the same, we hate and make mistakes, the same. Conversely, we all love, and we all can forgive the same. The ultimate truth is we have more similarities than we do differences. So, why are we fighting against each other?

Father Murphy appears very emotive in his speech saying, 'My son, in answer to your guilt and sorrow. I will impart to you this one lasting thought. Father murphy pauses then says, 'Just as Jesus Christ who was God's own son, carried his heavy cross on his shoulders which he was to be crucified on. Jesus bore this cross on his back and accepted this burden, as he walked up to

Mount Sion to death. In this life, it is not how heavy your burden is that you carry but the manner in which you carry it. It is the way that you carry your burdens that matters. No matter how big your troubles are, it is how you carry them through your life that really matters.

So my son, your burden may be heavy on your shoulders but you must carry it in the spirit of love and forgiveness. Guilt or hate cannot change the burden that you bear. Indeed, it can make your burden seem even heavier. However, you can change the manner in which you carry it through life's journey. Jesus Christ carried the heavy cross on his shoulders in the spirit of love and forgiveness for all of Mankind. Jesus suffered and died on the cross for us, for the forgiveness of our sins. God forgave us because of his love for us. God's only son, Jesus Christ died so we can be forgiven for our eternal sins. Jesus died because he loved us.

Father Murphy continues saying, 'By his death on the cross Jesus paid the debt incurred by our sins. We must all go back to the basic principles that the only truth is love not hate. The only answer is forgiveness, not revenge. It is that love for one another that will save us all. So, carry your burden in the spirit of forgiveness and love. John, you must let go of your guilt and hatred.

Father Murphy smiles at John, saying, 'My son with love and forgiveness for yourself and for your enemies, let go of your pain and sorrow.

Ask God for forgiveness and mercy for your sins. God has never left you my son. He has been walking beside you all this time and he is merciful. Just as forgiveness and love will set you free from bondage of pain and suffering. Ireland will only be free of pain through forgiveness and love for each other.

So John in the eyes of God right here with me will you now ask for mercy and forgiveness?

John, sceptical, says, 'If God loves us all so much, why does he allow so much evil in this world? Father Murphy ponders this question then says, 'Human beings perpetuate evil deeds through our free will, to choose. The good deeds in the world are not done by God but by good people. God has given us the right to choose for ourselves to do good or evil.

Father murphy continues saying, 'God, like a father, must allow his children to make their own way in the world. Like a father, God can guide but ultimately, human beings have free will. God, like a father, is always there for us regardless of their misgivings. God gives us freedom of choice and free will to choose to do good or evil. If God was to remove our freedom of choice, would we not just be servants of God rather than his children.

Whether God is real or not is irrelevant, it is the concept of what God stands for something. The idea of a higher purpose and moral standard that we can aspire to, an idea of love and understanding. The very existence of this concept, transcends us from savages to enlightened ones. Our enemies will try to destroy this concept but you cannot kill or break an idea or belief.

Father murphy passionately says, 'If you ask God for forgiveness, you follow the path of enlightenment and freedom. If you hold onto hatred and guilt, you are doomed to walk your path in darkness.

Father Murphy is focused intently on john saying, ' John, I ask you again. Will you ask God for forgiveness?'

John struggles to answer and then says, 'I cannot forgive those bastards for blowing up the cenotaph at Enniskillen and murdering all those innocent people.'

Father Murphy says, 'You must forgive them and yourself, John.'

There is an awkward silence

Father Murphy then continues saying, 'Harbouring resentment and not forgiving, is like being stabbed in the back and never removing the knife. It will constantly cause pain until it is removed. only then can your wounds heal. By forgiving, you remove the pain from inside and can heal yourself. So, forgive John, it is better to be wiser than wounded, forgive.

John ponders for a moment then says, 'Yes. ok'

Father Murphy smiles at John, saying, 'My son, do you renounce hatred and vengeance for your fellow man?

John says, 'Yes, I do.'

Father Murphy say,' Do you ask for forgiveness for your sins.'

John says,' Yes.'

Father Murphy continues saying, 'John, In the sight of God and through the Almighty himself. I now absolve you from all your sins and set you free to love and serve our Lord God, through the holy spirit. John, you have been found like the good shepherd who saves his lost sheep. You were lost but you are now found. God is with you always my son. Go in peace to love and serve the Lord.'

Father Murphy does the sign of the crosses, saying. 'I bless you in the name of the father and the son and the Holy spirit.'

Both John and Father Murphy simultaneously say 'Amen.'

John has been controlling his emotions but after Father Murphy's last words. The words reach so deeply into John's soul that they affect him Profoundly. In an express of relief, John lets out a torrent of emotions of tears and sorrow. All of the pent-up emotions of his guilt, anger and sadness seem to be released.

John cries uncontrollably and feels a sense of relief as if a weight has come off his shoulder.

A feeling of peace comes across John which calms him. John clears his throat and looks at Father Murphy who has been watching over John the whole time.

John says, 'Thank you' to Father Murphy.

The tall commanding figure of Father Murphy smiles down knowingly at john, calmly saying, 'You are very welcome my son.'

Father Murphy shakes John's hand saying, 'Now, we will begin the wedding to marry you and philomena, promptly at 10 am tomorrow morning.'

I will see Philomena separately before we start the ceremony. I have paperwork to prepare for your marriage certificate. I will catch up with Philomena tomorrow.

Sure, I have known Philomena since she was a young girl. I will leave you to reflect on our discussion. Praise be to God for our talk today and accepting the Lord back into your life.

John in a relaxed voice says, 'Thank you so much Father Murphy.' Father Murphy nods as he exits the room and leaves the safe house.

Some time has passed. Philomena enters the room, John is in deep thought about his conversation with Father Murphy. John feels different in himself.

Philomena says, 'How was your talk with Father Murphy?'

John smiles at Philomena saying, 'I feel more at peace with myself and my guilt.'

Philomena says, 'That is good john. You can't hold all that guilt inside you. You need to let go of the past. We have a chance for a new life in Spain. We just need to get out of here. God willing, with my brother's help, we will.

John touches Philomena on the cheek and kisses her gently saying, 'I Love you.'

Philomena smiles and says, 'I Love you too.'

Philomena walks towards the door of the room saying, 'Right, I am going to bed upstairs and you are sleeping on the sofa, down here.'

John says, 'Why am I sleeping on the sofa ? What have I done wrong ?'

Philomena says, 'You haven't done anything wrong. Have you forgotten already, It is bad luck for the bride and groom to see each other the night before their wedding.'

John raises his eyebrows and says, 'You are an old romantic at heart, aren't you?'

Philomena says, 'Yes, I suppose underneath my hard exterior is an old-fashioned Irish girl. Deep down, I just want the fairy-tale ending with my prince charming.'

John says, 'So, I am your prince charming am I?'

Philomena says, 'Well, you're a bit rough around the edges but you will do.'

Philomena smiles saying, 'Goodnight soldier boy.'

Before John has a chance to reply, Philomena has opened the door and disappeared upstairs.

John chuckles to himself at how happy he is right now. John then settles down for the night on the sofa.

New Years Eve 1993

Morning has broken into a bright fresh winter's day. Outside John's window, the sun melts the frost on the grass. A robin red breast bird briefly darts past the window. Stopping on the windowsill for a split second to look in, then moving on.

The frosted grass is steaming off in the air, as the temperature warms up.

John nervously waits on the sofa. John has been up early and has already washed and shaved himself, in preparation for his wedding. He sits patiently, waiting for his bride to arrive. John has changed from his old clothes. Thanks to Miguel, who has provided John with suitable clothing. John is wearing a dark grey suit, a clean white shirt, and blue tie.

John has a white handkerchief in the top left breast pocket of his jacket.

As John waits, he looks around the walls of the room to see a framed depiction of Jesus. The image shows Jesus with his arms open wide and the effigy of the sacred heart on Jesus's chest.

As John stares at this image, he cannot stop himself from picturing his dead army mates Kevin, Jocky and Tom. As he remembers them, he is overwhelmed with a sense of sadness at their wasted lives. This leads John's thought to all the lives that have been taken during the troubles in Northern Ireland. John's inner voice asks the question, what has been the point of all this wasted life? What has it achieved? John's gaze focused increasingly on the sacred heart of Jesus and the sorrow of loss. John feels a sense of acceptance that life is what happens between birth and death. As John reflects on his life. John realises that life is an uncontrollable roller coaster of occurrences, good and bad. All we can do is enjoy the ride.

Suddenly, the door opens. Philomena enters the room in a beautiful white dress. The dress is made of a silky material that flows over her body like the glistening mountain dew, flows over the hills. Philomena looks stunning. John's thoughts immediately turn to Philomena.

John says to Philomena, 'Wow, you look beautiful.'

Philomena smiles at John lovingly and innocently. John is in ore at Philomena beauty, as she stands in the room. John is amazed at how stunning she looks.

Behind Philomena there follows Father Murphy and Philomena's brother Miguel. Father Murphy on entering the room says, 'Now, here we all are.'

Miguel has agreed to be the witness for John and Philomena. Father Murphy continues in a jovial tone saying, 'John, it is a good job for your sake, that I have taken the vow or else I would be stealing this beautiful woman from you, to be my own.'

Father Murphy laughs in amusement at his own humour.

Philomena's brother smiles and reluctantly stands at the back of the room, as he witnesses his sister's wedding.

Father Murphy smiles and signs with his hands at John and Philomena to come together in front of him. Looking proudly at John and Philomena, Father Murphy says, 'We are here today to celebrate the wedding of Philomena and John, to honour the unity of marriage. These are extraordinary times we are living through. Subsequently, we find our ceremony not in church but here in this house.'

Father Murphy continues saying, 'But the divine Love of God is everywhere, not just in a church. So, today God is here with us in this house, joining us all together for this marriage'. Father Murphy pauses and looks at the image of Jesus on the wall of the sacred heart of Jesus. The same picture that John had been staring at early when he was in the room alone. Father Murphy moves over to where the framed image hangs on the wall. The Priest then says, 'I would like the bride and groom to stand over here with me in front of this image of the sacred heart of Jesus, our Lord.'

John and Philomena without hesitation move in unison over to Father Murphy and the picture of the sacred heart of Jesus.'

Father Murphy looking at the picture and continues saying, 'This image we look at is of the age-old effigy of the Sacred heart of Jesus. Many catholic churches and homes across Ireland have this image of the Sacred Heart of Jesus up on their walls. This image of the Sacred Heart of Jesus, developed out of the devotion to the Holy Wounds, in particular to the Sacred wound in the side of Jesus.

The first images of the Sacred Heart of Jesus were in the eleventh century in the Benedictine and Cistercian monasteries. The image of the sacred heart of Jesus represents Jesus's profound love for us all.

Father Murphy continues saying, 'The image of Jesus's heart, open and on display, demonstrates Jesus' willingness to sacrifice his life for our sake. The love from his heart motivated all his actions. It is God's love revealed in the pierced heart of his son.

It is the symbol of love and that only love conquers sin and transcends death. The symbol of Jesus Christ, who loved us to the end and sacrificed everything in the name of love.

The message of the sacred heart of Jesus is that we must love each other. To humbly turn to his heart and seek forgiveness. We must learn to love and forgive others as God loves and forgives us.

Father Murphy says, 'Do not let your past pain and suffering chain you. Be free to love as Christ loves you. Receive his love and healing. The Heart of Jesus calls us to be holy and grow sensitive to the matters that hurt and offend others. Finally, Love is the only truth.' Father Murphy pauses and allows the silence to prevail in the room. Father Murphy pauses before his tiny congregation to let them reflect on his comments.

Father Murphy with a warm smile, looks at the wedding couple and says, 'Through this union of John and Philomena today in the sight of God. We see the meaning of the sacred heart of Jesus demonstrated in reality. For a former British soldier and a catholic girl coming together in love and forgiveness, is a great example to us all. Transcending division and conflict and instead loving each other. The beauty and kindness they see in each other and the love they have for each other, is amazing.. This is a true testament to the meaning of the sacred heart of Jesus. We see the sacred heart of Jesus in action today at this wedding.'

John and Philomena are silent, like children looking at the priest with reverence.

There is silence as Father Murphy is quiet. Father Murphy is praying to himself, then says, 'Millions of years ago the land that makes up Ireland. existed on two continents known as Laurentia and Gondwana. These lands were separated by an ocean called Iapetus. The northern part of Ireland was located on the continent of Laurentia, as part of North America. The southern part of Ireland was located in Gondwana, as part of Europe. But then that ocean receded, and the two continents collided creating the Ireland we know now. A scar from Dingle on the west coast to Clogherhead on the east, shows the line along which the two continents collided with.'

Father Murphy looks at the bride and groom intently saying, 'Ireland's own birth came from division but conversely. Ireland's own creation came from the amalgamation of that division. Irelands birth was created from the unification of two opposing sides. Whether continents or religious ideologies. Ireland's differences make it the country that it is.

Conflict and division have always been part of Ireland's DNA. But in that same DNA, the coming together of division and resolution of enemies has also been the making of this Great Ireland of ours. Just as Great Britan deserves its name. Surely, the title of Great Ireland is warranted. Opposition and reconciliation have always been part of Ireland, but it is that Beauty and spiritual combination that makes it so uniquely special.

We can only hope and pray that the unconditional love that this couple has demonstrated, will one day spread to all the people of Ireland. To bring every man, woman, and child together in peace and harmony, through the spirit of love and forgiveness'

Father Murphy raises his hands in the air and loudly proclaims, saying, 'God is the greatest of all.'

With his hands outstretched, Father Murphy says, 'The two different parts of Ireland are like my hands, slightly different but yet the same. Just like my hands, the north and south are independent from each other but still attached to the one body. Like my hands as with the two parts of Ireland, it can be used to create or destroy, to hug or to hurt. Like my hands, as like this divided country, only when the two parts come together, unified can we truly give praise to God. Father Murphy put his hands together in the prayer position.'

Father Murphy smiles at the bride and groom. He then lowers his hands and looks up to the heavens.

Father Murphy begins saying, 'We are gathered here today for the marriage of John Terence Doyle and Philomena Margaret Martinez, in the presence of Philomena's brother Miguel Patrick Martinez.'

Father Murphy then looks at Philomena saying. 'In the presence of God. Do you, Philomena Margaret Martinez, take John to be your lawful wedded husband? Do you promise to love and cherish him, in sickness and in health, for richer or for poorer, for better or for worse, and forsaking all others, keep yourself only unto him, for so long as you both shall live?

Philomena looks at John and says, 'I do.'

Father Murphy then looks at John saying, 'In the presence of god. Do you, John Terence Doyle, take Philomena to be your lawful wedded wife? Do you promise to love and cherish her, in sickness and in health, for richer or for poorer, for better or for worse, and forsaking all others, keep yourself only unto her, for so long as you both shall live.

John looking at Philomena says, 'I do.'

Philomena and John look into each other's eyes and seem to forget everything around them. They have a moment which is timeless when two people capture the feeling of eternal connection and love for each other.

With a big grin on his face, Father Murphy says, 'It gives me great pleasure to now pronounce you man and wife, John you may kiss your wife.'

John raises his hands up to Philomena and holds her face gently. John leans forward and softly kisses her on the lips. The couple then hold each other in a long embrace. John and Philomena kiss again and hold hands. They look at Father Murphy and Philomena's Brother who are clapping their hands in approval.

For a moment in time there is a sense of normality, people celebrating a wedding and the warmth and kindness that comes from it. A glimpse of humanity against the harsh existence that John and Philomena have endured since they met.

Philomena's brother exits the room and quickly returns with drinks and a tray of food for everyone. They all share each other's company and for a few hours, they forget the world outside and enjoy themselves. Father Murphy then gives his blessing to the newly married couple saying, 'May God bless you and protect you. I wish you every happiness for you both. Goodbye and God bless.'

The newlyweds both shake Father Murphy's hand.

Philomena kisses Father Murphy on the cheek lovingly. Father Murphy looks at John saying, 'Look after this woman now John or I may renounce my calling to steal her away from you.'

Philomena blushes with embarrassment at Father Murphy's comment. Father Murphy is a big, handsome man that outside the life of ordained priesthood, would have surely stole many of the hearts of women.

John smiles at Father Murphy and says, 'Father Murphy, I cannot thank you enough for your talk with me,'

Father Murphy smiles back saying, 'Let me leave you both with an old Irish blessing, May god walk by your side and always be your guide. God's love bond you together and stick with you forever. So, it is said, so it is done, so it is written, so it is sung. God be with you.' Father Murphy smiles once more, then departs, leaving the safe house.

Philomena's brother says, 'Well, now you have made a decent woman of my sister. I suppose you will be wanting the bridal suite for tonight.'

John and Philomena are bemused by Miguel's warmth towards them.

Miguel continues saying, 'I have prepared a room upstairs for you tonight, to both stay in. I will sleep downstairs on the sofa.

Philomena kisses Miguel on the cheek and hugs him. John reaches out his hand to Miguel who this time accepts. The two men shake hands. Philomena's brother then exits the room. The married couple are left alone. In marital bliss, John and Philomena go upstairs to enjoy themselves in their makeshift bridal suite.

Philomena and John are in the bedroom. Miguel has left a bottle of wine on the bedside table. John opens the wine and pours them both a glass. Philomena is still in her wedding dress. John is still in his white shirt and grey trousers. Philomena is sipping her drink on the bed. She looks at John as he takes his shirt and tie off. The room is silent except for a clock ticking in the background. Philomena has a cheeky look on her face as she is so happy.

Philomena says, 'John, comes over here.'

John smiles at her and walks over to the bed. John has now taken his shirt off and is naked from the waist up. John is standing at the foot of the bed.

Philomena puts her drink down and sits upright in the bed. Philomena crawls to the end of the bed and grabs John's trousers.

She unzips John's trousers and pulls John's cock out. Looking at John, she then goes down on his penis and sucks it. John feels this pleasure. Philomena stops her blowjob and leans upright so she is face to face with John who is still standing. Philomena kisses John then says,' John, now we are married, there is something I have been wanting you to do for me.'

John curiously says, 'What is it?'

Philomena moves closer up to Johns face and whispers saying, 'I want you to fuck me up my arse.'

John is taken back by this unexpected request. John replies saying, 'Wow, I wasn't expecting that, but I have never done anyone up the arse before.'

Philomena laughs saying. 'Oh my word, you are an anal virgin.'

Philomena, excited at this, says, 'Well, tonight my husband. I will break your cherry. There is Vaseline on the bedside table. I want you to rub it on my arse hole and then stick you hard cock up it.'

John has a nervous excitement at the prospect of doing this. Aroused by this, John's cock is hard, erect and strong.

Philomena turns around on the bed and lifts her dress up to reveal she is not wearing knickers. Philomena then proceeds to bend down on all fours, in a doggy style position. Philomena raises her bum up for john. John has the Vaseline on his hands and appears nervous.

Philomena seeing this says, 'Tonight, I will tell you what to do' John smiles and nods at Philomena.

Philomena says, 'Rub the Vaseline on your cock and then on my arse hole. John does this with the Vaseline, to Philomena's arousal. Philomena says, 'Now, ease your penis into my anus. stick in right in me and fuck me in the arse.' Philomena shouts, 'Push your big hard cock in me.'

John still nervous but eager to fuck Philomena, holds his penis and slowly puts it in her arsehole. This visibly makes Philomena react with heavy breathing and groans. Once John feels his penis is comfortably inside her arse. John starts to fuck Philomena in the arse. John gets into his rhythm and starts enjoying fucking Philomena harder and with more force.

Philomena, still groaning, cannot see John's face as he is behind her. The noise of john panting and grunting excites Philomena who shouts, 'Fuck me harder, fuck me harder. Play with my clitoris and finger my vagina as well. Keep fucking me hard in the arse! Come on you bastard, fuck me hard.'

John reacts to Philomena's calls and bangs her like a jackhammer, pounding her anus. John puts his hand underneath and fingers her pussy, rubbing Philomena's clitoris. John can feel how wet Philomena's pussy is. The noise and smell of flesh slapping against flesh. Both their naked bodies glisten in the light from the moon outside shining through the bedroom window. These two bodies entwined in the fundamental urges of humanity.

In the throes of sexual intercourse. Philomena is still in her wedding dress, bent over on the bed. John with his trousers around his ankles fucking Philomena in the arse. Philomena is getting pushed back and forth with the weight of John behind her. Philomena's dress is pushed over onto her back and the rosary beads, John gave her, are hanging loosely from her neck. The rosary beads knock against her breasts as she enjoys sex. Philomena now with her eyes closed in pleasure, pulls her cleavage down to expose her tits. John sees her exposed bosoms and grabs, holds and squeezes them with both hands.

Philomena shouts out, 'Yes, yes,'

John groans in ecstasy. Philomena says, 'I want you to strangle me with the rosary beads, like you are choking me.

John, surprised by this, says, 'What?'

I want you to hold the rosary beads and make out you are strangling me with them. Act like I'm your bitch, like you are raping me. John unsure of this but still fucking Philomena from behind, says, 'Are you sure.'

Philomena shouts, 'Yes, yes quickly. I'm going to come.'

John grabs the rosary beads bouncing on Philomena's breast and holds it tightly around Philomena's throat. This sends Philomena's sexual arousal into overdrive.

Like crazy, Philomena screams and shout, 'Yes, yes fuck me, fuck me.' Philomena is in the sexual zone beginning to climax.

Philomena says, 'Tighter, Choke me with the Rosary Beads.

John, with excitement, pulls on the rosary beads around Philomena's neck. Philomena struggles to speak as the beads are obstructing her speech. Still panting she mutters, 'I am coming. let go.' John immediately releases the beads, as he does so, Philomena screams as she orgasms. John seeing and feeling her body convulse as she climaxes, spunks his sperms into her arse, as he too orgasms. John grunts with his ejaculation. Philomena breathes heavily and smiles saying, 'Yes, that's what I needed.'

John pulls his cock out of Philomena anus. John falls onto the bed next to Philomena, who is still in the doggy position. Philomena turns over onto her back and lays onto the bed beside John. They look at each other, both sweating, panting, and smiling. Philomena happily kisses John on the cheek and lays content on his bare chest. John says, 'Wow, I never thought you would be as wild as that.' Philomena says, 'I am a lady outside the bedroom but a whore inside it. John smiles at Philomena and says, 'As long as you will always love me. I am open to do anything you want to do.'

Philomena says, 'I will always love you, until the day I die.'

John says, ' I had died and you gave me a reason to live again. I will always love you forever Philomena.'

Philomena and John spend the rest of their wedding night in a loving embrace, at peace with themselves and the world.

New Year's Day 1994

The early morning is drenched in darkness on this winter's day. John and Philomena wake up to the welcoming smell of bacon and eggs, cooking downstairs. Still in the safe house. Philomena and John hope that today might be the day they can start a new life together. To make their escape to the port and then to Europe. They are excited but anxious for this new beginning. After sometime, they go downstairs into the kitchen. On entering the kitchen, Philomena's brother greets them with a smile.

Miguel says, 'Good Morning to the newlyweds and Happy New Year to you both. I hope you had a good night.'

John and Philomena smile at each other but say nothing. Miguel says, 'There is bacon and eggs on the stove, so help yourselves.'

There are other IRA operatives in the kitchen eating but they keep themselves to themselves and say nothing. Miguel continues saying, 'Eat heartily as you will have a long drive today. Later, I am expecting my contacts to arrive to take you to the Ringaskiddy Ferry Port in Cork and from there to Roscoff in northwest France'.

Philomena says, 'I am scared, Miguel'.

Miguel says, 'Don't be scared my little sister. I have it all arranged, from Roscoff in France, a contact will pick you up from the port and take you through France into Spain. Once in Spain, you will travel to the Basque region and back to our ancestral homeland of San Sebastian.'

Philomena says, 'It would be good to see our relatives and old friends'.

John says, 'Well, at least I will get a tan.'

Philomena says, 'You will need to let me do the talking, as where we are going, they hate the English.'

John says, 'Well, that is no surprise, coming from you and all the trouble I had with you. I would not expect anything less from your relatives and friends in Spain.' John and Philomena both smile at each other in amusement.

Philomena embraces her brother. Philomena hugs Miguel tightly and kisses him on the cheeks saying, 'Thank you so much, my brother. I love you so much.' Philomena looks seriously at Miguel saying, 'Miguel, look after yourself.'

Miguel says, 'I love you too my sister, say hello to everyone back in San Sebastian. Tell them I will see them soon.'

Philomena is tearful and smiles at Miguel saying, 'I will.'

John approaches Miguel, putting out his hand in friendship, saying, 'Thank you for saving me and your sister.' Miguel smiles at John saying, 'Promise me, you will protect my sister with your life'

John says, 'I would die protecting her, Miguel.'

Miguel warmly shakes John's hand in farewell.

An IRA colleague enters the room and whispers to Miguel. Miguel turns to Philomena and John saying, 'A car is on its way to take you to the port in Cork. Get only the basic things you need, for your journey. Once you get to Roscoff, go to this address, here is some money to get you there.' Miguel gives Philomena a slip of paper with an address on and a bundle of foreign money. Miguel continues saying, 'A good friend of mine will meet you there and will organise your passage to Spain.'

Philomena says, 'I cannot believe I am going back to Spain.'

Miguel says, 'Yes, my sweet little sister. It is back to the old country. You will be back with our old friends and relatives, and you will be safe.'

Miguel continues saying, 'Once you make it to my contact, they will travel with you all the way back to San Sebastian, they are from there.'

Philomena smiles lovingly at her brother, and they hug each other, again. Miguel kisses Philomena on the cheek as they separate. Philomena has a chill go down her spine and a sixth sense of impending doom. She looks at her brother like she will not see him again. Philomena says, 'Why don't you come with us Miguel? It is so dangerous here. I am worried for you.'

Miguel says, 'Do not worry my sister. I cannot leave my comrades in the fight for a free united Ireland. Besides, I am with my brothers in arms, I am in the safest place I could be.'

Philomena, still with a sense of unease, smiles begrudgingly as she leaves Miguel. John and Philomena have gathered their essentials in one small bag for the trip. A car has pulled up in front of the safe house, to take the couple to the port and safe passage to Europe.

The newlyweds leave out the front door of the safe house, waving goodbye to Philomena's brother. Philomena's brother is outside the house on the doorstep as the couple get in the car to leave. The car moves away slowly from the safe house. As the smiling couple start to leave, Philomena looks back at her brother to wave goodbye, again.

Miguel, standing on the doorstep of the safe house, is waving and smiling at the happy couple.

Suddenly, two men wearing balaclavas appear from behind Miguel in the doorway of the safe house. Philomena, seeing this, shouts out, 'Miguel.' but to no avail. Miguel is oblivious to his attackers. The men smother Miguel, by putting a clear plastic bag over his head and pulling it tight on his face, so he cannot breath. Miguel's face changes to terror and then to suffocation as the plastic sucks in on his mouth. Miguel gasps for air but it is futile. It is impossible for Miguel to breathe with the plastic so tightly pulled over his face. Miguel staggers back inside the doorway trying to desperately reach around to defend himself. The two masked men in complete control, unceremoniously yank and pull Miguel backwards inside the safe house. The front door shuts, sealing a fatal fate for Philomena's brother.

Philomena screaming grabs John who looks back to witness the unfolding betrayal. Instinctively, John looks around at the driver of the car they are in. John sees that the driver too, has a balaclava on. A man in the passenger seat, beside the driver also has a balaclava on.

This masked man is brandishing a gun, low down on the arm rest between the two front seats. The gun is pointing ominously at John and Philomena.

The balaclava man aiming the gun speaks, but only whispers saying, 'Did you really think you could escape the UDA, John? I suggest you both sit back. We are all going for a little ride.'

John and Philomena have no doubt of their impending fate. Death awaits them at their destination.

The car travels through the country lanes. It is only now, at the end of life, that life becomes so vivid in focus and clear. Death emphasizes how precious and extraordinarily beautiful life is, with all its ups and down, yet perfect. The landscape of Ireland looks especially stunning this winter's morning. Ireland and its proud mountains and rolling land, its multitude of colours and shade. This Ireland, scarred from endless conflict but despite this, so stubbornly stunningly. The splendour, spirit and tranquillity of Ireland will always endure.

The couple look at each other with impending doom. Yet they resign themselves to the inescapable fact that they are travelling together, to their execution. A peace comes over them both, like a burden lifted, an acceptance of the way of things, of the way of God.

They go from being tense in an upright position, to sitting back together holding hands, in the back seat of the car. Their car, which is now their hastily prepared hearse, proceeds along its procession towards the couple's shallow graves.

Calmly, Philomena and John contemplate their fate at the hands of their assassin's. No words are exchanged between the couple or the assassins, just an unspoken acceptance that it is, what it is.

As the car drives Philomena and John through the Irish countryside to their deaths. Simultaneously, there is a telephone conversation happening elsewhere. Somewhere in Belfast, there is a telephone conversation taking place between Steakknife and Bob. The IRA and the UDA.

Bob says, 'The package has been collected for disposal.'

Steakknife says, 'I appreciate your help in this matter.'

Bob says, 'We are always open to collaboration when both sides have a mutual mess that needs cleaning up. We can not have incidents of opposing sides living with each other, let alone marrying each other.

Steaknife interjected saying, 'What would happen if everyone decided they wanted to love their enemies? We both would be redundant.'

Bob says, 'Division between us, keeps us strong. Our mutual arrangement is beneficial to both of us.'

Steaknife says, 'I agree, we cannot have reconciliation. It is bad for business.'

Bob says, 'I will pass on your regards to the other senior UDA commanders. The UDA and the British government are always happy to help.'

Steaknife says. 'In return myself and my IRA superiors are always willing to return the favour. If any unruly or insubordinate IRA operatives start making it difficult for both our mutual interests. You know where to find me.'

There is a slight pause, then Bob says. 'Before I go, tell me, I'm wondering. Why did you want all of them killed ?

Steaknife says, 'My father told me this, many years ago. From the root to the fruit, everything grows. Meaning, like a fruit plant, if you cut the fruit away more will take its place. If you want to kill the fruit plant and prevent further produce, you must cut the root off to kill the line of succession.

Steaknife continues saying, 'Obviously, the pig feeder must die but John's wife, Philomena is pregnant. Therefore, if I do not kill her now, I will eventually have a vengeful son coming back for me, seeking revenge for killing his father. So, the wife must die.

Additionally, her brother must also be killed to completely remove the root. I do not want a vengeful brother trying to kill me for killing his sister. They must all be killed. From the root to the fruit it must be all cut away to prevent further problems.

Bob says, 'Wise words, I couldn't have put it better myself. It was a pleasure doing business with you again. As discussed, the arrangement stands, if the IRA needs any assistance to clear up any difficult stains in Ulster. We are happy to help in the future. If a stain becomes disruptive for both of us it must be eradicated.

Steaknife says, 'Conversely, if you need us to eliminate any unnecessaries, you can contact me again through the usual channels.

Bob says, 'Pleasure doing business with you, Steaknife'

Steaknife replies saying,' Pleasure doing business with you, Bob.'

As Bob puts the hand receiver back down onto the telephone, simultaneously the car carrying Philomena and John slowly turns into a field through an open gate.

A lush, deep green coloured field with beautiful mountains of Ireland opens up before the passengers of the car, as it enters the field. A scenery like a freshly painted watercolour with the dampness of the greens and blues still setting. The vehicle comes to a stop. Philomena and John are signalled by the assassin's gun to exit the car.

Philomena and John leave the car holding hands. Philomena's head resting on John's shoulder. They take in the view of the majestic mountains rising up as their backdrop on the stage of their final curtain call. Through the mist of the morning they watch the amazing beauty of life.

No one will live forever and life is such a blessing. John and Philomena turn to face the assassin, as the other assassin waits in the car with the engine running.

The assassin whispers saying, 'Make your peace with your God.' He gives the couple a final moment together.

Something catches Philomena's eye. It is a robin red breasted bird sitting on a branch of a nearby tree. Philomena admires its beauty, as the bird seems to watch Philomena.

Philomena is snapped back to her imminent execution with her hand being touched by john. John holds her hand lightly, looking into Philomena's eyes, John says, 'Thank you for loving me.' Philomena looks at John and kisses him gently on the lips.

Philomena and John take one last, longing look into each other's eyes. Philomena says, 'I'm scared, John.'

John smiles at Philomena saying, 'Close your eyes my love, I will see you again shortly.' They both turn to face their firing squad. They touch hands, locking their fingers together.

The assassin raises his pistol. Saying no words, he aims and fires two double shots at the couple in quick succession. First at John then Philomena. The shots ring out and echo through the mountains. like a death knell, it punctuates two lives have concluded.

Simultaneously, the red robin bird takes flight, flying up into the sky and disappears.

John falls over Philomena as he is hit by the assassin's bullets, then Philomena falls backwards as she is hit by the second bullets, a split second later. As they both fall, Philomena is left lying underneath John. They both lay on the grass, Philomena stretched out on her back with John slumped over her body, his head laying on her chest. John's arm is stretched out with his hand touching Philomena's face, lovingly, as if trying to protect her even at the end.

There is silence.

The whispering assassin turns his back on his victims, returning to the car which drives away.

The awe-inspiring views of the Irish countryside surrounds John and Philomena.

The dead couple lay silent and alone.

The heavens look down on them, laying together.

This solemn scene fades to black.

There is darkness.

Suddenly, Philomena's body jolts up, taking a sudden gulp of air.

The End?

'Love is the only truth'

In memory of the 12 innocent victims
of the Enniskillen bombing and
the countless killed on both sides
during the troubles.

I leave you with this one wish

May the souls of the dead all rest in peace.
May the souls of the living all live in peace.

Coming soon

The Sequel, 'The Pig Feeder's Wife'

Afterword

The information that inspired the story

Ireland has been occupied by England in one form or another, for the last 800 years. Most of Ireland gained indepencence in the early 20th century. It formed as a dominion called the Irish free state in 1922, except for six counties in the North. This Northern area was termed Northern Ireland. The Republic of Ireland gained complete independence as a nation state in 1949, as a result of the Republic of Ireland Act.

<u>The Troubles</u>

The Troubles was the name given to the civil war between nationalists and unionists in Northern Ireland. Predominantly, the main protagonists were the Irish Republican Army, the British government and the Ulster Défense Association. The troubles ran from 1969 to 1998 and the Good Friday Agreement.

During that time 3,720 people were killed as a result of the conflict. Approximately, 47, 541 were injured.

<u>The Enniskillen Bombing</u>

The Enniskillen bombings took place at the cenotaph on Sunday 8th November 1987. Killing 12 innocent people, 11 died at the time and one victim subsequently died 13 years later in 2000 after falling into a coma shortly after the bombing.

The bombing also injured 67 people.

The Enniskillen bombing was one of the most horrific losses of innocent civilian lives, through the period called the troubles in Northern Ireland. Its outcry changed the course of the troubles as after this atrocity, the IRA began looking for a peaceful solution to the troubles. Stating that they had made a mistake in allowing the bombing to happen. American support was never the same after the bombing. The bombing led to the British government passing an extradition bill, which they were not able to get through before the atrocity and subsequent public outcry.

Questions have been asked, could the injustice and indignity of such pointless loss of innocent lives have been prevented?

The youngest victim of the bombing was 20 years of age Marie Wilson. Her father, Gordon, also caught in the bombing.

Mr Wilson after this, stated that he forgave the murderers of his beloved daughter Marie. His selfless act of forgiveness and love stunned the world and brought Protestant and Catholics together, in an act of unity and show of support.

Mr Wilson's selfless act of forgiveness towards the IRA terrorist astonished the Irish people. This led to Mr Wilson setting up a foundation called the 'Spirit of Enniskillen' This foundation aimed at bringing reconciliation between enemies. The spirit of forgiveness brought people together and reduced division and conflict.

SAS British soldiers

Allegedly, SAS British soldiers operated in Northern Ireland during the troubles.

It is alleged that the SAS engaged in counterintelligence in Northern Ireland and over the Border into the republic.

Secret of Enniskillen

Under the thirty year rule, which is a ruling in the United Kingdom and the Republic of Ireland. It prohibits certain government documents from being released until thirty years have passed from when they were created.

After this thirty year rule, it emerged that in 2018, it was released by the Irish Government that a letter was sent to them after the Enniskillen bombing. The letter was sent anonymously to the Tanaiste and the Irish Minister of Foreign Affairs.

In this letter, it allegedly claimed that British intelligence had prior knowledge of an imminent attack of the Remembrance Day bombing in Enniskillen. However, it is alleged that they ignored this information and allowed it to happen. There was no evidence provided in the letter.

In the letter, the anonymous writer stated that the reason the attack was allowed to happen was to turn public opinion against the IRA. Due to the outcry resulting from such an atrocity against innocent civilians. Additionally, it would help push through new security legislation going through parliament at the time.

This novel is inspired by that letter.

The Romper Rooms
These were makeshift torture chambers set up to interrogate and execute its victims. These rooms were used from 1970. Allegedly, these terror rooms were not publicised by the media, as thought too disturbing for the public.

The Battle of Newry Road
This took place on 23rd September 1993. It involved IRA operatives and the British army, a British helicopter engaged in a running gun battle with IRA motorized vehicles.

The Butcher of Belfast
During the 1970, allegedly, a group of men kidnapped numerous innocent Catholics from the streets in Belfast. Once captured, they horrifically tortured and killed them. Their reputation became so terrifying and notorious that rumour circulated that they were called the butchers of Belfast and were allegedly mincing up the dead bodies of their victims and feeding them in meat pies back to the Catholics.

Steaknife was, allegedly, the code name of a man who was allegedly an undercover agent for the military intelligence unit called the Force research unit. It is alleged that steaknife infiltrated the top ranks of the IRA command and which was unknown to them. However, he was known for his ruthlessness.

The old man called Dagda - Daghgha
Dagda was an ancient mythical Irish God, who was the leader of all the Gods. This Irish ancient God could control Life and death and also fertility, time and the season amongst others. The Mythical father figure of Ireland.

www.ingramcontent.com/pod-product-compliance
Lightning Source LLC
Chambersburg PA
CBHW070946180726
48291CB00004B/1160